Sam Fisher must save one man's life to save his own country.

OUT OF THE FIRE . . .

"Holy shit."

That expletive had come from the SMI table, where Grim was bringing up Keyhole satellite surveillance footage, along with imagery captured by the U.S. Army's latest Vertical Take-Off and Landing Unmanned Aerial System dubbed the "Hummingbird."

Fisher reached the table and scanned the schematics of the drone, displayed on a data bar to his right.

Equipped with the ARGUS array composed of several cameras and a host of other sensor systems, the Hummingbird and her systems were capable of capturing 1.8 gigapixel high-resolution mosaic images and video, making it one of the most capable surveillance drones on the planet.

At the moment, the UAV had her cameras and sensors directed at a rugged, snowcapped mountainside with a long pennon of black smoke rising from it.

"What?" asked Fisher.

"That's Dykh-Tau," said Grim. "It means 'jagged mount' in Russian. It's about five klicks north of the Georgia border, and it's the second-highest peak in the Caucasus Mountains."

"That's a pretty big fire down there."

"That's not just a fire. Kasperov's plane just crashed."

TOM CLANCY'S HAWX

Tom Clancy's Ghost Recon

GHOST RECON
COMBAT OPS
CHOKEPOINT

Tom Clancy's EndWar

ENDWAR
THE HUNTED
THE MISSING

Tom Clancy's Splinter Cell

SPLINTER CELL	CONVICTION
OPERATION BARRACUDA	ENDGAME
CHECKMATE	BLACKLIST AFTERMATH
FALLOUT	

Created by Tom Clancy and Steve Pieczenik

TOM CLANCY'S OP-CENTER	TOM CLANCY'S NET FORCE
OP-CENTER	NET FORCE
MIRROR IMAGE	HIDDEN AGENDAS
GAMES OF STATE	NIGHT MOVES
ACTS OF WAR	BREAKING POINT
BALANCE OF POWER	POINT OF IMPACT
STATE OF SIEGE	CYBERNATION
DIVIDE AND CONQUER	STATE OF WAR
LINE OF CONTROL	CHANGING OF THE GUARD
MISSION OF HONOR	SPRINGBOARD
SEA OF FIRE	THE ARCHIMEDES EFFECT
CALL TO TREASON	
WAR OF EAGLES	

Created by Tom Clancy and Martin Greenberg

TOM CLANCY'S POWER PLAYS

POLITIKA	COLD WAR
RUTHLESS.COM	CUTTING EDGE
SHADOW WATCH	ZERO HOUR
BIO-STRIKE	WILD CARD

Tom Clancy's

SPLINTER CELL®

BLACKLIST™
AFTERMATH

WRITTEN BY

PETER TELEP

BERKLEY BOOKS, NEW YORK

THE BERKLEY PUBLISHING GROUP
Published by the Penguin Group
Penguin Group (USA) LLC
375 Hudson Street, New York, New York 10014

USA • Canada • UK • Ireland • Australia • New Zealand • India • South Africa • China

penguin.com

A Penguin Random House Company

TOM CLANCY'S SPLINTER CELL®: BLACKLIST ™ AFTERMATH

A Berkley Book / published by arrangement with Ubisoft Entertainment SARL

For information, address: The Berkley Publishing Group,
a division of Penguin Group (USA) LLC,
375 Hudson Street, New York, New York 10014.

ISBN: 978-0-425-26630-4

PUBLISHING HISTORY
Berkley premium edition / October 2013

PRINTED IN THE UNITED STATES OF AMERICA

10 9 8 7 6 5 4 3 2 1

Cover art and design by Ubisoft, Ltd.
Interior text design by Kristin del Rosario.

ACKNOWLEDGMENTS

Many talented and generous artisans contributed their expertise to this manuscript:

Mr. James Ide, chief warrant officer, U.S. Navy (Ret.), has worked with me as first reader, researcher, and collaborator on more than a dozen of my novels. His technical prowess and military experience have not only strengthened my manuscripts but have challenged me to strive for a level of authenticity that can pass muster with critical veterans like him.

Jackie Fiest knows more about the Splinter Cell universe than any reader or gamer out there. She's even had a character named after her in the novels. It was my great fortune to have her review this manuscript and offer her keen insights on it and the Splinter Cell canon. I'm truly grateful for her help.

I'm particularly indebted to Mr. Sam Strachman, Mr. Richard Dansky, and Mr. Patrick Redding of Ubisoft Entertainment for their support, encouragement, and enormous help in shaping the story line of this novel. I'm thankful, too, to many others at Ubisoft, including Jade Raymond, Yannick Spagna, Maxime Beland, and Christophe Martin.

Mr. Ron Cohen, Mr. Tom Jankiewicz, Mr. James "Johnny" Johnson, Mr. Adam Painchaud, Mr. Robert Hirt, Mr. Bud

Fini, Mr. Andrew Sands, and Mr. James Saltzman, along with the rest of the helpful folks at world-renowned firearms manufacturer Sig Sauer, provided me with technical support and hands-on training with their product line.

My agent, Mr. John Talbot, and editor, Mr. Tom Colgan, have allowed me to continue this awe-inspiring journey as a writer, and I'm thrilled that our teamwork has once more resulted in another rewarding project.

Last but not least, my wife, Nancy, and two lovely daughters, Lauren and Kendall, serve as my ultimate inspiration and most loyal fans, keeping me motivated and freshly stocked with peanut butter and coffee (writer fuel).

1

BOLIVIA'S North Yungas Road is known by the locals as El Camino de la Muerte, the Road of Death. It was constructed by Paraguayan prisoners of war back in the 1930s and is one of just a few routes through the mountainous rainforest that connects the country's seat of government, La Paz, with the northern regions some sixty-nine kilometers away. The road is barely wide enough for two cars abreast, with dozens of sheer vertical drop-offs lacking any form of guardrails. There is no margin for error. When it rains, rocks and earth grow loose from the towering hillsides above and tumble down along the switchbacks. As drivers round a hairpin turn, they're confronted by a mudslide or a wall of crumbling boulders that forces them off the ledge to plummet more than six hundred meters to the valley below, where the Coroico River rushes to join the Amazon. Even when nothing blocks the mostly unpaved path, dense fog often descends along the vine-covered cliffs, reducing visibility to zero. Numerous crosses and stone cairns mark the locations where, for two to three hundred loved ones each year, the journey ended and they became part of North Yungas's dark legend. Though some say it's cursed, clutched forever in the hands of the Devil, others have simply declared it the world's most dangerous road.

Sam Fisher knew all about North Yungas, and he knew the man he was chasing had deliberately led him up there to turn him into another statistic. The son of a bitch had no idea that he'd awakened America's newest and most formidable beast, a blacker-than-black special ops and counterterrorism unit known as Fourth Echelon, commanded by Fisher and free to sink its sharpened talons into men like him. Free to do whatever it took with impunity.

Fisher squeezed the stolen motorcycle's clutch lever, geared up, and accelerated. He gritted his teeth and cut hard around the next bend, the old Yamaha fishtailing and sending a bolt of anxiety up his spine. As he came out of the turn, the bike's rusting fenders rattled, and the faded sticker of Jesus affixed to the gas tank began peeling back. At once the headlight flickered through the gloom and heavy rain, and he found his prey just a few meters ahead, rooster tails of mud rising from the man's own bike. Fisher was out of gears, wailing now at full throttle.

The man known to intelligence sources as Hamed Rahmani, and with the known alias of Abu Jafar Harawi, saw something ahead and cut his wheel sharply, weaving around two pieces of rock appropriately shaped like coffins, one lying across the other. Fisher did likewise, his shoulder brushing along the wet stone. The bike's engine began to cough and sputter as they climbed toward nearly five kilometers above sea level. They sped by a wider section used for passing, then crossed onto a single-lane stretch running along at least a kilometer of cliffs whose ledges sent streams of water into the darkness.

Fisher's arms tensed, his triceps already sore from keeping a white-knuckled grip on the handlebars. He shifted gears again as Rahmani whipped around the next bend and vanished momentarily, only to reappear—his headlight sweeping along the wall to his right.

Seeing that Rahmani was widening the gap, Fisher leaned into the bike and accelerated, tucking in his elbows, trying to make himself a little more aerodynamic to bleed every bit of speed out of the machine.

Suddenly, he was thrown to the right, the front wheel having connected with a piece of rock that served as a ramp, and as both wheels left the road, he thought the chase was over and that he should've stopped like most locals did to pour libations of beer into the earth and ask the goddess Pachamama for safe passage—because in three seconds it might all end here.

As both tires slammed back onto the dirt, the impact reverberating up his spine, he gasped and recovered control, cutting the wheel to the left to avoid another section of larger gravel and by necessity taking the bike to within a tire's width of the ledge. He groaned and leaned to his right, guiding the motorcycle past the gravel, then back, closer to the wall. Yes, he'd earned himself a breath now.

What little he could see of the next ravine gave him pause, and he thought of the gear pack he'd left in La Paz, bulging with the rest of his weapons, along with his surveillance and comm equipment. He'd gone into the bar completely undercover, plainclothes. Somehow, someway, the bastard had been tipped off and had bolted. There'd been no time, no opportunity to get on Rahmani's wheel armed for bear. For the time being it was just the two of them, mano a mano, motorcycle to motorcycle. Fisher's custom FN Five-seveN semiautomatic pistol with integrated suppressor was tucked into a concealed holster at his hip, and he had to assume that Rahmani was packing at least one or more small arms.

Fisher checked the fuel gauge: about half a tank. If he couldn't overtake Rahmani, then maybe the thug would run out of gas first. Or maybe Fisher would. There was no way to tell, so . . . he would *have* to catch up and take this man alive. Rahmani was an army major and intel officer with MOIS, Iran's Ministry of Intelligence and Security. That alone made him valuable. However, he liked to moonlight as a thief who along with a select group of friends had gotten their hands on one hundred pounds of highly enriched uranium, or HEU, from Mayak, one of the largest nuclear facilities in the Russian Federation. After the theft he'd been spotted in Baghdad, then had vanished for a while until he popped up in Bolivia with some drug smuggling associates. He'd thought he was safe. Of course, he had no idea who he was dealing with now.

Blinking wind and water from his eyes, Fisher riveted his gaze on that dim light ahead, trying to follow Rahmani's trail in the mud, letting him have the more difficult job of picking the lines through, around, and across the debris washing onto the roadway.

After a relatively lazy turn to the right, with a curtain of vines extending three meters from the cliff wall to provide a few seconds of solace from the rain, Fisher's jaw dropped, and a curse burst from his lips.

A refrigerated shipping truck blocked most of the road. There was only a half-meter-wide track to the left of the vehicle, running along the broken ledge. The driver had, as many did, pulled over and parked to wait out the storm, fearful that the road ahead might be too dangerous and he'd have better judgment in the morning. These assumptions were borne out as the obese driver, a ball cap perched on his head, leaned out from his cab and shouted in Spanish for Fisher to stop and seek cover.

But there, off to the left, was Rahmani, one hand on his handlebars, the other sliding along the truck's side for balance as he finally reached the front bumper, gunned his engine, and was off again.

As Fisher slowed and carefully—breathlessly—guided his motorcycle around the back of the truck, coming alongside it, he reminded himself to keep his gaze on where he wanted to go. Don't look down. Damn, the temptation was too great, and as he coasted forward, he flicked his glance to the left. Through chutes of rain and the swirling gloom, he saw how the edge of the cliff was just a hairsbreadth away and dropped off into nothingness. Just then, his front tire shoved through some loose rocks that tumbled over the side. Fisher's heart was squarely in his throat.

Rahmani's engine whined as he once again raced along the wall, creating a sizable gap. Tensing, Fisher pushed off the truck, reached the front bumper, then geared up and took off, popping a small and unintended wheelie as he did so. They were nearing La Cumbre Pass, the highest point along the road, which was followed by a breakneck descent all the way to Coroico.

After a final push at full throttle that brought Fisher within an estimated fifty meters of Rahmani, the road veered left, then pitched forward, and abruptly they were barreling toward the next set of hairpin turns.

Wanting to check his speed but fearful of averting his gaze for even a second, Fisher clutched the handlebars a little tighter but maintained speed. A pile of rocks off to his left sent him hard toward the wall once more, but he'd gone too far and was heading for the rock when he turned back and overcorrected. He was about to lose control but jerked once more and came out of the turn while dragging one boot along the ground.

the cliff—indicated another sharp turn ahead. Fisher took a deep breath and held it. Bringing himself as close to the wall as he dared and locking his gaze on his headlight's meager beam, he soared around the turn, losing a bit of traction before easing up and letting the bike guide him into the corner. The old Yamaha was a true piece of crap, but she was growing on him now, his gear shifts a little more intuitive, the sounds of the motor communicating speed much more clearly.

Rahmani drew up fast on the taxi, and a second glance there showed he was trapped behind it. Fisher gritted his teeth and remained tight to the wall, his speed nearly twice that of Rahmani's. The cabdriver had to be confronting his own mortality, and for a moment, Rahmani looked back, his face cast in the pallid glow of Fisher's light. His eyes bugged out as he realized he'd failed to lose Fisher and was seconds away from being caught.

A faint thrumming of rotors sent Fisher's gaze skyward. Then another sound erupted, a large diesel engine, an engine much louder than the taxi's.

They were nearing another sharp turn to the right, and abruptly it was there: an old Volvo F6 delivery truck from the 1970s, its daredevil of a driver taking up the entire road and rumbling head-on toward the taxi.

The truck driver locked up his brakes, as did the cabdriver, but their tires had little traction across the sheets of rain and mud.

"Sam, we're back online, target locked on with FLIR, and Briggs is inbound," came a familiar voice through the nickel-sized subdermal embedded behind his ear.

Fisher wasn't wearing the subvocal transceiver, or SVT, patch on his throat, so he couldn't respond, but that hardly mattered.

The truck and taxi collided in a thundering, screeching explosion of twisting metal and fiberglass and shattering glass that stole his breath and sent debris hurtling toward him.

The taxi's front end crushed as though it were made of papier-mâché, and the truck kept coming, plowing the taxi back with the front wheels rising off the dirt.

Rahmani had no time to react. He screamed and struck the sedan's rear bumper. His front wheel folded like a taco as the bike slid sideways, and in the next second he caromed off the rear window and vanished beneath the vehicle—

Into the meat grinder.

The squealing and gurgling and crunching of metal grew to a crescendo as Fisher cursed and steered for the barest of openings on the left side, trying to skirt around the bulldozing truck. He swore again because the taxicab with Rahmani beneath began sliding toward the ledge, cutting him off. He crashed into the taxi and flew headfirst over the handlebars, went tumbling across the cab's trunk, and then the force of the Volvo's momentum sent him rolling off the side of the sedan.

A stretch of rocks and earth about eight inches wide saved Fisher's life.

He struck that patch shoulder-first, realized where he was—about to plunge over the ledge—and reflexively reached out with both hands, clutching some heavy weeds and grasses that sprouted along the cliffside.

His legs came whipping around, the force driving the grass through his fingers, his grip now tentative at best. He dug the tips of his boots into the mountainside, but there was no good purchase on the wet rock and mud, and his legs dangled. He groaned with exertion, his arms literally trembling under the load. Something flashed to his left, and there it was, the sticker of Jesus that had been peeling off his motorcycle's gas tank; it fluttered on a rock for a few seconds, then blew away.

Above Fisher, off to his right, the truck's rear wheels gave out, and the lumbering vehicle began sliding tail-first toward the edge. The driver tried to steer out of the slide, but it was too late.

The entire ledge quaked as the Volvo's rear wheels hung in midair while the undercarriage slammed down and was dragged along the stone. Finally, the front wheels left the road, even as the driver, a lean, bearded man in coveralls, tried to bail out, but the truck was already airborne. Fisher watched with an eerie fascination as the driver wailed and the vehicle's headlights shone straight up into the rain, then wiped across Fisher before the truck tumbled away, twin beams flashing and dancing, growing fainter, fainter . . . until a distant impact and whoosh of flames resounded from somewhere below.

The helicopter was overhead now, the rotor wash whipping through the storm. That would be a Mil

Mi-24 Russian-made helicopter gunship, one of a small fleet the government of Bolivia had purchased from the Russians to combat the drug trade. Fisher had sent Briggs to link up with the pilot and weapons system operator the moment their target had bolted.

A spotlight shone on Fisher, then the nylon fast rope dropped at his shoulder, within arm's reach. He reached out for the rope even as, from above, an African-American man dressed in full Kevlar-weave tactical operation suit and wearing trifocal sonar goggles came sliding down, looking for all the world like Fisher himself.

Clutching the rope, Fisher managed to climb back up and onto the road, then he guided the rope toward the wall so that the man, Isaac Briggs, could hop onto the mud.

Briggs was a kid, really, just twenty-seven, former U.S. Army intel officer, former paramilitary ops officer with the CIA, current member of Fourth Echelon—which he liked to call 4E because he hailed from a world of e-books and theories and military history, a world dominated by acronyms and PowerPoints that, in the world according to Fisher, didn't mean jack when you were in the field. Briggs was a good guy, handpicked by Fisher, and he was just now escaping from the clutches of theory and learning to trust his instincts. No more company man for him. He worked for Fourth Echelon now.

"Got here as soon as we could," Briggs cried, tugging up the goggles and lifting his voice over the sound of the chopper.

Fisher shrugged. "Doesn't matter. This thing's gone to shit."

Ignoring the needling pain that seemed to come from every part of his body, Fisher led Briggs back toward the taxi, which was now hanging partially off the ledge. The stench of leaking gasoline and oil still rose through the rain as they drew near.

"Damn," Briggs gasped.

The taxi's engine was somewhere in the backseat. The driver's head—just his head—was lying on the rear dashboard, his severed left arm jutting from a rear window.

Fisher frowned at Briggs. "You're not gonna be sick, are you?"

"I was already sick of chasing this bastard around the world."

"Well, you got your wish. It ends here. And not well for us." Fisher glared at the chopper. "Call that bird. Tell him to bug out for a few minutes till we're ready for him."

Briggs nodded and barked orders into his radio.

Tensing, Fisher dropped to all fours, called for Briggs to hand him a flashlight, and let the beam play under the wreckage. He spotted one of Rahmani's legs, IDed by the color of the man's pants, shoved up into the cab's transmission, but the rest of him was missing.

Releasing another string of curses, Fisher sprang to his feet and directed the light across the road, the beam slowly exposing a trail of body parts near the wall, one they'd missed walking over because it was hidden in the shadows. They found the torso with the head still attached; it was lying among some rocks, the blood washing off in the rain.

Fisher was ready to strangle someone, and Briggs sensed that. He kept his distance, and without a word, they began a meticulous search of the body and scoured the rest of the road for anything Rahmani might have been carrying. Fisher found a small pistol, a beat-up old Makarov, but nothing else. Briggs snapped as many photos as he could before they gathered up the body parts in a "glad bag" and sent them up to the chopper when it returned.

Rahmani had been the best lead they'd had in locating that stolen uranium. That his group had pulled off the robbery was nothing short of miraculous, which had the world's intelligence communities assuming that it was an inside job. The general public had no idea what was happening, and the Russians were thus far tight-lipped about the entire affair. Sorry, nyet, this is state secret information.

The Mayak facility was two hours south of Ekaterin-burg, at the end of unmarked back roads, near a forested plateau of lakes and small rivers. It was protected by chain-link barbed-wire fences and a deforested strip of land that provided no cover. The facility had just been updated with a new electronic surveillance system provided by the United States and a radiation monitoring system that was well-nigh impossible to defeat—unless your name was Sam Fisher. The rest of its defenses were classified, but it was not reckless to assume that the Russians had a keen interest in guarding their nuclear material—especially when they'd been backed by the U.S. Congress to the tune of 350 million dollars to build a heavily fortified warehouse or "Plutonium Palace" to store approximately 40 percent of their military's excess fissile material.

Nevertheless, Rahmani and his unidentified cronies had not only broken into the facility but had managed to escape from it with their pockets glowing green. Their smuggling route was still a point of conjecture. Kazakhstan was only a four-hour drive to the south, but that course would've taken them through Chelyabinsk and many border checkpoints. They had more likely gone southwest, traveling some 1,200 miles or more to the Caspian Sea, with the goal of smuggling the uranium through Azerbaijan and into Turkey.

What's more, it took the Russian government more than three days to officially report the incident, giving the thieves ample time to escape the country. Whether the Russians were doing their own damage control or the theft was entirely unnoticed by their staff at the facility was a second point of conjecture.

A tip from the National Intelligence Organization of Turkey—Milli İstihbarat Teşkilatı, or MİT—led to a raid on a small machine shop in an industrial sector of Istanbul situated near slums where the noise of constructing a nuclear weapon was easily masked. And yes, Fisher had learned long ago that the process of nuclear bomb making was, in fact, quite loud, which seemed rather fitting, given the nature of the device.

Their raid—a joint effort between the United States

and Russia's own foreign intelligence service, Sluzhba Vneshney Razvedki, or SVR—had turned up little. Rahmani's group had already pulled up stakes before they'd fully moved in and begun constructing their weapon. The SVR agent operating with them was a sour-faced mute who offered little more than shrugs between playing on his smartphone. Fisher had suggested that Istanbul was merely a diversionary stop along their route. The SVR agent had agreed. Then shrugged. Then agreed again.

Bottom line: Rahmani had known where to find the uranium. And if he hadn't, he would've at least known the players who could point Fisher and his team in the right direction.

For now, though, all Fisher could do was stare through the rain as he was hoisted up to the chopper.

The mountainside seemed darker and even emptier now. El Camino de la Muerte had claimed three more victims, and Fisher should have been grateful that he hadn't been the fourth, but he wasn't. He felt only anger—knots of anger—tightening in his gut.

2

"**MONEY** is like alcohol," Igor Kasperov was telling the reporters from the *Wall Street Journal* as they toured his Moscow headquarters. "It's good to have enough, but it's not target. I'm here to be global police and peace-keeper. I'm here to do charity work everywhere. I'm here, I guess, to save our world!" He tossed a hand into the air and unleashed one of his trademark smiles that had been featured on the cover of *Time* magazine. The two gray-haired, bespectacled reporters beamed back at him.

Kasperov was no stranger to entertaining the press in the old factory that was now the headquarters of Kasperov Labs, one of the most successful computer antivirus corporations on the planet. That was no boast.

According to *Forbes*, between 2009 and 2012 retail sales of his software increased 174 percent, reaching almost 5.5 million a year—nearly as much as his rivals Symantec and McAfee combined. Worldwide, he had over 60 million users of his security network, users who sent data to his headquarters every time they downloaded an application to their desktops. The cloud-based system automatically checked the code against a "green base" of 300 million software objects it knew to be trustworthy, as well as a "red base" of 94 million known malicious objects. Kasperov's code was also embedded in Microsoft, Cisco, and Juniper Networks products, effectively giving the company 400 million users. His critics often quibbled over the accuracy of those numbers. He'd send them cases of vodka with notes that instructed them to relax and simply watch as Kasperov Labs became *the* world's leading provider of antivirus software.

To that end, Kasperov took enormous pleasure in employing hundreds of software engineers, coders, and designers barely out of college. This motley crew of pierced-and-tattooed warriors created a magnificent dorm room atmosphere that was, no pun intended, infected with their enthusiasm. They'd seen pictures of the playful Google offices in Mountain View, California, and had become, in a word, inspired. These reporters could sense that, and Kasperov played it up for them, joking around with the staff, high-fiving them like a six-foot-five rock star with unkempt sandy blond hair that he constantly tossed out of his face. His daily glasses of vodka had turned his cheeks ruddy, and last year he'd begun wearing bifocals, but he was still young enough for an American girlfriend barely thirty-two who'd modeled for Victoria's Secret among others. Surrounded by his youthful staff and his lover, he would defy time and live forever because life was good. Life was fun.

Without question, these uptight American journalists would refer to him as an oligarch in their reports, a continent-hopping mogul who'd made his fortune after the fall of the Soviet Union. They'd say he was a wild man who had the president's ear and was, like the country's other oligarchs, heavily influencing the government because of his connections and wealth. He would dismiss those shopworn claims and give them something more impressive to write about that would enthrall their readers. To begin, he would discuss the ambitious nature of his new offices in Peru and the great work he was going to do there.

They stood now on a balcony overlooking the hundreds of individually decorated cubicles and walls of classic arcade games. Banks of enormous windows brought in the snowscape and frozen Moskva River beyond. "It is wonderful, is it not?" he asked.

The reporters nodded, issued perfunctory grins, then launched quite suddenly and aggressively into their questions, as though the sheen of his celebrity and success had suddenly worn thin.

"What do you think about social media websites like Facebook, Instagram, and others?"

Kasperov refilled their vodka glasses as he spoke. "Freedom is good thing. We all know this. But too much freedom allows bad guys to do bad things, right?"

"So you don't like Facebook."

"I'm *suspicious* of these websites. We have VK here, right? It's like Facebook clone, very popular, even my daughter who's in college has account. But these websites can be used by wrong people to send wrong messages."

"You said freedom is a good thing. But exactly how much freedom do *you* have?"

"What do mean? I have much freedom!" He gestured with his drink toward the work floor. "And so do they."

Kasperov knew exactly what they were getting at, but he preferred not to discuss it.

In Russia, high-tech firms like his had to cooperate with the *siloviki*—the network of military, security, law enforcement, and KGB veterans at the core of President Treskayev's regime. Kasperov worked intimately with the SVR and other agencies to hunt down, expose, and capture cybercriminals who'd already unleashed attacks on the banking systems in the United States and Europe. In turn, the Kremlin had given him enough freedom to become the successful entrepreneur he was, but their arrangement was their business—not fodder for American journalism.

"You work very closely with the intelligence community here, don't you?"

"What is it they say in *Top Gun* movie? I could tell you, but then I must kill you, right?" He broke out in raucous laughter that wasn't quite mimicked by the reporters.

"Mr. Kasperov, there have been some allegations

linking you to the VK blackout during the elections. Some say you helped the government bring down the social media website to help quell the opposition. After all, they *had* struck a rallying cry on social media."

"I've already commented on that. I had nothing to do with this. Nothing at all. We detected no attacks on VK. None at all. We don't know what happened."

"And you don't find that—to use your word—*suspicious*?"

"Of course I do, but it's all been investigated and put to sleep. Don't you have any more fun questions? If not, I have some stories to tell you."

The journalists frowned at each other, then the taller one spoke up again: "Your company is valuable to the Kremlin, so do you think you can ever really be independent of it?"

Kasperov tried to quell his frustration. He had been told this would be an interview, not an interrogation. "There's no problem here. We work together the same way other companies work with American government. Executive orders by your past presidents provide exchange of data between private sector and government. Your Homeland Security regulates critical infrastructure, same as we do. We're very happy in this marriage."

He took a long pull on his vodka, then tipped his head and led them across the balcony to his office door. He ushered them inside, and they gasped over the mementoes of his past and world travels: an African lion mount from one of his safaris; thousands of rare artifacts and gem stones meticulously arranged in glass cases; walls of software boxes written in German and Chinese; Persian rugs splayed across the floor; a basketball jersey from the New Jersey Nets in a glass case, the NBA team owned by a Russian billionaire friend; photos of himself with celebrities and world dignitaries, including American President Patricia Caldwell and the pope; and finally, his dark green dress jacket from his tenure as an intelligence officer with the Soviet Army. His desk, which was loosely copied from the one located in the reception area of the British House of Commons building and cost more than a three-bedroom house in Liverpool, had an opaque glass top and a limestone front. On it sat a picture of himself with his parents before their house, a meager shack on the outskirts of St. Petersburg.

He gestured toward a sprawling leather sofa that, when the reporters sank deeply into the cushions, made them look like dwarves. Kasperov gesticulated more wildly now as he spoke: "Welcome to my life. A poor boy from St. Petersburg. I got lucky. But you know story, right?"

One of the reporters glanced at his notes. "At sixteen you were accepted into a five-year program at the KGB-backed Institute of Cryptography, Telecommunications, and Computer Science. After graduation, you were commissioned as an intelligence officer in the Soviet Army."

"Yes, but reason I'm here is because one day, I'm like on my computer, and it's virus there. This is long time ago, 1989. Every time I find new virus, I get more curious. I spend hundreds of hours thinking about them, working on them. This is how I made name for myself in Soviet Army." Kasperov glanced to the doorway, where, in the shadows, a man appeared, a familiar man whose presence suddenly dampened his mood.

"Mr. Kasperov, you've been touted around the world as a generous and remarkable businessman, but you have to admit, you're surrounded by others in your country who might not be quite as honest as you are. Oligarchs, mafia . . . How do you keep yourself above all the corruption?"

Kasperov glanced once more at the doorway and tried to keep a happy face. "I keep pictures of my family close to my heart. I keep pictures of children all over the world I've helped close to my heart. I know they need me and believe in me. I know this company can help me do great things because I believe in it."

"Do you think your company can help foster better relations between our nations?"

"Oh, I think it already has."

"I can see why you say that . . . Your girlfriend's an American. Any talk of marriage?"

He blushed. "No marriage yet. Now, gentlemen, you'll have to excuse me, I have another visitor. If you'll go downstairs, one of my best managers, Patrik Ruggov—we call him Kannonball—will show you exactly how we work with customer."

The journalists rose and Kasperov escorted them to the spiral staircase, then he returned to the man who'd been waiting for him in the shadows.

"Hello, Chern," Kasperov grunted in Russian.

"Igor, I see you are massaging your ego again."

Kasperov ignored the remark and stormed back into his office. Chern followed.

"Shut the door," Kasperov ordered him.

Chern smirked and complied.

Kasperov knew this man only by his nickname, "Chernobyl," aka "Chern." Leonine, with a prominent gray widow's peak and fiery blue eyes, Chern contaminated everything he touched and was often the bearer of bad news. While officially he was a member of the SBP, the Presidential Security Service, he served unofficially as President Treskayev's personal strong arm and courier.

"How is your daughter doing?" Chern asked.

"Very well."

"She's away at school, yes?"

"She just flew home for a short visit."

Chern grinned over that, then moved to the window at the far end of the office. He spent a long moment staring at the snow through the frosted glass, then lifted his voice. "There's someone else who needs to go home."

"And who's that?"

"Calamity Jane."

Kasperov nearly spit out his vodka. "Excuse me?"

"You heard me."

"That can't be possible."

Chern's eyes widened. "Are you that naïve?"

"I was told from the beginning that it was a deterrent, a deterrent that would *never* be used."

"Then you *are* that naïve."

Calamity Jane, named after the famous American frontierswoman, was created by Kasperov and a few of his lead programmers, most notably his man Kannonball. It was, in their estimation, the most malicious computer virus in the world; it not only would bring down the American banking system but would also render the country's GPS system useless by exploiting a systemic problem with the cryptographic keying scheme. The virus would take advantage of this weakness before Raytheon delivered to the U.S. Air Force its Next Generation Operational Control System, or OCX, with the GPS III, third generation, satellites. With banks and GPS offline, the virus would move on to major utilities. Of course, he and his team were the best people to construct such a piece of horrific code because as antivirus champions, they knew the enemy better than anyone.

"I need to think about this," said Kasperov.

Chern snorted. "There's nothing to think about. You're a brilliant man, Igor. You follow the news and world events. You understand the pressure. You know why it's come to this. All the other elements are falling into place."

Kasperov closed his eyes. Every time he consulted one of his news websites, there was a new threat to the motherland's interests.

The merging of local European missile systems into a NATO defense system now put each country's weapons under NATO command and standardized the command and control, along with local radar access and tactical communication systems. This gave NATO HQ the ability to launch each country's missiles. The system was coming fully online, and the Kremlin feared it would interfere with Russia's ability to launch their own preemptive strikes. The military had been threatening to attack the European sites for months . . .

The U.S. Navy's decision to home port many of its Aegis missile system–equipped ships throughout key Mediterranean ports served as a bold parry to Russia's opposition to American land-based missile defense installations in the region.

And then, of course, there was the recent surge of American natural gas being exported and sold to European nations at less than half the cost of the Russian natural gas those nations had been buying.

However, there was an even larger economic threat, one Kasperov himself had noted to the Kremlin:

European nations were aggressively developing thorium reactors, the so-called green reactors with their low levels of radiation, minimal waste materials, and outstanding safety features. Thorium, a white radioactive metal with nonfertile isotopes, was proving a viable substitute for nuclear fuel in reactors, and its demand was ever-increasing. In fact, the United States had just struck a deal to sell its current stockpiles of thorium, which were stored in Nevada, to European nations. These stockpiles would be used to bring hundreds of liquid fluoride thorium reactors—FLTR, pronounced *flitter*—on line throughout Europe, ultimately making Europe fossil fuel independent and destroying Russia's customer base there.

Finally, recent U.S. sanctions against countries like Syria and Iran, where Russia had strong economic interests, continued to tax the motherland's ability to sustain herself.

If this was a new cold war, it was one of economics under the umbrella of MAD—mutually assured disruption. There had to be a better way to address these problems.

Kasperov locked gazes with Chern. "This doesn't come from Treskayev. It comes from the men controlling him. They've forced him into this. They don't think he'll stand up to the Americans."

"And they're probably right. But that doesn't matter. We have our orders. We do our duty."

"I want to speak to the president."

Chern smiled weakly. "He won't take your call now. Igor, you've danced your little dance for long enough. And, from what I understand, you'll be able to walk away from this. The virus hides our involvement. We blame it all on the hackers you love to put in jail, the Estonian hackers and others. Sure, your company will suffer a blow, but you'll survive."

Kasperov averted his gaze, his stomach growing sour.

Suddenly, Chern was clutching his arms. "Igor, we must all make our sacrifices for the motherland."

"You're not asking me to guarantee an election here. You're asking me to cripple the economy of a nation that has been very good to me."

"No one's *asking*. You know what to do."

A chill began at the base of Kasperov's spine and wove

its way upward, into his chest. "I'm sorry . . . sorry for my reluctance. I was thinking of my employees and of all the families that would be affected by this."

"They will be okay. Will you?"

Kasperov steeled his voice. "You don't need to threaten me. We've come from the same place. We have the same heart. Do we have a timetable?"

"Yes, I'll be communicating that to you directly. I would expect sometime tomorrow. Now, it was good seeing you. I have a plane to catch."

Chern reached the door, hesitated, then glanced back at Kasperov. "We're trusting you, Igor." He nodded, opened the door, and left.

Kasperov fired his empty vodka glass across the room, spun around, then bit his fist, trying to hold in the scream boiling at the back of his throat.

Last week he was in Cancun, Mexico, speaking at a convention. He had Bill Gates to his left and former President Clinton to his right. Colleagues.

Two weeks ago he and his girlfriend, Jessica North, were in South Beach at a fashion show and enjoying cocktails.

Three weeks ago, he was having lunch in San Francisco with Virgin empire mogul Richard Branson and discussing his ticket aboard one of Branson's spacecraft.

The fairy-tale life would end today. No more rock star.

He began to lose his breath, eyes burning with tears. He glowered at his old Soviet uniform, then looked to the picture on his desk, the little boy there, the innocent little boy who would grow up to destroy the world.

They were asking too much. Their plan would not work. The truth would emerge and the motherland would become the pariah of the global community.

But if he failed to obey now, they would systematically tear apart his life. They would start with those he loved, then move on to the causes he loved, undermine and destroy the humanitarian work, punish him until he was a broken, bleeding, and bitter old man who'd "disappeared" but was, in truth, lying in a gulag and hunting roaches for dinner.

Again, this was not coming from the president. Kasperov knew this in his heart of hearts. Yes, Treskayev was a nationalist like his father, but he was also a pragmatist, spending much of his administration mending fences with the United States and Europe, earning him the ire of the imperialists. He wanted to call the man, beg him to stop this, but Treskayev might not even know what was going on. This could be bigger than all of them.

Kasperov backhanded the tears from his cheeks. If he did not comply, he, like the malicious objects identified by his own software, would be quarantined . . . then erased.

3

THE C147-B, call sign Paladin, had become Fourth Echelon's mobile headquarters and was cruising over the Atlantic at thirty thousand feet, traveling at a speed of Mach 0.74, or 563 mph. She was a fully customized C-17 Globemaster III with special composite matte gray fuselage that functioned as a Faraday cage, shielding her cutting-edge components from electromagnetic pulses. Her interior was TEMPEST certified up to and including NATO SDIP-27 Level A standards. Her avionics/comm circuits met RED/BLACK separation standards, and her computers were shielded against electromagnetic eavesdropping techniques called Van Eck phreaking. These countermeasures had been phased in after the jet's flight controls had been hacked, and Fisher had made damned sure that would never happen again.

With a length of 174 feet and wingspan just shy of 170 feet, Paladin was originally designed for heavy lift military cargo and troop transport and was powered by four fully reversible Pratt & Whitney F117-PW-100 turbofan engines similar to those used on commercial Boeing 757s. Her original cargo compartment was 88 feet long by 18 feet wide, with a ceiling height of over 12 feet, but now much of that open space had been converted into living quarters, a galley, a fully stocked armory with more than a thousand pieces of ordnance, an infirmary with complete surgical center, and a holding cell.

Located at the bay's core was Fourth Echelon's control center—a cocoon of flat-screen computer monitor stations, along with giant displays affixed to either side of the hatch leading to the infirmary. Cables lay like piles of spaghetti beneath the flickering glow of computer stations, and dim starlight filtered in through the circular portholes above them. The desktops of several junior analysts were piled with hard-copy files and seemingly every portable electronic device known to mankind: Kindles, iPads, iPods, and tablets of varying sizes, colors, and shapes. Heavily padded computer chairs sat on tracks bolted to the deck, and you could tell where Charlie Cole was working based upon the coordinates of a jar of extra-crunchy peanut butter with a fork jutting from it. The kid said Skippy helped him think.

Positioned at the center of this technological nest was

a rectangular-shaped table about nine feet long and six feet wide constructed of magnesium and titanium to support a glass touchscreen surface. This table with its linked processors was Fourth Echelon's Strategic Mission Interface, or SMI, an advanced prototype analytics engine capable of news and Internet data mining, predictive analytics, and photo and video forensics. The SMI enabled them to have backdoors into foreign electronic intelligence, or ELINT, systems, as well as facial recognition integration from the CIA, NSA, DHS, and FBI. They were linked directly to the National Counterterrorism Center and to the watch teams inside the White House Situation Room. In the blink of an eye they could pull up surveillance video from a hundred different locations simultaneously, analyze those videos, and issue a report.

Opposite the SMI, Sam Fisher leaned back in one of the computer chairs, pillowed his head in his hands, and reflected on his new life. Talk about a reboot. A breath ago he'd quit Third Echelon—once a top secret subbranch within the National Security Agency—but then he'd been caught up in a 3E conspiracy that had resulted in the entire covert ops organization being grounded and gutted, dismantled forever. Fisher assumed he'd never again be a Splinter Cell. He was done.

But then President Caldwell had come to him with an operation that required a man not only with his skill set but one with the internal fortitude to get the job done:

A coalition of rogue nations had come together to bankroll and support a terrorist group called the

Blacklist Engineers, who were bent on forcing the United States to withdraw its military forces from around the world. Their leader was Majid Sadiq, a former MI6 deep cover field agent and sociopath. The group's plan involved a "blacklist" of American targets that would be hit if the Americans did not comply.

Caldwell had sweetened the deal, told Fisher the entire op was off the books, no NSA jurisdiction, no open government involvement. She had granted him "the fifth freedom" to use any means necessary to take out the terrorists with no fear of prosecution. The freedoms of speech and worship, along with the freedoms from want and fear, had first been articulated by President Theodore Roosevelt. The fifth freedom was the freedom to protect the first four. Fisher had the right to defend our laws—by breaking them; the right to safeguard secrets—by stealing them; and the right to save lives—by taking them.

No more bureaucratic bullshit. No more politics. No more red tape. It was a covert operator's dream come true. Clandestine backing from the government without interference.

That Majid Sadiq had been dispatched and members of his group were dead or on the run was an important victory in the never-ending war on terrorism because it had proven that Fisher and his team were a viable asset.

Indeed, this was Fourth Echelon, and Fisher answered only to the President of the United States. He no longer worked alone in the field but relied upon his team. He'd come a long way since his early days of hanging out in a ventilation shaft at the Tropical Casino in Macau. However, the ghosts still hovered at his shoulders, the ghost of his old boss Lambert, a man whose life he had once saved but then had been forced to take . . .

"We're going over the files from Istanbul," came a voice from behind Fisher, jarring him back to the present. "But you still want to go back there?"

Fisher swung his chair around to face Anna "Grim" Grimsdóttir, her strawberry blond hair pulled back in a ponytail, her blue eyes narrowing with skepticism. She wore a black striped blouse and the shoulder harness for a SIG P229R 9mm pistol.

When he'd first met Grim, she never carried a weapon. She'd been secretly watching him run a CIA obstacle course at "the Farm," Camp Peary, Virginia. Her spying on him should've been his first clue that he couldn't trust her, but as they say, hindsight is twenty-twenty. She'd begun her career as a programmer, hacker, and analyst, providing assistance for Fisher while he was in the field. Over the years they became friends, sharing jokes about the use of lasers being so 1970s and hi-fi versus Wi-Fi in such globetrotting locations as skyscrapers in New York and banks in Panama City. Grim relished reminding him that he was "old," but her taunts were good-natured, and Fisher never took them lying down; in fact, he usually took them while suspended, inverted, from a rope.

Then, regrettably, their relationship had taken a very dark turn. They'd told him that his daughter, Sarah, was killed by a drunk driver.

That was a lie.

Grim had known the truth. For three long years he'd thought he had no reason to go on living, and she'd done nothing. Then, when 3E became gripped in conspiracy and corruption, she began working as a mole inside the organization, reporting directly to President Caldwell. Grim had used the promise of Fisher being reunited with his daughter to manipulate him into a mission he didn't want to take.

He'd thought what she'd done to him was unforgivable, but she'd apologized, told him she'd had little choice, that it was all for the greater good and that she'd do it all again if necessary. The venerable nickname "Ice Queen" had been used to describe her before, but that seemed insufficient. He'd never known she'd go to such great lengths to protect their country. He'd never known her at all, and the emptiness he felt over that revelation ached every day.

He studied her now, acutely aware that she had *not* wanted him in this position, that Fourth Echelon had originally been her initiative and she'd wanted to be its commander. She hadn't trusted his motives, but he thought he'd proven himself to her during the Blacklist mission.

"Grim, I know it's a long shot, but maybe we missed something. There has to be another connection."

"If there is, we'll find it. Charlie's acting like he's possessed right now."

"I'm glad you guys are getting along."

"I wouldn't go that far."

"I'm telling you, Grim, when we worked for Victor, the kid was amazing. And you have to admit, the SMI would be nothing without him."

Fisher was referring to his time working for his old Seal Team Two buddy Victor Coste, who'd formed Paladin 9, a private security firm. That's where Charlie Cole, the twenty-five-year-old technophile and brilliant programmer, had gone to work after Grim had booted him out of Third Echelon's R&D department—they'd been working on the SMI together—and that's where they'd taken the call sign for their aircraft after Vic was injured in the first Blacklist attack and closed up his firm. The name "Paladin" was a tribute to him and a historical reference to chivalrous and courageous knights.

Grim shook her head. "Charlie hasn't changed a bit. Still an uncompromising know-it-all who almost got us killed—"

Fisher frowned. "What're you talking about?"

Grim winced, as though she'd let something slip. "Look, he's great at what he does—"

"But what?"

"But I still don't know if I can trust him."

"Give him a chance."

"Oh, I will. That doesn't mean I'll take my eyes off him."

"Maybe I never earned your trust, but he will."

She took a deep breath. "Sam, we've been through a lot together. And we'll go through a lot more. The work always comes first."

"You're preaching to the choir."

"I know, but we can't let the past come between us."

"I'm glad you finally said that."

"Really?"

He smirked. "Yeah, because it's the understatement of the year. You think we'll ever trust each other?"

"We're gonna have to." She started off.

"Hey, Grim?"

She paused and glanced back.

"You made me realize I belong here. Not Vic. Not anyone else . . ."

A sheen came into her eyes before she turned and headed back to the SMI table.

Her reaction surprised him. It always seemed that her warmth and sympathy had been accidently uploaded and stored in the cloud instead of her heart. And admittedly, she was often a far better strategist than him, yet at the same time she was risk averse, unable to call an audible, and too worried about the consequences of going with your gut. But he needed her. More than ever.

Before he could ponder that further, the seal of the President of the United States appeared on their big screens, and Charlie came rushing out of his chair, tugging on the strings of his hoodie and raising his voice: "Got the POTUS on the line!"

"Good morning, everyone," said the president.

Patricia Linklater Caldwell was an absolute rarity in American politics, having reached the highest office in the land while single. Her husband, Tobias Linklater, had lived long enough to see Caldwell become a senator before he'd succumbed to pancreatic cancer. In many ways Caldwell was a survivor, having suffered the loss of her husband even as she weathered a tumultuous bid for the presidency and an assassination attempt after she'd been elected. As chief executive, she was results driven, did not frighten easily, and her willingness to get things done by taking quick action had easily won over Fisher. Knowing she lacked Fisher's perspective from the ground, she wasn't afraid to listen to his advice.

"Hello, Madame President. If this is about Rahmani, let me assure you—"

"I'll cut you off right there, Sam. I know you're on your way to Istanbul, but there's been a change of plans."

The SMI began flashing with imagery and data bars, and the big screens above the infirmary hatch displayed images of a handsome middle-aged man with long sandy blond hair and piercing eyes.

"I assume most of you recognize Igor Kasperov, founder and CEO of Kasperov Labs in Moscow."

"And one of the greatest antivirus programmers ever," added Charlie. "A legend like Gates, Jobs, and McAfee."

"That's right," said Caldwell. "And I've met him before. He's quite a character."

"What's going on?" Fisher asked.

"Just a few minutes ago his headquarters in Moscow abruptly shut down and his employees scattered. His offices around the world have been left hanging. No one knows where he is, but we just received some good HUMINT. Our agents in the Kremlin suspect that he wasn't taken prisoner by the government because a localized virus just infected security systems all over the city, bringing down surveillance cameras. They also report that the Federal Security Service has dispatched agents to all the transportation routes."

"I'm checking on all that now," Charlie said, drumming hard on his keyboard.

Fisher nodded. "Sounds like Kasperov is on the run."

"That's a pretty loud exit," said Grim. "If he wanted to bail, why didn't he sneak away?"

"Yeah, and why shut down the company—unless he was worried about reprisal or something? Did he want to save his employees? From what, though?" Fisher asked. "What's he running from?"

The SMI now glowed with a map of flashing blips marking the locations of Kasperov Labs offices around the globe. Grim tapped on Moscow and zoomed in on the Kasperov HQ.

Caldwell went on: "Between the robbery at Mayak and now Kasperov on the run, we've got something very dangerous going on in the Russian Federation, and maybe he knows what it is. Maybe he knows why the Russians are, as we speak, pulling their sovereign wealth funds out of American markets."

"You want us to find him?" Fisher asked. "We've still got a hundred pounds of weapons-grade uranium floating around out there—"

"Which I'm well aware of," she snapped. "It's time for a little multitasking. I want you to find Kasperov and extend my offer for protection and political asylum. While you're doing that, the Special Activities Division will back up your investigation to find the uranium. I need you to find that material *and* Kasperov."

"Madame President, sorry to interrupt," said Briggs from behind Fisher. "But if you want the CIA to back us, then let me suggest a few good operators."

"Excellent. You send me those recommendations."

"I will."

"But we're still off the books here," Fisher reminded the president.

"Of course. I don't think the CIA would have a problem with that, do you?"

Fisher cocked a brow at Briggs, who vigorously shook his head.

"Madame President, you think there's a link between the missing uranium and Kasperov?" asked Grim.

"That's what I need to know. As usual all our intel assets will be available to you."

"We're on it," said Fisher. "We'll get to Turkey and refuel there. Hopefully by the time we land we'll have a lead on Kasperov's location."

"Stay in touch. I'm counting on you."

The president's seal reappeared, then the screens went blank.

"Charlie, full profile on Kasperov," Grim ordered. "Right down to the brand of vodka he likes. Briggs, see what you can dig up on his employees, people from his past. We'll have the SMI analyze possible escape routes."

"Got something good already," said Charlie, who'd already been diving into his databases while the president was speaking. "He was married for thirteen years, but his wife died of ovarian cancer. They have a daughter, Nadia, now twenty. We'll locate her. Right now he's got an American girlfriend, Jessica North, super hottie. We can follow up with her entire family. Also, he was a Soviet intel officer. I'll search for old buddies. Says he attended the Institute of Cryptography. Could find an old teacher or somebody providing a safe house."

"Go for it," said Fisher.

Briggs chimed in: "Kasperov's right hand was a young guy named Patrik Ruggov, aka Kannonball. Big Russian bear. I'll see if I can find him. In the meantime, the NSA's telling us they've already flagged Kasperov's family members' and known intimates' landlines and cell phones for intercept. They've been logging in every incoming and outgoing phone call for the last couple of years."

"I'll get the SMI on that, too," said Grim.

Fisher was working through a sidebar on the SMI, sifting through magazine articles on Kasperov. "Jesus, this guy's been everywhere. He sponsors an F1 race team: Kasperov-McClaren. Maybe he's got contacts in one of the race cities. And look at this, he's hung out with rock stars all over the UK, going on pub crawls and taking his people on lavish company retreats in Costa del Sol, Monte Carlo, and Cancún. Says here he threw a New Year's Eve party with over a thousand guests. His company operates in more than one hundred countries. Gonna be tough to narrow down this search."

"No kidding," said Grim. "And that localized virus? It's affecting ATC over Moscow right now. Look at these reports."

Fisher scanned the airport map and the transcripts from intercepted radio transmissions. Domodedovo, Sheremetyevo, Vnukovo, Myachkovo, Ostafyevo, Bykovo, and Ramenskoye Airports were all reporting radar service disruptions, distortion, false blips on radar, and other unexplained interference.

"Like I said," Charlie began, "he's a genius. He won't do anything stupid like use a credit card or allow his face to be photographed. He knows where the security cameras are, and he knows all about facial recognition software. Hell, he wrote some of it. If he wanted to run, then he planned it well, used his expertise with computers and viruses to cover his ass. Maybe he's had an escape plan in place for years. The airport disruption suggests he flew out. We'll pull up every flight plan we can."

Fisher turned to the image of Kasperov glowing now on one of the big screens. "So, comrade, where are you going? Are you going to pull a Bin Laden and hide in the open? Or maybe something completely different."

"You've gone underground before," said Grim. "Where would you go if you were him?"

Fisher thought for a long moment but didn't answer.

4

MAJOR Viktoria Kolosov—code-named Snegurochka, the Snow Maiden—had tied her long, black hair into a neat bun. This was not because she preferred it that way, but because most times when she knifed a man he tended to flail about, reaching violently for anything he could grasp—and she liked her hair, thought it was one of her best features, didn't want any dying bastard to mess it up.

Unsurprisingly, Boris reached out as she punched the folding blade into his neck, ripped it free, then stabbed him in the heart, which was her original target before he'd turned and spoiled her whole attack.

As he fell to the asphalt with a gurgling "Why?" she raised the stolen PSS silent pistol at Oleg.

She cut loose with a pair of 7.62mm rounds that traveled at two hundred meters per second to impact squarely with his forehead, a textbook double tap that kicked him back into the old subway's crumbling wall.

The knife attack on Boris was quieter than the gun and gave her enough time to shoot Oleg before he realized what was happening. Besides, she liked variety when it came to killing. Blade, pistol, weak arm, strong arm. Also, a combination knife/gun attack was riskier than just shooting both of them in the back of the head. There was no sport in that.

She leaned over, wiping the bloody blade on Oleg's chest and thankful she had remembered her gloves, always a good idea when you planned to murder your partners. Was she insane? Of course not. This was an important operation with career advancement at stake, too important to share credit, so now the extra baggage was gone. Never mind the investigation into their deaths. There would be none. She would ensure that, too.

The Glavnoye Razvedyvatel'noye Upravleniye, or GRU, the motherland's foreign military intelligence agency, was headed by Sergei Izotov, who'd called upon any SVR operatives in the immediate area. They were to capture Igor Kasperov's twenty-year-old daughter, Nadia, after the girl had made the fatal mistake of posting a status update to her VK page, saying good-bye to Moscow. She was, the SVR had assumed, rushing to the airport to link up with her father.

While a domestic job like this ordinarily belonged to the FSB, the Snow Maiden, Boris, and Oleg had been heading out to their airport themselves to catch a plane to Poland when they'd picked up the daughter's limousine. Nadia and her four bodyguards had either spotted the tail or been tipped off.

The Snow Maiden had enjoyed taking out both tires on the limo and forcing them off the road, but it seemed the bodyguards had already planned an alternate escape route and had reached it in the crippled limo. They took Nadia on foot into the "third basement" of Moscow State University, entering Metro-2, the informal name for the secret underground metro system that paralleled the public Moscow Metro. The Snow Maiden wondered if Kasperov and his people were also privy to the Yastreb Complex, that highly classified subterranean fortress beneath Red Square. These were all part of an interconnected system supposedly built during Stalin's reign and code-named D-6 by the KGB. The tunnels, subway, and secure bunkers provided a fast and secure means of evacuation for leadership through concealed entryways and into protective quarters beneath the city, helping to maintain national command authority during wartime. The trains themselves were safeguarded by electronic surveillance and a small garrison of troops. Nadia's bodyguards seemed to know about that, too, and they were escorting her down a series of abandoned access tunnels that ran adjacent to the tracks and well out of sight and earshot of that garrison. This section lacked any security and was, in effect, a dilapidated maze leading toward the VIP terminal at Vnukovo Airport.

The Snow Maiden sprinted off and turned left into

the first arching entranceway, spotting the shifting lights in the distance. The bodyguards had improvised on the fly, using the flashlight apps on their smartphones to lead the way. The Snow Maiden did likewise. She grimaced as the musty scent grew thicker and the cobwebs wafting down from the ceiling blew across her face. The concrete walls were scarred by rust and mold, and the floors alternated between dirt-covered concrete and what felt like mushy earth.

One of the bodyguards broke off at a T-shaped intersection, turning right while the rest of the group went left. He knew exactly what he was doing, thinking he'd ambush her from behind as she was forced to go after the others.

She ran straight up to the intersection, dropped to her stomach, then shifted the pistol to her weak hand and peered around the corner, her cheek just off the floor.

His light shone on her. She answered with three rounds, the clicks barely echoing as she sprang up and saw he was down, his head blossoming with blood. The other two rounds had struck him in the chest, but he was wearing a vest, probably an old Level IIIA. He was middle-aged and former military, judging from his weapon, crew cut, and tattoo on his wrist. She snatched up his 9mm pistol, an MP-443 Grach, the latest standard issue military sidearm with a seventeen-round magazine. She tucked the pistol into her belt and winked at the dead man. That he'd been killed by a woman had probably annoyed him to no end. She'd bet on it. If he would've known she was just the daughter of a simple schoolteacher and car transporter from Vladivostok— not some assassin prodigy raised by a military family— he'd feel even worse.

Three to go. She raced back through the intersecting tunnel, the group's footfalls unmistakable ahead. The tunnel grew narrower, the concrete support structures turning to wooden beams that resembled railroad ties for a long section, the floor speckled with rat feces.

Nadia was wearing a strong perfume that stood out sharply, and the Snow Maiden reached another intersection where for a moment she thought she'd have to rely on only her sense of smell until a slight thump to the right set her off again toward two more intersections.

They were staging another ambush. She could feel it.

Suddenly, dead silence, only her footfalls.

She stopped, waited, then shifted to the wall and crouched down, slipping her phone into her leather jacket's inner breast pocket. She let her eyes readjust.

With both hands, she clutched her pistol and aimed for the intersection.

Still nothing . . .

Back in the car, on the way here, Boris had been smoking a cigarette and asking why they called her the Snow Maiden. She'd never worked with him before, and it'd been interesting to explain it to him, even as she was plotting his death.

Snegurochka was the Snow Maiden in Russian folklore. In one tale she was the daughter of Spring and Frost. She fell in love with a shepherd, but when her heart warmed, she melted. In another narrative, falling in love transformed her into a mortal who would die. In a third story she was the daughter of an old couple who created her from snow. She leapt over a fire and melted.

Major Viktoria Kolosov felt a special attachment to the character that stemmed from something deep in her subconscious. Never warm your heart? In this business, maybe so.

She was holding her breath now, thinking about the single round left in her magazine, the spare six-round mag still tucked in her hip pocket, and the bodyguard's Grach pressing against the small of her back. She should change guns now but feared making even the slightest movement.

The shadows seemed to collect on the left side of the intersection, and then she saw the silhouette of a head peering around the corner.

She fired, a spark leaping off the wall, damn it. There wasn't even time to curse. She was already rolling across the floor while reaching into her waistband for the Grach. By the time she came out of her roll, she had the pistol and was raising it while the bodyguard returned fire, three rounds booming and stitching across the floor, extending from her ghost to her current position hunkered down at the opposite wall.

Going asymmetric in a gunfight was not a technique for amateurs or veterans turned bodyguards, men too often married to their conventional tactics. She proved that to this oaf by sensing his pause to check fire.

She sprinted straight up the tunnel in the pitch

darkness, spun right, and caught the whites of his eyes as he was just lifting his gun.

Simultaneously, she grabbed his pistol and shot him in the head.

Not a half second later, she dropped to the floor as the guy behind her, the guy whose curse of surprise had given him away, fired above her head.

With her chin buried in her chest, the pistol down low near her knee, she squeezed off two rounds that sent him staggering back.

But he didn't fall, and the shots must've gone high or wide, striking him in the arm or shoulder. She fired once more and he finally dropped.

Thump. Silence again.

She was panting and wincing over the stench of gunpowder. Her ears rang from all the close-quarters gunfire.

Shuddering over how much time she'd wasted here, she sprang up, ejected and pocketed the magazine from one of the bodyguards, then tugged free her phone, its narrow beam now lighting the way.

The last bodyguard would present the greatest challenge. She had to eliminate him without inadvertently killing Nadia, the spoiled little rich girl who, of course, was a research student at ETH Zurich's Swiss National Supercomputing Centre, CSCS. ETH was considered one of the finest schools in Europe, and daddy had footed the entire bill. Poor baby was having a bad day, wasn't she?

The Snow Maiden snorted and raced up the tunnel

for some thirty meters where it terminated at another T-shaped intersection. Straight ahead hung a small hatch cracked open. She shone the light on the door's hinges, the rust freshly caked off. She hustled through, emerging into a much broader tunnel at least six meters wide where piles of old railroad ties rose several meters and pieces of track lay in dusty piles. At the far end of the conduit was another opening, the hatch removed from the doorway and propped up against the wall. She assumed that the final bodyguard would want to keep moving, no doubling back to ambush her, so the Snow Maiden picked up the pace. She practically blasted by the doorway and followed the tunnel to the right, where at the far end, some fifty meters away, a faint cry echoed off like a dying bird.

And there it was again. That perfume.

Gritting her teeth and tucking her arms close to her sides, she ran a marathon up that tunnel, the light bobbing wildly, the ceiling suddenly rumbling from a train passing overhead. Dust and debris flitted down as she gasped, wondering if the entire tunnel might collapse.

The next passage bore to the right, the walls closing in like a compactor, just wide enough for one person now. She slowed and held her light high above her head like a lantern—

And there they were, twenty meters ahead. The bodyguard was helping Nadia off the floor from where she'd fallen. Her jeans were torn at the knee and bloody, and her dirty blond hair hung down in her face, just like her father's.

The bodyguard spotted her light, shoved Nadia forward into a side tunnel while at the same time opening fire.

The Snow Maiden crouched as two rounds pinged at her shoulder, the sparks on her periphery, the bullets so close she felt their wind.

Damn, it'd be a bitch to die here. She was just a few months away from marrying Nikolai Antsyforov, a physician ten years her senior who'd not only swept her off her feet but who appreciated her job, her position, her strength. At the moment he was in Paldiski, Estonia, treating workers involved in a reactor accident. He was fresh out of medical school, and his passion, like hers, knew no bounds.

Remembering all she had to lose was wrong and weakened her. She was better than this, better trained. She blinked away the thoughts and burst forward, crossing to the opposite side of the tunnel. He fired again, this time hitting the floor not a finger's length from her boot.

Just as he doused his light, she hit the ground again, heard their footfalls. They were making another break.

She reached the side tunnel and hunkered down. She peered around the corner and saw them charging away, the bodyguard shielding Nadia.

Holding her breath, the Snow Maiden came around the corner, raised the gun with both hands, and took aim.

The pistol cracked, and the single round struck the bodyguard in the right thigh.

Good enough. She charged like a pole-vaulter ready to launch herself into the air.

As he collapsed and then rolled back to fire, she dug her right boot into the side wall, then flew forward, the bodyguard trying to get a bead on her before she collided with him.

Together, they fell back onto the floor—which abruptly collapsed, this entire section reinforced with rotting wooden beams that she noticed at the last second. Nadia, who'd been just behind the bodyguard, fell through the hole as well, and all three of them plunged some five meters into yet another tunnel, this one flooded with inky black water rushing up around them.

Never losing her grip on the bodyguard, the Snow Maiden felt the concrete bottom slam into him. As the impact reverberated into her arms, she kicked out and realized she could stand, the water barely more than a meter deep. With Nadia coughing and screaming behind them, the Snow Maiden wrapped her gloved hands around the stunned man's throat, then drove him back into the water. His hands locked around her own wrists. He tried to kick with his one good leg, the other still bleeding profusely from the gunshot wound.

The Snow Maiden raged aloud, her own cries echoing down the tunnel. The bodyguard was twice her size, twice as strong, and he was beginning to tear free of her grip—when he suddenly went limp. She screamed and shoved him back into the water, where he floated, inert.

She spun around to face the crying college girl, who stood there, trembling. She was barely visible in the faintest of light from their smartphones shining down through the jagged hole above.

"What do you want?" the girl managed.

"You," the Snow Maiden snapped.

"My father has a lot of money. He'll take care of you. Okay?"

Narrowing her eyes on the girl, the Snow Maiden started toward her. Nadia shifted a few steps back, sloshing through the water, but the Snow Maiden kept coming.

"Please, you obviously know who I am. We can settle this right now. I'll pay you whatever you want. Just get me to the airport. Whatever it is you want, no matter how much, we'll give it to you."

Lifting her hand and shushing the girl, the Snow Maiden approached and said, "You haven't worked for a thing in your entire life, have you?"

"That's not true."

"You think you can buy your way out of anything."

Nadia's lip quivered. "You police are all corrupt, aren't you?"

"I'm not the police. I'm much worse."

"If you do anything to me, my father will find you. He'll find you, and your family, and everyone you care about."

The Snow Maiden couldn't help but grin. She drew a little closer, then suddenly clutched the girl by the throat with both hands. "Where money speaks, the conscience is silent."

"Stop . . ."

It took everything she had not to kill this little bitch with her endless supply of rubles, a girl who had no idea what squirrel meat tasted like because her father's business was hurting, who'd never shivered at night under four blankets because her house had no heat.

The Snow Maiden tightened her grip. "Now tell me. Where is your father?"

Before the girl could answer, shouts came from above. That'd be the garrison, drawn by all the gunfire. The Snow Maiden glanced up the hole, then back to Nadia.

She shoved the girl back into the water, then lifted her fingers to form a gun. "Bang, bang, bang—just like that you die. So where is he?"

Nadia trembled violently. "I don't know."

FISHER took another long pull on his cup of coffee, then rested his palm on the back of Charlie's computer chair. "Anything else?"

"Well, I thought I got past the virus Kasperov used to infect the security camera systems, thought it was an old spaghetti code variation—some old-school trick—but it must've been on a timer and just shut itself down. Interesting. Looking at Kasperov's duplex now; it's in a gated community bordering a park in Moscow." Charlie raked fingers through his short black hair, then pointed to a satellite map shimmering on one of his screens. He zoomed in to a 3-D view showing the buildings. The screen to the left was the black-and-white security camera feed, with a half dozen men posted outside the main entrance. "Looks like the police are getting their party on at Kasperov's house. Same deal at his headquarters. They're moving all the hardware into trucks, confiscating everything."

"You thinking about going in there?" Briggs asked from his station opposite Charlie's.

"Be a waste of time," Fisher answered. "Like Charlie said, he's planned this well, wiped all of his hard drives. There's nothing to find there."

Grim lifted her voice from the SMI table. "I'm sure if he's left the country they've got the SVR looking for him, but they'll take it one step further and bring in Voron."

Fisher looked at her. "I was thinking the same thing. And if that's the case, we'll play our ace in the hole."

Voron, which meant "raven" in Russian, was a clandestine group within the SVR whose existence was known only by a select few within the government. They were tasked with sabotage, corporate theft, and "talent extraction," as well as other tasks from which even the SVR wanted to distance itself. Fisher had initially classified the group as a mirror image of the old Third Echelon, but more recently, when 3E's assets went dark all over South India, Fisher and Grim realized that Voron had gone fully rogue and had access to Third Echelon's intel—a frightening thought. Still, the team hadn't been without leads. Fisher knew a former Voron operative who'd become a valuable asset, a man left for dead but who was now very much alive.

Mikhail Andreyevitch Loskov, whose code name was

Kestrel, had run a joint operation with a Splinter Cell known as Archer; however, Kestrel was betrayed by Tom Reed, Third Echelon's corrupt leader. Shot in the head and left for dead, Kestrel was destined to live out his days as a prisoner in Russia, placed in a medically induced coma, and would only be awakened when the men controlling him needed something, such as intel on Third Echelon's operations or other Federation secrets Kestrel might know. It had been up to Fisher and Briggs to rescue the man—and they had.

Consequently, Fisher had made a deal with Kestrel. Once he'd learned what Kestrel had given up to Voron, he released the man. Kestrel said he was returning to Russia. He planned to settle the score with those who'd been using him and who'd forcibly extracted that intel.

Kestrel owed his life to Fisher and Briggs, but he was not a man who could be owned by guilt or gratitude. He'd suffered a lot of hardships in his life, had lost his parents in a terrorist attack, and had watched his army teammates being tortured and killed by Chechens. He was a stubborn Russian bastard, but he'd vowed to keep in touch with Fisher, even offered to sell him information when he acquired it. The last time they'd spoken, Kestrel had said he was "freelancing" in the Federation, ever prepared to exact his vengeance.

"Any luck getting us into the SVR?" Briggs asked Charlie.

"Are you kidding? Kasperov helped design their firewalls. It'll be the hack of the century. But I'm not giving up. Some files are air gapped, but I may have found a backdoor that actually takes us through a front door, then it lets us sit there through a rootkit application."

"Tell me more about this backdoor," Grim said, raising a cautious brow.

"Oh, you don't want to know."

Grim cleared her throat. "Excuse me, I need to know."

Fisher leaned closer to Charlie and said, "Play nice."

Charlie alternated his gaze between Grim and Fisher, then finally sighed. "All right, so the SVR's pumping tons of cash into R&D with a focus on social media networks like VK and Facebook. They've got a three-tiered program for the future of the Internet. They call these tiers Monitor-3, Dispute, and Storm-13. That last one, Storm, involves an army of spambots that'll flood social networks with propaganda to influence public opinion."

"So how does that get you inside?" asked Fisher.

"Well, there's a double connection here. Kasperov's boy genius, the guy named Kannonball? He was tagged as the lead programmer on this project."

"So he was working for the SVR and Kasperov?" asked Briggs.

"Yeah, sure, it's like the SVR is a client. What's more interesting, though, is that after he created their spambot army, he was tagged by the SVR as being a member of a hacktivist group known as Redtalk. They've been leaking secrets about corruption within the Russian government and military."

"Like another WikiLeaks," Fisher concluded.

"Yeah, but smaller and more specific. They probably

didn't touch Kannonball because he was so close to Kasperov."

"I guess this is the long explanation of how you intend to get into their computers," said Briggs through a yawn.

Charlie grew more animated, waving his peanut butter fork at Briggs. "Kannonball's already hacked in, and he's left his signature on some of the code for the social media spambots. In fact, I have to study it some more, but he may have left more clues there."

"You mean like passwords to get in?" Fisher asked.

"Exactly. That's Redtalk's MO. That's our front door into the SVR."

"Or we could just call Kestrel," Fisher said with a smile. "Old-school wins again. Grim? Find me Kestrel."

"Will do."

Charlie snickered. "You're a real thread killer, Sam. I was on a roll!"

"I know. And still, there's no guarantee the SVR or Voron are doing any better than we are right now, but we need to keep tabs on them."

Grim raised her voice. "Charlie, I want to see everything you're doing to get in there. Don't make a move until we're both sure they can't track us."

Charlie nodded, then lowered his voice and turned to Fisher. "Can I talk to you for a minute?"

Fisher nodded and Charlie rose, leading him out of the command center, down a narrow hall, and toward the living quarters. He opened a small hatch and invited Fisher into his tiny room, replete with narrow bed, notebook computers, and a few posters for alternative rock bands that Fisher had never heard of. Charlie shut the hatch and quickly said, "If you want to find this guy, you gotta cut me loose. I can't work with her breathing down my neck."

"She's not breathing down your neck."

"Are you deaf?"

"Look, you know where she's coming from."

He rolled his eyes. "It was hard enough taking the job in the first place, knowing she'd be here."

"I thought you guys were getting along."

"It's nothing that interferes with the job, but—"

"But you have a problem with authority figures. I get that. So do I."

At twenty-five, young Charlie Cole was still grappling with remaining calm under fire—especially when the incoming came from Grim. During the time he and Fisher worked together at Vic's old agency, Fisher had learned a lot about the kid, learned why he had the attitude and why he'd become a hacker. Charlie had lost his father when he was just eleven, and his mother remarried a man who ruled with an iron fist and had ridiculous expectations for him. He buried himself in his room and retreated into computers. While his mother supported his interest, by the time he was fourteen, his stepfather had shipped him off to Choate Rosemary Hall, the prestigious boarding school in Connecticut, where he'd terrorized administrators with his hacking exploits. They forced him through the program because it was easier than kicking him out. He was a classic genius underachiever. He went on to the Rochester

Institute of Technology because his grades wouldn't get him into MIT like the rest of his friends, and after that, some of his online exploits had caught the attention of the NSA and he was quickly rolled into Grim's R&D group at Third Echelon.

He didn't last long. He was immature, had an uncompromising vision for what the SMI should be, and Grim summarily fired him. That he'd flipped her a double bird on the way out didn't help. He'd tried a few scrub jobs, even moonlighted for two weeks as an IT temp under false credentials, until some of the people he'd hacked in the past came looking for him, including members of a Mexican drug cartel he'd once helped expose, or "dox," by revealing all of their personal information online.

Vic's private security firm had rescued him from all that, literally saving him when the Mexicans had sent two hit men to teach him a final lesson. Vic took him under his wing, and Charlie helped support some deftly executed operations for private clients. Despite his youth, his defiance of authority, and his often brash and animated demeanor, Charlie possessed a rare combination of go-with-your-gut instincts coupled with a cunning and always up-to-date knowledge of complex computer systems and code.

And if you wanted to get deeply psychological about it, you could say that he'd become all of these things because he was searching for his lost father, wanting answers for why the man had left him so long ago.

Charlie rubbed the corners of his eyes and nodded. "Grim's intense. I get that. But sometimes she's gotta back off. I'm afraid to say anything—because I know you'll take the heat for it."

"You just do your job. She'll keep you honest."

"I got the feeling that when you first came on board, you didn't want her around."

"This was her initiative, nonnegotiable with the president."

"So why didn't you walk away?"

Fisher steeled his voice. "Because they need us. The country needs us. Remember that."

"Hey, Sam?" came Briggs's voice from the hallway. "Got something else here. Apparently, the Russian government just pulled Kasperov's license. His company is officially shut down. At least for now."

Fisher met up with Briggs and followed him back to the command center with Charlie in tow.

"Sam, we're still analyzing all the flights out of every airport around Moscow at the time Kasperov might've bolted," said Grim. "The radar distortion has made that tough."

"So did any of Kasperov's jets take off?"

"Well, not according to the flight plans, but I'm sure he didn't file one. And he probably didn't take his own plane. Maybe a friend's with falsified docs."

An alert screen flashed in the upper right corner of the SMI's main screen. Grim dragged and dropped a new data window into the center of the display then opened it. "Well, it can't be this easy, can it? We've just confirmed that one of Kasperov's private jets did take off from Vnukovo Airport, actually just *after* the radar interruption. Flight plan indicates that the jet's bound for Tbilisi, the capital of Georgia. Says there's three passengers on board, along with two crew members."

"That doesn't make any sense," said Charlie. "Again, he wouldn't use his own plane and wouldn't file a flight plan."

"I agree," Grim answered.

"Decoy?" asked Fisher.

"Hard to say. Maybe a decoy to buy him time? Divert forces away from him?"

"Yeah, he's a smart bastard, because he knows that jet's a decoy we can't ignore. No matter what, we have to check it out."

"I'll see what assets we have in Georgia, get some people to Tbilisi before that plane arrives."

"I've got the rest of the flight plans for that bird," said Charlie. "Looks like his daughter, Nadia, was on board, flew back home from school in Zurich a few days ago."

"Maybe that's not his escape route but hers?" asked Fisher.

"Why wouldn't he cover her exit as well as he covered his own?" asked Grim.

"I don't know."

"We'll have to follow that plane."

Fisher nodded, then crossed over to Briggs. "You dig up anything else?"

"His girlfriend was born and raised in Orlando. She attended the University of Central Florida. She's got parents and a brother still living near there in a place called Winter Springs. We've got eyes on the house, and the NSA's got the comms covered."

"Any other possibilities?"

"In one of his gazillion magazine interviews, he spoke very highly of one of his old teachers from encryption school, a Professor Halitov. He retired in a little town called Peski, southeast of Moscow."

"So if he went there, he's hiding right under their noses."

"Yeah, but you know if we found it this easily, so did they. We'll keep an eye on it, though."

"Hey, Sam?"

Fisher ventured back to the SMI table and stood opposite Grim. "What do you got?"

"A crazy thought. What if this whole thing's a hoax? What if Kasperov staged this event with the government's help? They're in on this together."

"For what purpose?"

"The company's in bed with the FSB. Maybe there was a breach, and they staged this to contain it."

"Well, if that's the case, we're taking the bait."

"Or maybe there *is* a Mayak connection and this is their first stage in dealing with it."

"Hey, excuse me, but Nadia Kasperov has a VK account," Charlie said. "I hacked it and her last post was her saying good-bye to Moscow."

Fisher cocked a brow. "So she bolted, too. If we find her, maybe we'll find him."

"Holy shit."

That expletive had come from the SMI table, where Grim was bringing up Keyhole satellite surveillance footage, along with imagery captured by the U.S. Army's latest Vertical Take-Off and Landing Unmanned Aerial System dubbed the "Hummingbird."

Fisher reached the table and scanned the schematics of the drone, displayed on a data bar to his right.

Equipped with the ARGUS array composed of several cameras and a host of other sensor systems, the Hummingbird and her systems were capable of capturing 1.8 gigapixel high-resolution mosaic images and video, making it one of the most capable surveillance drones on the planet.

At the moment, the UAV had her cameras and sensors directed at a rugged, snowcapped mountainside with a long pennon of black smoke rising from it.

"What?" asked Fisher.

"That's Dykh-Tau," said Grim. "It means 'jagged mount' in Russian. It's about five klicks north of the Georgia border, and it's the second-highest peak in the Caucasus Mountains."

"That's a pretty big fire down there."

"That's not just a fire. Kasperov's plane just crashed."

"Was it shot down?" asked Briggs.

"Don't know," answered Grim. "No reports of aircraft scrambled, nothing on radar."

"What's our ETA over that site?" asked Fisher.

Grim brought up the maps, worked furiously on the touchscreen, and then the SMI drew the line and displayed the data bars. "If we divert from Incirlik right now, it'll be eighteen minutes at top speed."

"The Russians will send in some S&R crews. Think we can beat 'em?"

Grim consulted the SMI and pinpointed the locations of the nearest military bases and local authorities equipped with air power. "That location's pretty remote. You've got a shot. But the sun doesn't set for another two hours, and if you HALO jump right in there, they'll spot your descent."

"I know. I've got a work-around."

"What about getting out?"

"That part always gives me a headache. You mind calling us a cab or something?"

Grim rolled her eyes. "I'll see what I can do."

Fisher hustled away from the table. "Briggs? Come with me. We've got a lot of prep and no time."

The man rose from his station. "Sam, you mind if we make sure our extraction plan's in place before we . . ." The young man drifted off, and wisely so, because Fisher was already ignoring him—

But he did turn back and fix Briggs with a hard look. "Is there a problem?"

"Uh, no."

"Good. Because the jump alone might kill you. Let's go."

6

PALADIN'S cargo bay had been sealed off from the rest of the pressurized aircraft so that the side door and rear loading ramp could be opened to take on cargo or make hasty departures. The bay was still large enough to stow a small helicopter with the rotors removed but significantly smaller than an unmodified C-17 capable of carrying more than 100 paratroopers and 170,000 pounds of cargo.

Fisher stood near the door, double-checking Briggs's gear while Briggs did likewise for Fisher. The loadout was always the same, each item meticulously chosen and inspected by Fisher before it was ever stowed on board the plane. They each wore an HGU-55/P ballistic helmet, tactical goggles, an MBU-12/P oxygen mask,

Airox VIII O2 regulator, Twin 53 bailout bottle assemblies, tac-suits, gloves, and high-altitude altimeters.

The final piece of gear was, of course, the topic of conversation:

"How do you like that squirrel suit?" Fisher asked Briggs over the radio.

The man extended his arms to reveal the black wings. "I'm proud to wear it."

"You look like a dork."

Briggs raised his brows. "That makes two of us."

Fisher repressed his grin. "Your record says you've made a few jumps."

"A few."

Fisher nodded. "So . . . two hundred twenty-six miles per hour . . ."

"What's that?"

"That's the world record speed for the fastest wing-suit jump. I think we can beat it."

Briggs's eyes widened from behind his mask. "Do you mind if we don't?"

Fisher spun the man around, giving his MC-5 parachute rig a final inspection. The chute added considerable bulk and cut down on aerodynamics but tended to come in handy if they chose to actually survive their HALO—high altitude low opening—jump. Briggs checked Fisher's suit and flashed him a thumbs-up.

"All right, gentlemen, stand by," said Grim. "Thirty seconds."

Fisher levered open the side door, then slid it over until it locked in place. The icy wind whooshed inside and nearly knocked him off his feet. He immediately joined Briggs on one knee to clutch metal rungs attached to the deck. Leaving the aircraft even a few seconds too soon or too late would severely affect their infiltration. Grim was using the SMI to calculate their entire jump, from the second they left the plane until the second they should, in theory, touch down on the surface within a quarter kilometer of the crash site—if not closer. The SMI factored in all the data such as the "forward throw" while exiting the aircraft; the "relative wind"; the air temperature, wind speed, and direction; the barometric pressure; and how much pizza Fisher had eaten for lunch—well, perhaps not that last part.

Out beyond the door, the clouds were backlit in deep orange and red, and the setting sun coruscated off the wing tip. Fisher cleared his mind of the clutter, the past, the pain, the torn loyalties, the nightmares he'd had over that time Grim had shot him in the shoulder, which had been part of her plan to undermine Tom Reed.

On cold days like this the shoulder still ached. But that was okay. He'd told her to do what she had to do. And he was still here, ready to show Briggs the ride of a lifetime.

"Okay, stand by," said Grim. "Remember, radio blackout once you pop chutes. In five, four, three, two . . ."

The flashing red light above the door turned green.

Without hesitation, Briggs vanished into the ether.

Fisher shivered through a breath, the adrenaline coursing through his chest. No matter how many times you did it, every step into oblivion was a tremendous rush.

The loadmaster was there to shut the door behind him. He gave the young airman first class a curt nod, which she returned, then he threw himself out of the aircraft.

The wind struck a massive blow to his body, wrenching him far and fast. The disorientation was normal and no reason to panic. Reflexes and training took over, muscle memory causing him to extend his arms and legs so the wingsuit would catch air. The roar of the wind deepened as he straightened his spine and pushed his shoulders forward. Since his entire body was now acting as an airfoil, he need only adjust his arms, legs, and head to maneuver deftly through the air.

Briggs was down below, appearing as a black hourglass against a mottled backdrop of snowcapped mountains and an almost imperceptible thin line of smoke. He, too, knew they needed to cover a great distance, so like Fisher, he was now lowering his chin against his neck, rolling his shoulders even farther forward, and pushing the wingsuit into a head-low position downwind while narrowing his arms. Decreasing the amount of drag always increased velocity, and you always sacrificed altitude in order to gain speed. Indeed, HALO jumps were dangerous enough, but a wingsuit insertion from nearly thirty thousand feet opened a whole new world of hazards, including unrecoverable spins that led to blackouts and unhappy endings. Moreover, they hadn't had much time to pre-breathe 100 percent oxygen beforehand, so the possibility of getting the sort of "bends" that sometimes accompanied scuba diving was still there.

Briggs banked to the left, aiming for the smoke and mountains, and Fisher began twisting his arms and legs in small but appreciable movements to drop in behind the man. The key was to make gradual changes, no sharp or chaotic moves that could result in a loss of control. As a former SEAL, Fisher likened the maneuvering to swimming underwater and shifting one's body to change direction. Flight was simply the relationship of four opposing forces: weight, lift, thrust, and drag, and as expected, Grim adroitly reminded him of those facts:

"Sixteen thousand feet and falling. Airspeed 191. Your glide ratio looks excellent. On target."

They might be on course, but that airspeed was too slow for Fisher. "Tighten it up, Briggs. Let's get in there a little faster."

"Roger that."

Briggs narrowed his position even further and dropped like a missile, picking up so much speed that Fisher found it difficult to follow his lead.

"Airspeed 210," reported Grim. "Take it easy, Briggs."

"I'm good. I'm good."

"Sam, you're up to 215. Slow down! You can't afford to get sick."

Fisher rolled his wrist slightly inward to check his altimeter and airspeed, verifying it against Grim's report. He shifted his arms a little wider. No, he wasn't going to break any records today. They'd never get reported anyway. And who knew if that speed record still held? He'd read that report a few months prior. Better to just take a deep breath and enjoy the ride.

He soared in behind Briggs, and they swooped down like a pair of vultures, tiny against the mountains, impossible to see by most distant aircraft whose radar systems would filter out slower moving blips like themselves, mistaking them for birds.

His breathing grew even as they approached the mountainside and the long rings of talus and scree scattered like broken necklaces across the valley. The peaks thrust up in crystalline white arches that made him feel insignificant. These were the Caucasus Mountains, a broad range considered the dividing line between Asia and Europe, with the northern section in Europe and the southern in Asia. The region was split between Russia, Turkey, Iran, Georgia, Armenia, and Azerbaijan, and it was bounded on the west by the Black Sea and on the east by the Caspian Sea. This was a land of rugged people and even more rugged terrain.

Briggs turned again, coming in for their final approach, but the wind was suddenly gusting. He adjusted quickly, once more pulling away from Fisher. It seemed the younger man was schooling Fisher in wingsuit drops, and it took everything Fisher had to stay with the man.

"Ten seconds, Briggs," Grim reported.

"Just say the word," he answered.

The treetops were visible now, blurring by in a dozen shades of green.

"Five."

Fisher ticked off the seconds and watched as Briggs released his drogue then main chute and suddenly shot upward. Good opening.

"Ten seconds, Sam," came Grim's warning.

He didn't know exactly why it was, and he'd discussed the issue with other paratroopers, but during free fall there was always a tingling sensation at the back of his neck that urged him to tempt fate and delay his chute opening. The adrenaline pumped harder, and the thrill magnified as he whispered in death's ear: *"No, not today. You can't have me."*

Even so, if for some reason Fisher became incapacitated or listened too intently to the siren's call, the CYPRES would kick in and save his life. An acronym for Cybernetic Parachute Release System, the CYPRES was an automatic activation device, or AAD, that could open the chute at a preset altitude if the rate of descent was over a certain threshold.

"And three, two, one!" cried Grim.

Bracing himself, Fisher reached back, deployed the drogue chute, then, three, two, one, *boom!* The main chute deployed, ripping him upward and swinging him sideways for a few seconds until he took control of the toggles and began to steer himself down, once more falling into Briggs's path.

Relief warmed his gut like a good scotch, although at the moment, he'd rather have the scotch. During his SEAL days he used to joke that his uncle was the navy's greatest parachute packer: no operator ever came back to complain that the chute didn't open.

"Nice work, gentlemen. Continue on track," Grim reported. "Radio blackout now."

Fisher wanted to tell Briggs how impressed he was with the man's jump, but that could wait until later. They floated at a painfully slow rate now, drifting in toward the smoke directly ahead, and as they descended to within a thousand feet, Fisher's chest tightened.

His reservations were voiced by Briggs, who'd suddenly broken radio silence: "Dense canopy down there, Sam. I can't . . . I can't find a good opening."

"You'll need to call it at the last second. We're on our own here."

"Shit, the wind's knocking me all over the place."

Fisher grimaced. "Just get off the channel and focus. You own this landing."

"Roger that." Briggs cursed again and then, out ahead of Fisher, with the smoke about a quarter klick north of them, Briggs was swallowed by the canopy.

Even as Fisher was tugging his lines, buffeted hard by the wind and fighting for a spot between two giant pines, a long string of curses erupted from Briggs, followed by a breathy groan . . . and then . . . silence.

"Briggs, you all right?" Fisher cried, just as he came slicing between the trees, his seven-cell canopy missing the branches by only inches before he thumped down hard on some patches of snow and beds of pine needles. He ejected his parachute and pack, then turned back and gathered up the chute. "Briggs, you there?"

No reply. *Shit.*

He unbuckled his helmet and oxygen gear and buried

them in a pile of snow, then did likewise with his chute and pack. Holstered at his right hip was his FN Five-seveN, which he immediately drew, and on his left hip he'd packed a secondary weapon, one equally impressive and having a lot of sentimental value: his SIG SAUER P226 semiautomatic 9mm pistol, the one he'd carried as a Navy SEAL. The gun was now known as the P226 MK25 and was one of the most reliable firearms in the world.

Fisher's updated OPSAT, or operational satellite uplink, was strapped to his left wrist, facing inward. The full-color screen, which could also be set to dim green stealth mode, glowed and provided real-time data integration with field intel collection. Fourth Echelon comms and onboard access to the SMI analytics engine up on Paladin were newer additions to the software. The OPSAT was like having a powerful computer, a satellite phone, and a smartphone in one device. It even offered ambient sound readings to check his own movements, along with light and temperature measurements. As its name implied, the OPSAT also linked Fisher to Keyhole spy satellites and drones like the Hummingbird wheeling overhead. He was capable of downloading data directly from them and from Grim on Paladin. The device even offered a rudimentary alarm system in the form of a T-shaped rod that nudged his wrist.

Willing himself into a moment of calm, Fisher worked the touchscreen, keying in on Briggs's GPS location. A satellite map with glowing grid overlay marked each man's position. He sprinted off in the direction of Briggs's landing zone, with the OPSAT serving as navigator, muttering course corrections to him via his subdermal.

The OPSAT screen flashed with an encrypted message from Grim, and Fisher slowed to read it:

> No RF jamming of those enemy birds yet. As soon as we begin jamming, they'll be onto us. I've plotted your course to Briggs. Keep heading straight. I've told him to shut down his beacon, so if you lose it, just stay on the coordinates of his last signal. Then you shut down yours. Total blackout now.

Fisher raced around a pair of trees, spun, then checked his OPSAT while trying to catch his breath in the much thinner air of the mountains. The beacon was gone, meaning Briggs had to be conscious. However, Fisher was on top of his last signal. He moved around the largest of two pines, then spotted the man's helmet off to his right. He winced and looked up. "Aw, shit."

Briggs was dangling nearly ten meters above the forest floor between a pair of thick, snow-covered limbs, his lines caught in the web of smaller branches. He was trying to swing himself back toward the nearest tree, but he was too far out.

Fisher sent Grim a three-word status report: Briggs in tree. Then he holstered his pistol, took a deep breath, and began hauling himself up and across the sticky bark, wrapping his legs around the tree trunk until he reached the nearest branch. After that, he ascended much more quickly, reaching Briggs within a handful of seconds.

He immediately got to work, digging into a pouch on his belt near his spare magazines to produce a twenty-yard length of 550 paracord. He unraveled the cord, broke off a small branch, then tied the rope around the branch so it would serve as a weight or small anchor. He reared back and tossed the branch to Briggs, who caught it on the first try and reeled in some line.

Fisher ascended even higher into the tree, drawing the rope with him. Once he neared the branch on which Briggs's chute had become tangled, he began drawing in the rope, then wrapped it over another, thicker branch to serve as a winch. Bracing himself, he began hauling Briggs back up toward the limb above.

With both of them gasping and grunting, Briggs finally got his hand wrapped around the branch, and then, with his free hand, he triggered his quick release, breaking free from the chute.

Coaxed by Fisher, he swung his legs up and did an inverted log crawl toward the trunk. Fisher hauled him to safety on the supporting limb, and Briggs took a deep breath. "Thank you, sir. Sorry, sir."

Fisher nodded. "We need to move." He glanced at his OPSAT. Grim reported the launch of two Mil Mi-8 transport choppers/gunships from the new Russian military base in Tskhinvali, Georgia, 120 kilometers southwest of the crash site. Their ETA was approximately eight minutes.

They descended the tree, and once on solid ground, Fisher helped Briggs remove and hide his jump gear.

As the sun disappeared behind the ice-slick canopy and their breaths turned heavy on the air, they tugged down their trifocal goggles with high-frequency sonar detection and sprinted for the crash site.

7

AS part of the team's investigation into Kasperov's disappearance, Fisher had reviewed a lengthy catalog of the software giant's personal assets—jets, yachts, vacation properties, and even an automobile collection that rivaled talk show host Jay Leno's. In regard to planes, Kasperov had a fleet of seven private aircraft that ran the gamut from smaller luxury jets to a giant Airbus A380 fit for an Arab sheik. Two years prior, Brazilian aerospace conglomerate Embraer S.A. had constructed for Kasperov a Legacy 650 they described as an airborne palace and state-of-the-art mobile business suite. The plane had a crew of two with optional flight attendant and total capacity of thirteen passengers plus one in the cockpit jump seat. The 650 was eighty-six feet long, with a wingspan of sixty-eight feet, and was powered by two Rolls-Royce AE 3007/A1P turbofans. Her max speed was 518 mph, with a service ceiling of 41,000 feet.

The price tag? A whopping thirty-one million dollars.

Kasperov probably had great insurance, too, and he'd need it, because as Fisher and Briggs ran parallel to the burning trees cordoning off the wreckage like giant torches, they thought the plane had entirely disintegrated, leaving only a blackened slash mark across the valley. Finally, in the middle of a clearing below more pines littered with debris that resembled metallic confetti, they observed a large portion of the tail section and fuselage, both miraculously intact.

Briggs shot HD video of everything, while Fisher slid his goggles up onto his forehead. The burning trees were doing an exceptional job of lighting the scene, with waves of heat billowing into his face.

He picked his way around the shattered fuselage, navigating between the twisted and charred seats, then he directed a powerful LED penlight into the cabin, whose bulkheads had been blackened. He was searching for charred skeletons, imagining one appearing in his light, but found only mangled metal and melted plastic.

With the stench of all that kerosene-based Jet A fuel and a dozen other chemicals wafting in the air and beginning to get to him, he hustled back outside and jogged forward, following the ragged edge of a huge furrow until he found a small portion of the cockpit lying inverted and jammed between two trees.

The seats were still attached. Seat belts thrown off. No pilots. Had they bailed out? Fisher examined the seat belts again: no signs of tearing, stretching, or strain.

"Hey, Sam? Over here!" cried Briggs.

Fisher raced away from the cockpit, back along the furrow toward Briggs, who was holding a backpack with a large logo embroidered on the outside pocket: four red squares forming a diamond pattern with gray shadow boxes behind them. Beneath the image were the letters "CSCS." Briggs proffered the bag, and Fisher zipped it open and rifled through textbooks and notebooks.

"The daughter went to school in Zurich," whispered Fisher. "We got her bag, but where'd she go?"

"Yeah, and if they wanted to fake their deaths, then where are the bodies?" asked Briggs.

Grim, who'd been analyzing the video Briggs had sent, chimed in over the radio. "Break radio silence now, guys. I've been monitoring the Russian army's transmissions, and they're onto us. Picked you up with infrared before Charlie could start the jam and GPS spoofing. Those Mi-8s are three minutes out now."

"Sam, it's Charlie. Like I mentioned, if you can deploy the drone, I'll remote operate it from here. I'll be another set of eyes and ears."

"He's got soldier envy," said Briggs.

"What he's got is our backs," Fisher corrected. "Charlie, roger that. Deploying the drone."

From a custom-designed holster sitting low on his right hip, Fisher slipped free another of Charlie's prototypes: a micro tri-rotor drone even smaller than the first

one they'd fielded during the Blacklist mission. Fisher
simply tossed the UAV into the air like a softball. The
drone's rotors automatically unfolded and purred to life.
After gaining some altitude, the tiny bird boomeranged
back toward Fisher, now controlling it from his OPSAT.
He plucked two CS smoke grenades from his utility belt
pouches and attached them to the drone's undercarriage
via custom release clips that served to pull their pins so
the canisters could be deployed down on the enemy. The
drone was also equipped with a self-destruct system and
served as a remote sonar beacon to watch enemy movements. The larger model could be fitted with a micro
9mm semiautomatic gun on a pivoting mount, but
Fisher had chosen the smaller model since the plan here
was to go in "ghost," evade detection, and not engage
the enemy. The CS gas would both screen them and give
the Russians a tearful moment of pause as it wreaked
havoc with their respiratory systems.

"Okay, Charlie, the drone's all yours."

"Sweet. I bet that S&R team will fast rope into the
crash site. The best time for you guys to extract would be
while they're infiltrating."

"Yeah, in a perfect world," said Fisher. "Not sure we
can get to the LZ in time. You keep them busy with that
drone. I want SITREPs every couple of minutes or
sooner," said Fisher.

"You got it, Sam."

Fisher looked to Briggs. "Take the backpack. Spot
anything else?"

Briggs shook his head. "You know, the bodies

could've been ejected far away from here, could be dangling from trees, hard to spot now . . ."

"Pilot seats were empty. They weren't torn free and the seat belts were unbuckled," said Fisher. "Either the pilots bailed out, or the jet was fitted with some kind of remote with a pilot on the ground transmitting to the tower while the jet took off."

"So they flew it out here and deliberately crashed it? Man, that's an expensive diversion."

"What does he care? He's got more money than God. Grim, we need to know if the pilots bailed out."

"I'm already on it, Sam. Best we can do there is gather HUMINT from witnesses on the ground who might've spotted their chutes."

Fisher gritted his teeth in frustration. "I want to know what happened here."

Briggs turned around to regard the wreckage. "I still say if Kasperov was really smart, he would've planted bodies. That would buy him a little more time until the corpses were ID'd and ruled out."

"Agreed, but maybe he ran out of time. Just like us. Let's go!"

Fisher took off running to the west. Their rally point lay .8 kilometers away in a depression where the mountainside grew more level and the trees tapered off into a more barren belt of ridges and ravines. The LZ—landing zone—was just wide enough and just flat enough for their UH-60 Black Hawk with Turkish Air Force insignia and an American flight crew to set down. The chopper's call sign was Paladin Two.

"Sam, one of the Russian choppers is breaking ahead," said Grim. "Past the crash site."

Fisher glanced up as the whomping troop transport cut overhead like a black cloud, running lights flashing. "ETA on our extraction helo?"

"Another fifteen minutes. We kept him on the ground to avoid being intercepted."

"Sorry for the delay, Sam," Charlie cut in. "I usually have no trouble disrupting the Mi-8's radar system. I'm jamming their FLIR now, sending phantom blips to get them off our extraction bird. Two soft kills to be sure, but if those pilots visually ID the Black Hawk, there's not much I can do about their door-mounted guns, which, according to the specs, have a thousand rounds apiece."

Confusing a radar electronically was what Charlie called a "soft kill." The method Fisher preferred, the "hard kill," involved ramming a Hellfire missile down their throats.

He watched the chopper fly ahead of them, then wheel around and hover. "Shit, they're trying to cut us off."

"Exactly," answered Grim.

"All right, tell our pilot business as usual. We'll worry about those troops. Charlie, you pick the drone's targets very carefully. You gotta buy us time."

"It's cool, Sam. Looks like the Mi-8 can hold up to twenty-four troops, so the odds aren't bad at all: forty-eight to four! We got this!"

Charlie wasn't much of a math major, it seemed.

Fisher knifed past two more trees, broke hard left, and kept moving, with Briggs hard on his heels.

They both had activated their sonar systems. The deep hues of the forest dissolved into the black-and-white contrast of an X-ray. The system relied on sonic pulses, combined with an advanced AI controller, to penetrate through objects and walls so that they could literally see through them to mark targets. Downtime between echoed bursts along with jamming vulnerabilities and distorted images while they were on the move were the system's chief weaknesses, but the sonar did come in handy when obstacles and terrain made threat assessment difficult.

Through that stark imagery Fisher watched as the chopper descended another twenty meters, then the crew chief lowered a pair of ropes. Two teams of troops came zipping down the lines like beads of crude oil across gleaming gossamers.

"Sam, if I can say so, this shit is *not* good," gasped Briggs.

"It's not bad, either," Fisher snapped.

"Are you serious?"

"Yeah, because if we get out of this, we got one hell of a story to tell."

"A story? Who're we gonna tell? We don't exist."

"Don't overthink it. Now, come on, pick it up." Fisher raced up and over a small rise, kicking up ice and gravel.

"Sam, Charlie here. I count nineteen on the ground behind you, range six hundred meters. They've fanned out in three squads with an officer and some other logistics dickhead hanging back. We called them a search and rescue team, but these guys look like Spetsnaz, Special Forces, man. Hard-core mothers."

Fisher snorted. "That's perfect. They've got bigger egos, so when we escape it'll piss 'em off even more."

They were sidestepping down another slope, heading to the southwest, but Fisher swore as the forest broke off, and they would soon be forced to cross a series of rock-strewn hogbacks whose drop-offs on the left side brought flashbacks of Bolivia. The ledge was about thirty meters long but barely two meters wide, and above it, outcrops of stone jutted like awnings layered with snow, their bellies sharpened by icicles. On the other side lay more forest, and off to the northwest, their rendezvous point with the chopper.

"Wait a minute," said Fisher, raising his palm. "Perfect. Absolutely perfect."

Briggs arrived at his side, panting and confused. "You found us a good place to die?"

Fisher hoisted his brows. "Not us, Briggs. *Them.*"

8

LESS than three minutes later, they were crouched low behind two fir trees nearest the hogbacks. They each had a fragmentation grenade in their strong hands, pistols in their weak. Training, equipment, and terrain were all force multipliers, and Fisher had recognized that. Briggs, a student of military history, had agreed and reminded Fisher of the ancient battle between the Greeks and the Persians at the pass of Thermopylae. A mere 7,000 Greeks held off between 100,000 and 300,000 men for seven days in one of the most remarkable battles ever fought.

"Here they come," whispered Briggs.

Like their comrades to the east, these troops had formed three squads, six men in each, with two squads hustling through the forest toward the pass. The third was holding back in overwatch positions along the out-croppings above the pass.

"Sam, I've just deployed the CS canisters," reported Charlie. "Probably took out at least six or seven of them, but the wind's picking up again. Looks like the rest are converging on the crash site, at least for now."

"Roger that. Do a sweep over the tree line surround-ing the jet. Double-check for bodies."

"No problem."

"Sam, it's Grim. One of you needs to move ahead, pop smoke, and do some combat control for the chop-per. GPS coordinates are a little off, and the pilot's hav-ing a hard time seeing the LZ. It's real tight down there."

"We'll get on it," answered Fisher.

"Uh, and yeah, uh, excuse me, you've got twelve hos-tiles inbound with another six overhead," she said.

"I know, Grim."

"Why aren't you moving?"

"You'll see."

The first squad of Spetsnaz ventured tentatively onto the cliff, the point man hunkered down and waving his assault rifle toward the shadows ahead. His comrades followed, their spacing well practiced, their fingers at the ready to cut loose volleys of superheated lead.

All six were passing through the hogback now, and then came the second squad, one by one. The mountain-side grew so quiet that Fisher thought he could hear every piece of ice crunching under their boots. Even the wind seemed to be holding back, waiting for something to happen.

Fisher zoomed in with his trifocals. The Spetsnaz wore dark green camouflage uniforms with balaclavas tugged down over their faces. Frost was forming on the areas around their mouths. He got a better look at their weapons now, flicking his glance between them and his OPSAT, which ID'd the rifles as Kalashnikov AK-12s, the latest derivative of the Soviet/Russian AK-47 series with a curious lower number than 47. The 12 referred to the year the rifle went into production. What a shame. These were excellent new toys in the hands of men relying upon conventional tactics. They might be hard-core, as Charlie had mentioned, but they needed a hell of a lot more creativity if they were going to capture or kill Fisher and Briggs.

Zooming back out, Fisher noted that the point man was only a few meters away from what he and Briggs had dubbed the "rock of no return"—a small stone about the size of a volleyball they'd placed along the ledge as a landmark.

He glanced over at the young man hunkered down at his side. Briggs's eyes were covered by his trifocals, and Fisher let his gaze drift down to Briggs's gloved hand. Was he trembling? Was his pulse bounding? Could Fisher trust him enough to react and carry out the plan as discussed? There'd been a moment during the Blacklist operation where Sadiq had been clutching Fisher and it'd been up to Briggs to take the shot, end it right there, but the kid just couldn't do it. Fisher had, in effect, fired him after that. They'd come to terms with the incident, and while Fisher forgave, he never forgot.

Briggs must've felt the heat of Fisher's gaze, and he glanced over and nodded.

The point man lifted his hand, halting the squad.

"Shit," Briggs whispered.

Fisher leaned toward Briggs. "Take it easy."

A few of the troops craned their heads at the sound of the Black Hawk's rotors approaching from the west.

The point man shouted in Russian, "Double-time!"

And they took off running—

Right into Fisher's trap.

9

NO plan ever survived the first enemy contact, and if you believed otherwise, you were an armchair general who'd never set foot on a battlefield. The plan of going in ghost, reconnoitering the crash site, and getting out without ever being detected had already been abandoned. Taking out enemy troops while still remaining stealthy was a tactic most often employed by Fisher, one he'd recently begun calling "panther." Going in "ghost" or going in "panther" was shorthand he used with Grim.

Going in "assault"—loud and offensive—was a last resort. They were information gatherers, not direct action specialists, but they were always prepared to bring the fight to the enemy when they had to, and bring it they had.

The point man broke the laser trip wire they'd set up on the ledge near that rock.

Fisher held his breath.

The small C-4 charges with wireless detonators that he and Briggs had emplaced along the ledge went off in a thread of echoing booms, instantly killing the point man and the two men behind him, their shredded bodies arching through the air and disappearing into the chasm below.

Fisher and Briggs hurled their grenades up and onto the outcroppings. While some troops up there and below hit the deck, others were so disoriented that they either ran or were blown right off the ledge. In the next heartbeat, the outcroppings exploded, raining down tons of rock onto the pass, crushing a few troops while a handful of others narrowly escaped back toward the forest. One man doing overwatch tumbled from the cliff above the pass, the rock beneath him having suddenly given way. The screaming and random salvos flashing from AK-12s, along with the still flickering light of burning shrapnel splayed across the cliff, cast the entire scene in a weird otherworldly glow.

As the miniature mushroom clouds of fire expanded above, rising from columns of dense black smoke, the injured appeared, a couple of troops missing appendages, crawling with what limbs they had left, scraping forward across the ice.

Before Fisher and Briggs could assess any more of their ambush, they were on their feet and hauling ass back toward the forest to circle around and above the pass. The sonar goggles revealed that there were at least five more troops left up top, all having fallen back to secondary defensive positions within the trees.

"Sam, the troops at the crash site—"

"I know, Grim," he snapped. "But we need to clear a path for Briggs so he can get to that helo."

"Well, you'd better move. I count at least ten sprinting toward your position."

"Charlie, can you run interference?" Fisher asked.

"I'll see if I can offer the drone as bait, let 'em take some potshots to keep 'em distracted. And Sam, I haven't spotted any bodies in the trees."

"Okay," Fisher answered, fighting for breath. "Just slow down those bastards for me."

He and Briggs scaled a hill so steep they were forced to lean forward and clutch at the earth and snow. At the top, Fisher's quads were burning, and the altitude was really getting to him now. Briggs was crouched again, scanning with his trifocals. He gave Fisher a hand signal: got two guys to the left, three to the right.

Fisher gestured for Briggs to go left, take out those two quietly. Fisher slipped off across the snow and toward the other three, holstering his pistol and drawing the karambit from its sheath attached to his waistband just behind the holster.

The knife was a curved blade variant, a "tiger's claw" endemic to Sumatra, Central Java, and Madura. Over his long career, Fisher had studied with many close-quarters combat experts, among them world-renowned edged weapon master Michael Janich, who'd taught Fisher to use the blade with expert and deadly efficiency. The karambit's design made it more easily concealable in the hand as well as offering more leverage while dragging it across the neck, with the ultimate goal of opening an enemy's head like a PEZ dispenser. The karambit's outside edge was sharpened, its back blade nearest the handle heavily serrated to be flipped and used to hack through thicker objects or pieces of flesh. By slipping your pinky or ring finger through the ring attached to the bottom of the knife's hilt, you could switch between forward and reverse grips in a lightning-fast 180-degree stroke. Fisher owned two karambits, one with a silver uncoated blade, the other featuring a DLC, or diamond-like carbon, coating that gave the blade a matte black appearance for better camouflage and protection against reflections that could betray his position.

Knowing most of this op would be run at night, he'd taken the black blade—which now jutted from the bottom of his fist.

At the next tree he paused and marked the positions of each troop, their weapons trained on the valley to his left. He zoomed in once more with his trifocals. The nearest troop peered out from behind a more narrow pine, his rifle at the ready, a pair of night-vision goggles clipped to his helmet and slid down over his eyes.

After plotting his path, Fisher stepped as gingerly as he could, coming in from behind the man, who turned back as he approached, but all he saw was the next spruce behind him. He didn't realize Fisher was so close, placing a gloved hand over his mouth to try to stifle his warm breath. Once more Fisher examined the ground between his position and the soldier's. No, not good. Broken patches of ice, pine needles, and a few brown leaves scattered on top of it all. A soundless approach would involve antigravity boots. He'd have to get Charlie on that. For now, though, it was all about reaching the troop before the man could fire and alert his comrades.

Reaching the troop . . . that was one way to do it. The other involved bringing the troop to him . . .

Taking in a long breath, the air stinging his lungs, Fisher stood and began to walk in place, the snow and leaves crunching loudly under his boots.

Then he froze, got back down on his haunches, and doused the green lights on his trifocals.

As expected, the troop clambered to his feet and left his position to investigate the noise. His movements were tense; in fact, Fisher had never seen a young man more puckered up.

As he came toward Fisher's tree, Fisher cautiously maneuvered to the side so he could still attack from the rear. Again, the most important part of the assault was getting the troop's finger away from his trigger. After that, the karambit would communicate Fisher's will in a way words could not.

Fisher rose and came up on the troop like a camouflaged extraterrestrial, once part of the mountainside but now morphing into a lethal, three-eyed combatant.

In that half second when Fisher sensed the troop would whirl around, he reached out and seized the man's right wrist, yanking it away from the assault rifle.

The blade was already tearing across the man's throat before he could yell, and as he fell back toward the snow, Fisher eased him silently to the ground. While grisly, it was necessary to stab him twice more in the heart before he was sprawled out on his back and flinching involuntarily.

Men did not die instantly from knife wounds the way Hollywood producers wanted you to believe. It took a while to bleed out, but flooding an enemy's throat with blood ensured he wouldn't be screaming for his brothers as, in the minutes to come, he finally, inevitably, drowned.

Fisher took the man's rifle and slung it over his shoulder. He was about to open the man's belt pouch to draw some spare magazines when he spotted movement farther up the mountain. He dashed off, the thumping of the Black Hawk much closer and certainly welcome. With that racket concealing his footfalls, he wasted no time rushing up on the next troop and working the knife the way a symphony conductor instinctively works his baton. The troop saw nothing, felt only a hand, the edge of the blade, the warmth of his own blood spilling down his chest.

As Fisher silently finished the job with two more blows, he caught sight of the man's painfully young eyes, and that youth reminded him of a moment after he'd had a few drinks and his guard was down. His daughter, Sarah, had asked, "Is it easy to kill a man?"

He'd considered the question for a long time, then finally told her, "When it's for our country, I try not to think about it. But most of the time I do. And it's never easy. Or fun. Or anything that should be glorified."

Breathing a heavy sigh, Fisher traded his blood-soaked gloves for the troop's, then hustled out of there.

"Hey, Sam, Briggs here. Two down, nice and quiet. But they're coming up fast from the east. If you want me on combat control for that helo, I need to roll now."

"Go. I'll be right behind."

Following a deep cut in the mountain formed eons prior by glaciers, Fisher abandoned his assault on the last troop, who was just north of his position.

Maybe they could lure that soldier into following, then double back to take him out once they were near the LZ. Getting to that troop now would take Fisher too far off the trail and leave Briggs more vulnerable to those attackers from the east.

With his lips chapped and nose sore from the cold, Fisher dragged himself up another ten meters, the grade nearly 40 percent now, his breath ragged. He had to stop, find some air, find some way to actually catch his breath.

And that's when the grenade went off.

The white-hot blinding flash, followed by the ear-rattling *ka-boom* sent him crashing forward and burying his face in the dirt. Grim and Charlie were screaming in his ear for him to move, and for a moment, the world seemed to tip on its axis.

There was no rush of imagery from his past, no reflections on his divorce, or anything else—just that terrible ringing and white noise, the blinding flashes like old flashbulbs going off repeatedly in his face.

One of those flashes turned into a lightning bolt with

still images printed along its surface, each cell depicting Sarah receiving the news of his death. No, he couldn't put her through that . . .

Muted gunfire stitched up the mountainside, and he could feel the rounds thumping into the earth behind him. Was he hit by shrapnel? Was he okay? Where the hell was he?

The moment came down like an avalanche, and barely conscious of his movements, he was already on his feet, digging in deep, charging up the mountain, with more gunfire trailing. He ripped free a grenade, pulled the pin, and tossed it over his shoulder without looking.

To his left rose a stand of pines, and he darted toward them, boots sliding as he fought against the incline, his ears ringing loudly from the explosions.

Those sons of bitches were coming up behind him, but *he* had the high ground, if nothing else.

He had two more grenades left. Tugging down his trifocals, he went to sonar, marked the positions of nine men now who were fanned out in a semicircle within the trees, with several more, three or four, in the distance.

Night-vision mode allowed him to zoom in on the nearest troop. Seeing an opportunity, Fisher shoved up his goggles and got behind the AK-12's attached scope. As a rule of combat—and if you had a choice—you never trusted an enemy's rifle. He sighted the forehead of the nearest troop, then panned right to the next three about a yard back. The second man was there, leaning out from behind the trunk. Fisher knew that once he fired the first round, the second guy would switch positions, ducking for cover—but his tree wasn't quite wide enough, and so when he did try to hide, Fisher would exploit that reaction.

The moment seemed perfect, and firing down at a sharp angle decreased the amount of bullet drop, placing the odds of a better shot in his favor.

If he did it right, gripped the weapon firmly with his left hand, gently with his right, then exhaled halfway, every shot would be a surprise. There was no conscious pulling of the trigger, only pressure until the round exploded from the barrel. It did. The troop's head snapped back as Fisher was already shifting fire to the second one—who moved exactly as predicted. Fisher caught him in the side of the head.

The other troops detected his muzzle flash and sent volley after volley of automatic weapons fire in his direction. Rounds tore apart the pines and ricocheted off the rocks behind him.

At the next pause in fire, he was on his feet, gritting his teeth and clambering for the next stand of trees back to his left, the gunfire resuming and ripping past him now. The bullets sounded like sand thrown into a fan, and a round or two might've struck his legs, he wasn't sure, the Kevlar certainly protecting him at this range, but he wasn't sticking around to tempt fate any further.

A blur raced over his head and zoomed back down the mountain. He recognized the buzzing of the drone's rotors and sighed with relief.

"Goddamn, Charlie, you're a little late!" he cried.

"Sorry, Sam, the drone took fire. Lost one rotor. Had to reboot. Just get out of there!"

"That's the plan."

"Sam, don't move," cried Grim. "There's another squad. They just got in front of you. They came up on your flank. You're about to be surrounded!"

"Then, Grim, I need to move!"

"Sam, I have an idea, but you won't like it," said Charlie.

Fisher reached the next tree, dropped to his knees, then leaned over, stealing more breath. He was a few seconds away from collapsing. "Charlie, what're you thinking?"

"The Black Hawk's armed with Hellfire missiles—"

"Absolutely not!" shouted Grim. "He's too close and while I can explain away a Black Hawk off course, I can't account for missiles fired on Russian ground troops."

"Forget the missiles," said Fisher. "I'll slip past that squad ahead. Briggs, what's your ETA to the landing zone?"

The man's voice came broken and breathless: "Uh, just a minute or two, I think."

Fisher activated his sonar and wished he hadn't.

His heart sank, and a string of expletives slipped from his lips. He was surrounded, all right, with six strung out above him, seven or more moving up from behind, a couple more on each flank, with his perimeter narrowing from thirty or so meters to twenty and decreasing by the minute. Not an ingenious way to capture someone, given the risk of cross fire, and there was an opportunity for Fisher to get them shooting at each other, but he'd rather just get on the move. Somehow.

"Sam, I'm looking at sonar now," said Briggs. "You won't make it."

"Sure, I will."

"Look, you've told me there's nothing more important than the mission. Not you, not me, not anyone."

"That's right."

"Well, I get that. I respect it. But all we got out of this drop was a backpack. And we're not going to lose you over a backpack."

Fisher grinned weakly over the irony. "All right, Briggs, I see your point."

"Good. I'm going after the three guys east of your position."

Fisher could almost hear the smile on the man's face.

Just then the drone returned to Fisher's side and Charlie was barking in his ear: "Attach your last two frags, Sam. I'll light 'em up!"

Fisher tugged out the grenades and got to work. Clip one, clip two. "Okay, rock 'n' roll, Charlie."

"Sam, break to the left," said Grim. "The widest gap between the troops above you is there."

"Right along where the trees thin out?" he asked.

"That's it."

Fisher clutched the rifle to his chest, broke from the trees, and sprinted off toward the next patch of cover: a small mound with a large shoulder of mottled rock rising to knee height behind it. He trudged up through the snow, getting about ten meters ahead, when the first salvo of rifle fire split wood like a dozen hatchets in the trees ahead. He craned his head back as a few more rounds thumped into his boot prints. Cutting a serpentine path while crouched down, he reached the rock, his pulse drumming in his ears.

"Get down, Sam!" cried Charlie.

The kid had control of the frags, and if he said to "get down," then Fisher sure as shit wouldn't argue. He threw himself behind the rock, and not a second too soon. An explosion tore across the hillside only a few meters back, the ground trembling and erupting, waves of flying dirt reaching as far as the rock. At the same time, shrapnel cut through that dirt storm to strike with metallic snicks against the stone.

The shrieks that split the night were bone-chilling but quickly cut off by the second grenade, which Charlie had deposited atop the troops even farther back, the burst more distant, the echoing cries sounding inhuman at first before they, too, were lost in the reverberating thunder.

The sound of Briggs's P220 .45ACP pistol cracking in the distance sent Fisher springing from his cover behind the rock and scrambling back up toward the three men waiting for him in the trees ahead. While the canopy was thinning out, the remaining branches were thrashing about in the rotor wash as the Black Hawk banked hard just a dozen or so meters above them.

And then, much to Fisher's shock, the chopper's door gunner opened fire on the tree line with his M240H, a classic and supremely badass machine gun sometimes known as the "240 Hotel." The weapon was capable of delivering up to 950 rounds per minute of 7.62x51mm ammo out to a range of nearly 1,800 meters. Splintering branches and hunks of bark flitted down and were churned up by the rotors as he targeted the three Spetsnaz troops pinning down Fisher.

Those troops answered the door gunner with rifle fire of their own.

"Charlie, what're you doing?" cried Grim.

"You said no missiles," he answered. "You didn't say anything about machine guns!"

Fisher understood Grim's fury; he also understood that not only were the troops distracted, but they had just given up their positions and sent Fisher into a flow state where there was no more thinking, only action and reaction. He bolted up to the first man, who swung his rifle down from the sky. Fisher already had his Five-seveN pointed at the man's forehead.

The man's gaze averted in defeat a second before Fisher shot him.

While that troop tumbled, the next one came rushing up from the west at the sound of the shot.

Fisher rolled behind the nearest tree and waited. Just as the man jogged by, Fisher swung around and stabbed him in the neck, bringing the karambit down, into the man's clavicle, then stirring his insides with the blade.

At the same time, he had his pistol in his left hand and fired over the shoulder of his victim, striking the final oncoming troop in the chest at a range of nearly fifty meters. Some of his old navy instructors would've been proud of those shots . . .

However, the man jolted back, stepped drunkenly

toward the trees, but still managed to return fire like a relentless Russian cyborg. He was obviously wearing a vest and clearly a pretty good shot, the rounds drumming into the soldier Fisher now used as a shield.

A pistol cracked jarringly close to Fisher's right ear, and the troop ahead fell with a spasmodic jerk to the snow. Fisher craned his head.

"We're clear, Sam," said Briggs, lowering his weapon.

"You took out all three of your guys?"

"Yeah."

"And now one of mine?"

Briggs frowned. "We keeping score?"

Fisher was impressed. "Shit, maybe we should!" He burst off after the man, and together they raced across the top of the hill, then once more were sidestepping along the mountain, finding better purchase in the denser sections of forest where the snow had barely filtered through. What could be described as a bang and not a true explosion resounded from somewhere behind them, and Fisher paused beneath a tree that had fallen and lay at a forty-five-degree angle across two more.

He got back on the radio. "How many left, Grim?"

"Got four still on the move, with another two or three pretty far back but en route."

"Charlie, can you at least buzz 'em with the drone?"

"Wish I could, Sam, but the drone is toast. Lost all rotors. In order to avoid it being confiscated and reverse engineered, I hit the self-destruct. For what it's worth, I did manage to blow it up in one guy's face."

"All right, this is it. We're hitting the LZ."

They drifted down the mountainside and within a minute were nearing the clearing. It felt like the temperature had dropped twenty degrees, and Fisher's teeth were literally and uncontrollably chattering. Briggs popped red smoke, indicating a hot LZ to the chopper pilot, but she had already assumed that, bringing the helo in low across the treetops to avoid both radar and small arms fire. The rotors turned the smoke into crimson corkscrews as the helicopter descended.

Next came the most breath-robbing part of the mission: the final sprint to the chopper. When he was in the SEALs, this was the time when most men bought it, when they were celebrating a successful op and all they had to do was hop on a helo—

Because there was always some sniper or small squad waiting in the wings to take terribly cheap shots at those trying to escape. And Fisher could feel those rounds on the back of his neck as he told Briggs to go off first, he'd cover.

Briggs put his strong legs to work, bridging the gap between them and the hovering bird in all of five seconds.

The tree beside Fisher practically exploded with gunfire, showering him with bark as he hit the ground, rolled, then came up firing with the AK-12. He emptied the magazine at the trees in a simple wave of covering fire, spotting the silhouettes shifting between them, fluctuating like wraiths.

He tossed the rifle aside, drew his pistol, then fired once more, emptying the entire twenty-round magazine and holstering the weapon with one hand while drawing his secondary weapon, the P226, with the other.

"Sam, circle around the clearing and I'll have the door gunner lay down suppressing fire for you," said Charlie.

"Good call," said Fisher.

He stole off away from the trees, racing at full tilt around the edge of the clearing—just as the door gunner went to town, the big gun thudding and spewing brass.

Instead of boarding the chopper, Briggs took up a position beside the door gunner, his goggles over his eyes, arms extended, pistol winking.

"Sam, they look dug in," said Grim. "Make your break now!"

Knowing he couldn't wait any longer, lest one of the troops hurl a grenade at the helo, Fisher sprang into the clearing, and while it would take just a handful of seconds to reach the bird, the moment swept by in a noiseless vacuum of slow motion.

He glanced to his left and saw the troops' muzzle flashes within the trees. They resembled a string of broken holiday lights poking holes in the shadows.

He turned right, spotted Briggs waving him over, his mouth working, the words swept away by the powerful rotors.

The chopper's running lights strobed in an almost hypnotic rhythm as the snow and dirt beneath it fanned away into miniature tornadoes. Fisher stomped through the wash, fully conscious that this was it, the final sprint.

He hoped he hadn't pissed off the gods of war, lest a bullet make contact with the back of his head.

He reached the chopper's open bay door and did a flying leap inside, then turned back and thrust out his arm, hauling Briggs inside—just as the helo lifted off.

They banked hard and away, the pilot sweeping over by staying tight to the trees, avoiding any more chances of potshots and flying nape of the earth to keep them hidden.

The gunner handed them headsets with attached microphones, and Fisher got on the intercom. "Thanks for the lift," he told the pilot.

She glanced back and smiled. "I'm sorry, sir, I have no idea what you're talking about."

"Me, neither," said Fisher.

Briggs climbed into one of the jump seats and buckled himself in. Fisher joined him and said, "Nice work."

Briggs patted the backpack lying across his lap. "Just wish we got more."

Fisher closed his eyes and threw his head back on the seat. "We had to follow up here. So we did."

"Hey, well, there was something small. I forgot to mention that one of her textbooks still had the receipt inside. Had the address to her apartment in Zurich. Might be worth a shot."

"We could've found her place without that."

"Probably, but either way we should check it out."

"Let's run it by Grim and Charlie."

"Roger that. And oh, yeah, I wanted to show you something." Briggs tugged up his sleeve to expose his wrist altimeter. He thumbed a few buttons to bring up his data file, then showed the glowing screen to Fisher—

MAX SPEED: 227 MPH.

Fisher's eyes bugged out.

Briggs smiled crookedly. "I guess Grim's data was a little off. When she told me I was doing 210, I was already up to 221. That's a world record no one will ever know about."

10

THEY rendezvoused at Incirlik Air Base in Turkey, which had a U.S. complement of nearly five thousand airmen. There, Fisher and Briggs returned to Paladin to debrief while the crew took care of refueling operations.

After dragging themselves up the rear cargo ramp and passing through the hatch, they entered the command center to the concerned looks of Grim and Charlie.

"Whoa, you guys got in deep," said Charlie, gawking at the bloodstains covering their tac-suits.

Briggs sighed. "If it were easy, they would've hired someone else."

"Grim, any word back from Kestrel?" asked Fisher, crossing directly to the SMI table.

"Not yet. Should I activate one of his trackers?"

"Call him again. We'll give him the benefit of the doubt. Give him a few hours to answer. If he doesn't respond, then yeah, we'll go after him."

Briggs placed the backpack on the edge of the SMI. "This is all we got."

"We'll have Ollie and the rest go through that stuff," said Grim. She regarded Fisher. "You told me the daughter has an apartment in Zurich?"

"Yeah, I want to check it out," he said.

"I already have," said Grim, bringing up surveillance camera video from the surrounding apartment buildings and college. "This street here is Via Trevano. The college is right here in Lugano." She tapped a screen and brought up traffic footage showing an impressive four-story glass office building nestled in a valley. The snow-capped Lugano Prealps loomed on the horizon. The image switched to a luxury apartment building, then to a closer shot of the sidewalk outside the main entrance.

"See there, that's Nadia getting into that Bentley Flying Spur," said Grim.

"Nice set of wheels," remarked Charlie.

Grim went on: "She's wearing the backpack you guys found. She's on her way to the airport to visit her father."

"Any new intel on where she is now?"

"Nothing. We have more cam footage of her arriving in Moscow, but not much after that."

"Any HUMINT on the pilots bailing out of the plane?"

Grim sighed even more deeply. "Still working on that, too, plus I've got a cleanup crew that'll hike back into the mountains to pick up your jump gear. I just sent them the GPS locations."

"Good. Now, here's what I'm thinking," Fisher began. "Kasperov decides to bolt. He sends off the daughter's plane to confuse and divert us. She was planning on flying back, which is why she just left her backpack on board, figuring she'd study during the flight back."

"That makes sense," said Grim.

"Charlie, we get anything else on Kasperov's friends, family, the old teacher, military buddies?"

"No red flags, Sam. Plus the FSB has operatives scoping out all those people, too."

Fisher turned to back to Grim. "You said the plane was headed to Tbilisi. Any connection there?"

"Just that he's flown through before. Attended a few conferences over the years. Again, nothing out of the ordinary."

"Well, we do have this backpack," said Briggs.

Fisher stood there, looking at them all. He opened his mouth, hesitated, then blurted out, "Let's go to Zurich. Get inside the daughter's apartment. Maybe there's something there."

"I doubt it, Sam. Have a look."

Grim fast-forwarded through more security camera footage and slowed down on two sedans pulling up outside Nadia's building. Four men got out and hurried inside the building. Grim switched to the hallway cameras. The men rushed forward, reached a door, and a fifth man, either the landlord or a maintenance guy, opened the door for them. They burst into the apartment like wolves.

"We can assume the SVR's already ransacked the place," Grim said. "Footage doesn't show them taking anything outside, but I can't tell if they removed smaller items and just put them in their pockets."

Fisher stepped away from the table, rubbing his stubble in thought. "The POTUS said it herself: Kasperov is quite a character. And he's a genius, so he's anticipated the search. He won't go to any of the obvious places. It'll be someplace much more obscure, but it won't be a place unfamiliar because he still needs to maintain security, and that's tougher in an unfamiliar environment. He wouldn't leave himself that vulnerable."

"All that does is rule out all the places associated with him, his background, his family and friends," said Grim. "And it leaves the rest of the world wide open."

"Let's take a look at his daughter's place. What'd they do, leave an agent or two behind for surveillance?"

"We've picked up two watching the apartment," said Grim.

"And Kasperov's place in Moscow?"

"They tore it apart, Sam," said Charlie. "I mean literally moved everything out of it, furniture, everything. It's all gone to a warehouse in Moscow, along with everything from his headquarters. Security there is ridiculously tight."

Grim shrugged. "I think we'd have better luck getting to Kestrel, see if he can tap us into Voron's search—"

"But then we're always a step behind them," Fisher said. "We need to be out front on this—"

"Sam, this time I think Grim's right," said Briggs. "I don't think we'll find much there."

"All it takes is one thing, something Kasperov over-looked that'll give him away." Fisher faced Grim. "How many scumbags have we taken out because they made one tiny mistake? It's all about the details—the ones they've overlooked."

"You trying to suck up so I'll go along?" she asked.

"Flight time from here to Zurich?"

She consulted the SMI. "Little over three hours."

"It's worth a shot, come on," he said.

"It's your call, Sam," she reminded him. "Why don't you just order us there?"

His tone softened. "Because we're a team."

Charlie tugged nervously on the strings of his hoodie. "So maybe we lose half a day in Zurich. If we pick up something, it'll be worth it."

"And maybe by then the SMI will have something for us," said Grim. "We're checking out the flights of all of Kasperov's friends and business associates, having the computer run through every piece of terminal data, the cam footage, scanning faces for Kasperov, his girlfriend, and Nadia. We're talking about thousands of hours of footage across thousands of airports. Plus we're looking at as many private airstrips as we can, but the enormity of this is just mind-boggling."

Fisher nodded. "You know, we do have one more resource we haven't tapped . . ."

"What's that?" Briggs asked.

Fisher widened his eyes. "Kobin."

"Aw, hell, are you kidding me?" Briggs cried.

Fisher nodded. "Let's go get cleaned up. Then I'll go have a word with the little man."

ANDRIY Semyon Kobin was a fast-talking runt and the son of a Ukrainian American shipping clerk from Baltimore. His black hair was slicked back and now graying at the temples to match the soul patch beneath his lower lip. He had a penchant for bling—gold necklaces in particular—as well as large-collared silk shirts and dress slacks that made him resemble some oddball Euro-pimp-wannabe-gangster, even though in his own mind he was trying to flaunt his wealth. He'd fallen in with the Ukrainian mob, smuggling drugs and weapons, then graduating to his own "business," where he'd established worldwide connections within the underworld. He'd been uncovered and captured by Third Echelon, then kept on as a useful and deniable asset. Fisher's old boss had come to trust Kobin so much that he'd asked the man to provide a body to substitute for Fisher's daughter, Sarah, when they'd faked her death. Kobin had, in effect, pretended to kill Sarah, allowing Grim to have leverage over Fisher. Lambert had thanked the man by setting him up with a smuggling operation in Malta. Kobin's network expanded, but then he began to lose control as a life of wealth and excess took its toll; consequently, when Fisher hunted him down to learn more about Sarah, he'd barricaded himself inside his mansion in a coke-fueled frenzy.

Much had happened since then. Kobin had been unwittingly caught up in the Blacklist attacks via an arms deal gone very bad, and he wound up turning himself in to the CIA for protection. When his safe house got hit, Fisher had gone in to rescue the man—more for the intel he carried than any particular love for the scumbag. Kobin did, however, return the favor when Paladin's flight controls were hacked, helping to get the plane restarted. His piloting skills and knowledge of the underworld were admittedly useful.

From that point on, Kobin took up residence inside Paladin's cell, sleeping in the shimmering glow of the nearby server lights. Given the number of enemies he'd made over the years and the fact that he'd sold arms to the Blacklist Engineers, he'd probably spend the rest of his life in prison. Thus, he'd begged Fisher and Grim to let him stay on board so he could offer up what intel he could. He was actually working on Charlie, trying to convince him that he should be a new member of their team, even trying to teach the kid about weapons and the jet's flight control systems.

"Hey, asshole," Fisher said as he approached the holding cell.

Kobin was lying on his bunk, hands folded behind his

head, staring off into space. Charlie had loaned him some clean clothes, so the ostentatious outfit was gone, replaced by a slightly grunge look that Kobin had whined about but accepted until they could find him more silly silk duds.

He finally glanced up from his trance. "You know, Fisher, back in the glory days they used to call me King of Assholes!"

"I'm sure they did." Fisher unlocked the cell and stepped inside.

Kobin shook his head. "I told you, you don't have to lock the door. I wanna be here."

"Grim thinks it's a good idea. Sometimes I sleepwalk and kill scumbags."

"Like a PTSD thing?" asked Kobin.

"Yeah."

"So it's for my own protection."

Fisher grinned crookedly. "Yeah."

"So I take it you've come to the master seeking knowledge?" Kobin sat up, gazing emphatically at Fisher. "It's gonna cost you."

"The fact that you're not dead means we can run a tab for as long as we want."

"Dude, I'm just kidding. Why do you have to be so intense?"

"Because we've still got a hundred pounds of stolen uranium out there, along with a Russian software geek who's just gone missing."

"You talking about Kasperov?"

"You know him?"

"I went to one of his parties—and that bastard knows how to throw a party!"

"Any idea where he might've gone?"

Kobin snorted. "The fuck do I know? Why the hell did he run in the first place?"

"We're not sure yet. We need to get into the SVR's comm network—and even deeper, right into Voron."

"Well, good luck with that shit."

"You know, I'm so glad we're keeping you here, free room and board, so you can tell us, *good luck with that shit . . .*"

"What do you want from me? If I knew something, I'd tell you."

Fisher's smartphone beeped, and he answered.

"Sam, I just activated the beacon to find Kestrel, but it's dead," Grim said. "No signal. He must've found it."

"Shit, all right, thanks."

"Did I hear her say Kestrel?"

"That's right."

"Why is that fucker not dead? I thought your people hauled away the body."

"They weren't my people . . ."

"So where is he now?" asked Kobin.

Fisher bit back a curse. "Last I heard he was in Moscow, settling some scores."

"You let me make a few calls, and I'll find him. If he's on the hunt, then he's asking a lot of questions, and that's how we get him. I know the network in Moscow better than anybody."

"Tell you what. If you find him, you'll move up the

espionage ladder from worthless piece of shit to unreliable scumbag who can sometimes help."

"I'll take it. And with a nickel pay raise, too. You motherfuckers are too generous. I'm crying with tears of joy over here."

Fisher held open the door. "Shut up and get to the control room. Start making your calls."

As Kobin walked past the cell door, he paused to sniff Fisher's neck. "You just take a shower? You smell nice—like a three-dollar whore."

11

SVR agent number one, the gray-haired operator Fisher had nicknamed "Uncle Harry," sat in his idling Volkswagen rental, crushing the seat with his considerable girth. A rather mundane surveillance op like this was led by a more seasoned—see "ready to retire"—agent while his two more youthful colleagues braved the early-morning temperatures on foot patrol. Grim had initially spotted only two agents at Nadia's apartment, along with the two requisite private security guards posted at the front desk and at the gate near the parking garage. Fisher dubbed these rent-a-cops the "puppy patrol." Meanwhile, Briggs, operating from a rooftop opposite the five-story building, had picked up a third SVR agent

street side and looking oh-so-clandestine with a Bluetooth receiver jutting from one of his ears.

While Harry and his associates were here to appre-
hend and question Kasperov, his daughter, or anyone
else who returned to the apartment, they had obviously
grown bored with their duties. For his part, Harry spoke
only once on his radio while repeatedly adjusting himself
in his seat as though his legs were falling asleep or he had
a fiery case of hemorrhoids. He never saw Fisher, who
was under his car inserting the gas tube into the vehicle's
heating system to inject the halothane gas.

Fisher made the connection, threw the valve, then
slipped out from beneath the car, crawling to the parked
sedan behind the Volkswagen.

"He's adjusting the heat," reported Briggs. "He
knows something's up. In five, four, three, two . . . oh,
there he goes. He's out, Sam. Lying back on the seat."

"Roger that. Need to move fast now."

"Sam, Cousin Ivan is on the east side of the building,
smoking a cigarette near the parking garage across the
street," reported Grim. "Cousin Drago is still on the roof."

Rather than sitting in some not-so-discreet van, Grim
and Charlie were operating from a crowded Internet café
called Altro just one block down the street. They had a
window table, a couple of laptops, and access to some of
the most powerful software and best-tasting lattes on
the planet, according to Charlie.

They were surrounded by undergrads wired into their
own computers, yet Charlie and Grim still had privacy,
their screens out of view, their voices out of earshot. They

were fully patched into the surrounding security cameras as well as a video stream recorded by Briggs. Just before they'd arrived, Charlie had noted how several of the camera systems had been depressingly easy to bypass. He'd explained that inherent vulnerabilities existed in many of the top manufacturers' stand-alone CCTV systems as well as a substantial number of rebranded versions. Remote access capability via the web was a convenient feature that allowed guards and other administrators to view a location from off-site. Likewise it made the systems vulnerable to hackers if they weren't set up securely. If the remote access feature was enabled by default upon purchase—which many of them were—some customers didn't realize they should take steps to secure those systems.

However, even the systems that *were* security enabled came with laughably unsecure user names like "user" and "admin," along with passwords like "1234." They also failed to lock out a user after a certain number of incorrect password guesses. This meant that even if a customer changed the password, hackers like Charlie could crack them through a brute-force attack. Finally, because many customers who employed the systems didn't restrict access to computers from trusted networks, nor did they log who was accessing them, Charlie said that even the guards couldn't tell if a remote attacker was in their system viewing video footage from outside the network.

Interestingly enough, Nadia's building was the toughest to crack, and her father had probably had a hand in that. What Fisher found curious was why she'd opted for a penthouse in a five-story building instead of a private villa. The place was, after all, known as the "Monte Carlo of Switzerland," situated in the south of the country on the shores of Lake Lugano, with the city's waterfront forming a crescent around the bay between the Brè and the San Salvatore mountains. Fisher had read that Lugano was the largest Italian-speaking city outside of Italy, with an economy bolstered by business, finance, and tourism. It was one of the most popular tourist cities in Switzerland, as well as home to several universities and institutes, including Nadia's. A lakeside villa would've afforded her direct access to the waterfront and the collection of cafés and bistros that were crowded day and night. Perhaps she'd wanted to be closer to her colleagues, pretend to live a somewhat normal life. Grim had mentioned that several of her classmates lived in the building, and the SVR team had, according to the surveillance camera video, gone to their apartments to question them.

Fisher slipped away from the sedan behind the Volkswagen and worked his way along the line of cars. The sun was rising, the street and pedestrian traffic beginning to increase as the locals headed off to work. He darted across the street to the back of a public parking garage facing Nadia's complex. He vaulted over a four-foot-tall concrete wall, then hit the stairwell, heading up to the second level. He jogged across the garage, then reached another barrier wall. Keeping low, he eased up to the wall and glanced down. Cousin Ivan was directly below him, standing on the sidewalk and lighting up another cigarette.

Fisher set up his rappelling line, attaching its carabiner clip to the fitting of an electrical conduit spanning the ceiling. Given the fact that most pedestrians and drivers wouldn't necessarily be looking up at the side of the garage, and the fact that Ivan was pretty far from the nearest door, Fisher had devised a plan to make the agent disappear with minimal risk. A large oak tree on the corner provided additional cover.

"Briggs, you with me?" he asked.

"I'm here. You're clear."

"Okay, here we go."

Fisher eased himself headfirst over the wall, hooking one leg around his rappelling line that was paying out from the custom-designed mechanical descender box attached to his chest via a nylon harness. He slid down the side of the parking garage like an arachnid, using his weak hand to brake. The Australians called rappelling headfirst "Geneva" style, but Fisher had first experienced the technique while cross-training with the Israeli Hostage-Rescue Rappelling and Climbing Sections, also known as the "Terror Monkeys." They were acknowledged experts in climbing and conducting assaults from above, and they'd urged him to try the inverted drop in order to peek in windows and limit exposure. His trial efforts had resulted in a few mild concussions, but as he perfected his skills, he became so adept at the technique that he could do it unconsciously, focusing entirely on his target.

Just as Fisher neared Cousin Ivan, the agent glanced up. Fisher's descent was smooth and controlled, but it was well-nigh impossible to remain perfectly silent.

That didn't matter, though. In that second when Ivan

saw him, Fisher gripped the man in a windpipe-crushing choke hold. At the same time, he thumbed a remote jutting from his sleeve, and the line began spooling back up, lifting him and Ivan into the air. Fisher carried Ivan all the way to the second floor, over the barrier wall, then waited until the man went limp. He deposited Ivan's body onto the floor and detached himself from the line. The entire process took the better part of six seconds. Fisher dragged the body over to some plastic barriers cordoning off an area in the process of being repaved. He shoved the body between two of the barriers, where he'd lie temporarily out of sight until the construction workers found him later in the morning.

"Sam, the loop's up," Charlie said. "You're clear for the roof."

"Thanks, Charlie. On my way." The private security guard in the building's garage, along with the man posted at the desk in the foyer, were watching a video loop and would never see Fisher's approach to the building.

Fisher hit the stairwell and double-timed his way to the roof, eight stories above. He eased open the door to find a middle-aged businessman walking across the lot to his car, briefcase in hand.

"Hang on a second, Briggs, I've got a guy up here."

"Standing by."

The businessman got in his vehicle and drove off. The second he vanished down the ramp, Fisher sprinted to the opposite wall and gazed out across the street to the apartment's rooftop, where Cousin Drago stood near a vine-covered wall within the private garden. The agent stared down at the street through a pair of binoculars. Beyond him were the flickering lights of the city and a rather breathtaking view of the lake beyond, walled in by those deep-brown mountains.

Fisher slid down his trifocals and studied the terrace. He had a direct line on the rooftop door and the nearby palm tree, as he'd planned. "Okay, Briggs, got the target marked for my line. You're clear for the shot."

"Gotcha, Sam. Stand by . . ."

Fisher zoomed in on Drago, anticipating a round blasting through his skull and dropping him.

Tensing, Fisher detected the slightest crack from Briggs's suppressed sniper rifle from across the street.

But something had gone wrong. Drago jerked, lowered his binoculars, and was immediately on his cell phone.

"Missed the shot!" cried Briggs.

"Fire again!" Fisher ordered.

Losing his breath, Fisher watched as Drago darted for the back door.

He reached out for the doorknob, then slumped before ever applying pressure.

"Jesus, Briggs, you're giving me a heart attack," Fisher said.

"Wind shifted on me."

"It's cool, Sam," said Charlie. "Drago didn't call out. He only tried to dial Uncle Harry."

"Roger that. Heading over now."

Fisher fired a line and grappling hook across the

street. The hook struck one of three palm trees growing from enormous pots. The hook jammed between the heavy branches, and Fisher attached it to the undercarriage of the nearest car behind him. Next he slapped the ball-bearing guide belt over the line and zipped across, thumping softly onto the terrace. He turned back, thumbed another remote, and the carabiner attached to the line back at the garage automatically released the rope so he could retrieve it, leaving no evidence of how he'd entered the building. With that done and Drago's body dragged out of sight behind some shrubs, Fisher was prepared to pick the rooftop door's lock, but Drago was a fine lad and had left the door open. Fisher simply walked inside and reported that to Grim.

"At the next landing come out and make a left," she instructed him. "Her penthouse suite's door is at the end of the hall, straight ahead."

"I see it," said Fisher. He jogged quickly to the end of the hall, noting the security camera's light from the ceiling.

"Okay, we see you at the door," said Charlie.

"And the alarm?" Fisher asked.

"What about it?" asked Charlie. "I've gotten us into Gitmo. You don't think I can get us in here?"

"Right."

"So the alarm's yesterday's news. Completely bypassed and powered off so the monitoring company gets no call."

Fisher reached into his breast pocket and produced his lock-picking tools; they included a hook pick, a half diamond with steep angles, a snake rake, a half diamond with shallow angles, an S-rake pick, a double round pick, and a long double ended pick.

"Sam, you're so old-school," remarked Charlie.

"You got a better way?"

"Melt the lock off with a laser, and who gives a shit if we were there."

"That laser gives off smoke and a nasty smell. Good way to get your ass caught. You stick to firewalls and leave the locks to me." He went to work, first opening the dead bolt, then moving on to the handle's lock.

"Aren't you done yet?" Charlie asked.

Fisher snorted. "Three seconds . . ."

"Sam, you'd better make this quick. Looks like a police car has just pulled up behind Uncle Harry. Maybe they think he's a drunk fallen asleep in his car. Either way, you gotta move quickly."

The lock clicked. "I'm in."

Fisher pushed in the door and quietly shut it after himself. He switched on his penlight and moved through a hallway lined with tropical plants and into a broad living room with white leather furniture and an adjoining dining room with a black marble table. The décor was, indeed, rich and imported, and the paintings on the wall—all landscapes of Switzerland—were signed oil on canvas originals. Very mature furnishings for a twenty-year-old girl, and again, Fisher wondered how much her father had a say in this.

He crossed over to the spacious kitchen with ornate backsplashes of expensive glass and porcelain tiles. Every drawer had been pulled open and searched, every cabinet rifled through. He opened the refrigerator. Well stocked.

"How's it looking out there, Briggs?"

"The cops are knocking on Harry's door, but he's not responding. Rest of the zone looks clear."

"Roger."

Fisher left the kitchen and shifted across the living room. He reached a pair of sliding glass doors leading to a broad balcony with seating for four around an ornate wicker table set. The city and lake views were incredible. Hell, Fisher wouldn't mind retiring here himself. He shifted away, down another hall, then neared the bed-room, which looked a bit more like a traditional college girl's dorm with dozens of stuffed animals thrown off the bed and lying across the rug. The king-size bed itself had been wrenched apart, the sheets removed, the mattress slid aside to allow inspection beneath it. The nightstand's drawers were empty, their contents—books, pieces of jewelry, hair ties, and a few grooming products—splayed across the floor. He found the long dresser with attached vanity mirror equally torn apart, some of the drawers removed and sitting on the bed.

Fisher hurriedly inspected the items—tickets from concerts she'd attended, old ID cards from school, and a plethora of receipts from bars, restaurants, and cafés. She was big on saving her receipts. Nothing unusual or inter-esting caught his eye. He took a peek inside the walk-in closet. Her clothes had been shuffled apart, but most still hung from the hangers.

He moved on to the adjoining bathroom with the

large garden tub and stall shower. Her medicine cabinet and drawers had also been emptied, with makeup strewn across the white tile floor.

"What're we doing here, Sam?" Grim asked, her tone implying that they were, indeed, wasting their time.

"Details, Grim. Details."

"I hope so. The cops can't wake up Harry, so they're trying to pry open the door."

Fisher was about to leave when something flashed off his penlight. He crossed to the sink, where he found a very odd pendant on a gold chain. It was a glass orb encapsulating a bolus of clay-like material, and it reminded him of those once-popular sealed glass baubles containing mustard seeds. It was not the kind of fancy, stunning, ornate, or otherwise "flashy" jewelry he imagined a co-ed might wear. In fact, it appeared handmade, a souvenir from some vacation somewhere, perhaps. Fisher tugged open a Velcro pouch on his belt and slid the necklace and pendant inside. He left the bathroom and noticed Nadia's desk on the other side of the room. The monitor was there but the computer was gone. No surprise.

With no more time to waste, Fisher gathered up a few more items of mild interest—those receipts and tickets, and lo and behold, a diary she'd kept in the nightstand that had been wedged inside the drawer. He hustled out to check the other two bedrooms. One was entirely empty, no furniture prints on the carpet, just never used. The other, a guest room, had been searched as well, but the nightstand and dresser drawers were empty. He

checked the second guest bath, then the adjoining clos-
ets. Nothing.

He returned to the front door, stood there for a
moment, and sighed. Maybe the diary or the jewelry
would give them something. "All right, I'm coming
out," he said.

"Cops got Harry's door open. They've called for an
ambulance and are trying to revive him," Grim reported.

"Well, that's a nice diversion," Fisher said. "Briggs,
you there?"

"I'm here, Sam. Packing up my rifle, getting ready to
head down."

"Meet you at the rally point."

"Will do."

"Hey, Sam, we just got a call from Kobin back on the
plane," said Charlie. "Says he's got a good lead on Kestrel's whereabouts in Russia."

"Oh, yeah. Where is he?"

"Kobin's not saying. Says he wants to talk to you and
only you."

Fisher snickered. "You tell him he'll be spilling his
guts figuratively. And if not? Then literally."

"Nice. I'd buy tickets to see that."

Fisher returned to the roof, rappelled down the back
of the building, then took off running to link up with
Grim and Charlie.

WHILE in the SUV en route back to the airport, Fisher
showed Grim the diary and necklace.

"We'll have everything checked for DNA. Could even be a clue there, someone who was in her apartment, a friend we don't know about who's offering them a place."

Fisher lifted the pendant toward the window for better light. "It's weird, isn't it?"

"I've never seen anything like it. What's inside the glass?"

"That's for you to figure out."

"Hey, I picked up another piece of evidence at the café," said Charlie from the driver's seat.

"What's that?" asked Fisher.

"The cute barista's phone number." Charlie wriggled his brows as he held up a slip of paper.

"You idiot," said Grim, shaking her head.

Charlie seemed unfazed. "I have a Swiss girlfriend now. That's the way I roll."

Fisher turned to Briggs, who'd been deathly silent since entering the vehicle. "What's wrong with you?"

"Just replaying that shot in my head."

"Don't beat yourself up. Like you said, the wind shifted. You still got him."

Briggs sighed in disgust. "Not good enough."

"All right, then, make it up to us next time—don't miss."

Briggs's tone hardened. "I won't."

12

ACCORDING to Grim, Oliver "Ollie" Fenton, twenty-seven, was a graduate of North Carolina State's analytics program and the first member of his family to attend college. He'd assumed he was headed for a career in "big data," but after a rather serendipitous meeting with a CIA recruiter, he was quickly drafted into the ranks of the agency's young "quants." His analysis of the Arab Spring's effects on the nation of Qatar had caught Grim's eye, and his conclusions concurred with a recent report she'd read produced by the Kuwait Programme on Development, Governance and Globalisation in the Gulf States, a program based at the London School of Economics and Political Science. Of the handful of young analysts on board Paladin, he was the best, and Fisher felt comfortable with Grim giving Ollie the pendant and diary for analysis.

Meanwhile, she would go through the NSA's most recent report of comm intercepts, analyzing calls made by Kasperov prior to the man's disappearance, along with those received or placed by his girlfriend, by Nadia, and by a branching tree of dozens of others related to them.

Fisher took a seat beside Kobin, who was studying a map of Russia from one of Charlie's computer stations.

"Hey, asshole," Kobin said without looking up.

Fisher spun the man's chair around and leaned forward, getting squarely in Kobin's face. "I heard you got something for me."

"I'll need some guarantees."

"Guarantees?"

"I'm a businessman."

"Well, all right," Fisher began slowly, lowering his voice. "I guarantee that if you don't give me what I need, there's going to be pain in your future. A lot of pain."

"Come on, Fisher, you know what I'm saying . . . I'm just talking about him, Kestrel. I don't want him brought back here. I don't want to see him . . . *ever* . . . again."

"Because you shot him in the head?"

"I thought I was doing the right thing."

"Hard to tell anymore, right? Good guys . . . bad guys . . ."

"So, you're not planning to bring him back here, right?" A tremor had worked its way into his voice.

"Actually, my plan was to put the two of you in your

cell, stand back, and watch the smackdown. We could take bets on how long you'd last."

Kobin drew his head back. "Give me some fucking credit. Where Chuck Norris ends, I begin . . ."

Fisher couldn't help but grin.

"See, see, I made you laugh. Now you're amused and we can strike a deal."

"Tell me where Kestrel is, otherwise—"

"All right, all right!"

Fisher stood back and folded his arms over his chest. "Talk."

"He's not coming here, right?"

"I doubt it. But if he does, you won't have to see him."

"You promise?"

Fisher raised one brow. "Does a promise mean anything to a scumbag like you?"

"Coming from you it does."

"I'm flattered. Now . . . *talk*."

"Okay. Two of Kestrel's old army buddies used to work for me. Point is I hired a lot of those old Russian spec ops boys. The government doesn't pay 'em shit and then fucks 'em over in retirement, so they used to do a lot of freelance work for me once they got out. I even recruited a few of them right out of the exclusion zone."

"Oh, yeah," said Fisher. "Been there before. Long time ago."

Kobin turned and pointed to the map. "It hasn't changed. Twenty-six hundred square kilometers around Chernobyl—where the nuclear reactor blew and they have three-eyed fish and trees that glow in the dark."

"What the hell were they doing there?"

"If these guys couldn't find work in private security or something else, a lot of 'em got really desperate, turned to game poaching, illegal logging, and metal salvage operations inside the zone. Some of them got legit jobs giving tours, but a lot of them became criminals—especially the ones with a disability like a limp or something. They'd get help from the *samosely*—the people who refused to evacuate, like a lot of old people, or the ones who resettled illegally. You wouldn't believe how many people are still going in there, looking for a quick score."

"Nothing surprises me anymore."

"Yep, some of 'em are that desperate. If you've been there, you might remember the place is controlled by the State Agency of Ukraine on the Exclusion Zone Management. They call it S-A-E-Z. Of course yours truly—being a Ukrainian American—has friends in the agency. Good friends."

"So you picked up Kestrel there? I can't believe he's that desperate."

"He's not. I just talked to one of his army buddies, actually an old mentor who got him into special forces in the first place. He told me that before Kestrel moved to St. Petersburg, he spent some time as a kid with his foster parents in a little town called Vilcha; it's right there in the exclusion zone."

"So he's gone back to a contaminated town to what, reminisce?"

"No, here's where it gets good. Security's tight, like I said. You don't get past the checkpoint without papers.

So I talked to my friends at SAEZ, and they issued a temporary contractor's clearance pass to a man named . . . wait for it . . . Glib Lakeev."

"That's one of Kestrel's aliases."

"Bingo. And according to my contacts at SAEZ, he hasn't entered the zone yet. But the pass is only good for three days, so that Russian fucker is planning something— and we know where he's gonna be."

"And you think it's Vilcha?"

"Tell you why. He never worked in the exclusion zone like his buddies. Vilcha is his *only* connection to it. If he's going into the zone, I bet everything that he's going there."

"To do what?"

Kobin laughed through his big nose. "What the fuck do I look like? A mind reader? Maybe he's going in there for a beer with a radioactive corpse."

Fisher turned to Grim, who'd been eavesdropping on the conversation. "What do you think?"

"I think we can be in Kiev in less than three hours." She faced Charlie. "Can you get us into the SVR's comm network in less than three hours?"

"Are you crazy? I'm still sifting through Kannonball's code—it's slow going . . ."

"I thought so. Flight deck, prepare for departure. We're heading to Kiev."

Fisher crossed to the SMI table and frowned at Grim. "No argument?"

Her voice turned grave. "None—because I think I know why Kestrel's going to Vilcha."

13

TWO hours and fifty-one minutes later, Paladin touched down at Kiev's Zhuliany Airport, where Fisher and Briggs rented Suzuki C90T touring bikes for the trip over to Vilcha, with plans to arrive before sunset. The irradiated ghost town lay about seventy-nine miles northwest of Kiev and twenty-five miles east of Chernobyl in Ukraine.

Since its 1991 breakaway from the old Soviet Union, Ukraine remained a country vacillating between its past and uncertain future. The official language was Ukrainian, although Russian was the native tongue of a quarter of the country's forty-five million citizens and was designated an official language in thirteen of its twenty-seven regions. The country had a working partnership with

NATO yet remained home to the Russian Black Sea Fleet. Inside the exclusion zone, where all time had ceased in 1986, everything that was unequivocally Ukraine said so—only in Russian. The photos Fisher had reviewed during the flight over left a hollow feeling in his gut. Vilcha had been ripped straight from some postapocalyptic novel like *I Am Legend* by Richard Matheson. The place would make them feel like the last men on earth.

They reached the main checkpoint—a meager striped pole barrier along with a ramshackle guardhouse that had a familiar red stop sign in English hanging crookedly from its side wall. They slowed, then came to a halt, and Fisher lifted the visor on his helmet, wincing slightly at the frigid air. He handed the old man smoking an unfiltered Camel an envelope stuffed with greenbacks.

The man narrowed his gaze on Fisher before accepting the envelope.

Fisher returned a hard gaze of his own and said curtly in Russian, "Andriy Kobin sends his regards."

The guard seemed unimpressed—meaning he'd probably met Kobin before. He counted the money, turned back to his younger partner, then nodded. He faced Fisher and asked in broken English, "Why you go into zone?"

Fisher answered in Russian and without hesitation: "We're on vacation."

The old guard rubbed the corners of his eyes, removed his cigarette from his chapped lips, and revealed to Fisher the ugliest missing-toothed grin this side of Siberia. He turned back to his partner, then began to chuckle so violently that he broke into a fit of coughing. Once he finally cleared his throat, he beamed and cried, "Send postcard. Have fun! Good times!" He waved them on.

Fisher gave a quick nod to Briggs, the barrier lifted, and they sped on through.

The Suzuki was a far cry from the bike Fisher had stolen back in Bolivia, and the road, while glistening here and there with streaks of ice, had certainly not claimed more than two hundred lives this past year. However, it did present a different kind of danger.

They cut through a heavily forested area, the barren limbs already suggesting the lifelessness of the towns to come. Grim had gained them access into one of the satellites of the National Reconnaissance Office, or NRO, and while they'd only had the Keyhole on target for a few minutes, she'd been able to photograph a 2009 Renault Kangoo minivan heading into Vilcha less than an hour ago. Grim had photographed the tag; it was a rental signed out to one Glib Lakeev. Moreover, Kobin had confirmed that, yes indeed, Kestrel had gone through the checkpoint and was heading home.

Consequently, they were losing precious time. Fisher had planned to arrive at the town *before* Kestrel in order to stage an ambush, but maybe it was better they didn't spend additional time here. During the first five years after the catastrophe, the level of radioactive isotopes of cesium had reached 60 curies per square kilometer, with plutonium at 0.7 curies and strontium at 15 curies. Such radiation levels were deadly for humans; however, Grim had assured Fisher that while some of the radioactive isotopes, such as strontium-90 and cesium-137, still lingered, they were at tolerable exposure levels for limited periods of time.

The narrow road began showing signs of serious neglect as they left the forest and passed through several fields. Larger cracks and ruts rattled Fisher's bones, and weeds heavily encroached up from the embankments. Leaves and branches booted by high winds were strewn everywhere, cleared only by more winds, and in some sections Fisher found himself leaning hard into turns to navigate around a branch and even a few fallen trees. Soon the fields surrendered back to the more dense woods, with trees beginning to tower over roofless houses and barns whose pale white walls were streaked in heavy layers of rust visible even in the dim headlights. A few signs written in Cyrillic and English proclaimed: DANGER.

Fisher's skin began to crawl. He imagined he could feel the radioactive particles entering his lungs, then flowing into his bloodstream. He shuddered off the thought and checked his rearview mirror.

Briggs kept his bike about five meters back, allowing Fisher to pick the route across the potholes and debris. He'd been beating himself up over that missed shot, and while Fisher appreciated his determination, Briggs needed to accept and learn from setbacks. The lessons were sometimes bitter tasting, but you took your mental notes and moved on. Although he'd never admit it, Fisher thought that maybe, just maybe, Briggs was a better rifleman than he was. Fisher spent much more time firing pistols, perfecting his quick draw and close combat skills. Briggs did demonstrate an appreciable advantage with his various sniper rifles. One day they'd have to compete to see exactly where they stood.

As they neared the outskirts of the town, marked by a blue faded placard that read simply вильча, they pulled over, killed their engines and lights, then began walking their bikes quietly down the road, with the buildings lying about two hundred meters ahead.

For a moment, the pervading darkness and silence were overwhelming. The plinks and pings of their cooling 1,462cc engines, along with the scuffle of their boots, barely rose above the soft wind.

They seemed to be the only living creatures here.

But then out in the forest to their left came the half-muted chuffs and shuffling of an unknown number of four-legged animals. They paused to remove their helmets and slip on their trifocals, the twilight now pushed back by their night vision.

Grim had said she'd known why Kestrel had come to Vilcha, and it sure as hell wasn't to get nostalgic. A Voron agent the CIA and NSA were closely monitoring was found murdered in his hotel room in Kiev. A second agent operating in the same area was reported missing, according to their intel sources on the ground. That second agent was ID'd as Vasily Yenin, who, according to the CIA, had been a double agent working under former 3E director Tom Reed and possibly one of the men who'd been holding Kestrel prisoner.

If Kestrel was going into the contaminated zone, it was for one purpose, according to Grim: to interrogate and murder Yenin.

"Why get special permission and drive all the way into a contaminated zone just to kill a man?" Fisher had asked.

"It's quiet. No one to hear the sounds of torture. Easy to get rid of the body."

"If he killed one guy in Kiev, why would he take this guy to Vilcha?"

"Maybe Grim's right. Maybe he wants to drag it out," Briggs had suggested.

"And he's also got another reason for going there. Killing Yenin and dumping the body is convenient," Fisher had suggested. "He's killing two birds."

The answers were only minutes away.

They neared a row of shops emerging from the trees like broken teeth, their awnings shredded, their signs caked in a thick layer of dirt and dust. Fisher noted the briefest flash of light from a filthy window about midway down the row. A sign above read: МЯСО, or MEAT.

"Grim, he's gone into an old butcher shop."

"I'll try to confirm," she answered.

Running now, they reached the first alley and ducked into it to park their bikes. Fisher gestured for Briggs to head out across the street and climb up into the small church with Orthodox crosses rising from its stained steeples and what looked like a small, mold-covered balcony above the archway entrance.

Briggs took off with his SIG SSG 3000 sniper rifle

slung in its soft case over his back. The rifle was cham-
bered in 7.62mm and featured a modular chassis system,
making it perfect for an operation like this.

Fisher reached into his holster and deployed another
of their micro UAVs like the drone they'd used up in the
Caucasus Mountains. He reported the bird was in the air.

"Okay, Sam, I've got control," Charlie answered.

Fisher watched as the tri-rotors purred more loudly,
and the device flew away, rising high above the alley.

"I see Kestrel's van out back behind the old butcher
shop," Charlie said.

"Hey, Sam, it's Kobin here."

"What the hell's he doing on the channel?" Fisher
asked.

"I wanted him to monitor," said Grim. "Not talk."

"Yeah, but I got something else, comes straight from
Kestrel's old mentor. So that's not just any butcher shop.
Kestrel used to work there when he was fourteen. His
foster father made him lie about his age. It was all the
blood and gore that made him run away to St. Petersburg."

"It seems the blood and gore don't bother him
anymore."

"No shit. Do us both a favor and leave that fucker
there to rot."

Fisher groaned. "Okay, Grim, get him off the line.
Briggs, you in position?"

"Roger, up top, weapon ready in thirty seconds."

"Okay, stand by." Fisher skulked his way around the
corner, along the frozen earth behind the buildings,

then reached the butcher shop's rear door, whose tarnished brass handle and splintering wood around the knob were darkened by decades-old bloodstains. He slowly turned the knob, finding the door unlocked.

When noise of any kind was your enemy, you always came prepared. From his breast pocket he withdrew a pen-sized bottle of silicone spray and doused the door's hinges; the pump action was quiet enough to be dampened by the wind. He waited a few seconds more for the silicone to soak in.

Now, clutching his Five-seveN in one hand, he eased open the door, which pulled effortlessly aside, then he moved in, becoming one with the darkness. Holding his breath, he reached back and shut the door after himself.

A voice came from another room ahead, the Russian cadence at first strange, but then, as he pricked up his ears, Fisher recognized the voice.

Before advancing, he scanned his surroundings. He was crouched in a warehouse area of sorts where orders must've been wrapped and prepped to be delivered out the back door. The butcher-block tables had remained, the cabinets mounted to the walls emptied, the doors hanging open.

The narrow hallway ahead led straight out to the customer cases and butcher shop proper, with an intersecting hall lying between. Dim light filtered down from the right side of the intersection, with long shadows shifting across the wall.

"Sam, Briggs here. I got you on sonar. Looks like just

two ahead, right of your position. One guy might be standing on something."

Briggs had beat him to the punch. Fisher had been a breath away from activating his own sonar. He used his OPSAT to reply silently:

Good. Mark targets. Wait for me.

"Sam, Kestrel's too important to lose," said Grim. "And if he's got Yenin, they're both valuable assets."

He knew that, too, but Kestrel had assumedly found and removed his tracker, meaning he was not honoring his end of the bargain to feed Fourth Echelon information when they needed it. If he had gone completely rogue, then what would stop him from trying to kill Fisher? A whole lot of cash, maybe, but not much else. Kestrel might assume they were even now. He owed Fisher and Briggs nothing for saving his life. No more deals.

In truth, Fisher had no idea how Kestrel would react, and so as he eased forward, wary of every creak of floorboard, he shoved up his trifocals and held his breath. Once he reached the intersection, he brought himself to full height and clutched his pistol with both hands before turning the corner—

To confront the man.

14

STRAIGHT ahead lay an open meat locker door, and beyond came more of those long shadows, one shaped like a figure crucified against the corrugated aluminum wall. Cobwebs spanned the ceiling above the flickering silhouettes, and the walls rattled a moment as a strong gust came through.

Fisher took advantage of that noise to step forward as a stale, dry odor wafted into his face. He turned into the locker.

And froze.

His gaze panned up to the naked man suspended from four meat hooks.

Wow. He mouthed a curse.

The sharp ends of those hooks had been driven

through the soft flesh on the man's shoulders and slammed right through his palms, Old Testament style. Small incisions like slash marks from a whip covered his legs and rump, and blood pooled down across his ankles and dripped off his toes. He was a big man, six feet at least, probably two hundred pounds with biceps chiseled in the gym. From this angle, Fisher couldn't see his face and was glad for that. The panting and gasping that escaped his lips was hard to bear.

Since Vasily Yenin had been a double agent, the NSA and CIA had good records on him. Grim had shown Fisher the man's dossier and accompanying photographs. Once Fisher caught the man's profile, he nodded in confirmation, then tensed at the sound of creaking floorboards.

Kestrel came out from behind a row of metal shelving that ran along the far wall. He trained a Makarov on Fisher's chest.

"Fisher?"

"Yeah, it's me."

"What are you doing here?"

"Just picking up some roast beef."

Kestrel almost smiled. "Me, too."

Fisher took a step toward him. "We called. You didn't answer."

"You put tracker on me."

"We had a deal."

"You have no trust. Without trust, we have no deal."

"Sam, Briggs here. I got you covered. I'll take him out right through the wall if I have to . . ."

Fisher drew in a long breath, then gestured to Yenin. "Old friend of yours?"

"You know who he is."

"Get him down. I need him alive."

"Oh, you do? Maybe old friend of yours? Friend who kept me in coma? Maybe I have to kill you, too." Kestrel leaned toward Fisher, his heavily tattooed right arm flexing as he clutched his pistol with both hands in an aggressive thumbs-forward grip. He took another step, exposing an area behind him where the floorboards had been pried up with a screwdriver. On the table to his right sat a Nike gym bag covered in dirt.

"What's in the bag?"

"Pajamas."

"How much you got in there? Stashed it here for a rainy day?"

"Shut up, Fisher. What do you want?"

"Get him down. I want information on Igor Kasperov—and this guy can get us into the Voron database."

Kestrel shook his head. "He's no good now. He's like me. Ex-Voron. Passwords locked out. He can't get you shit."

"I don't believe you."

"Fool. Think about it. He went missing. As soon as that happens, they lock you out. They think maybe you have been taken prisoner. Simple."

"So you're leaving him here to bleed to death?"

"No, I leave him for the wolves. After Chernobyl, the wolves and wild dogs fed on roe deer, and when the deer were gone, the wolves fed on dogs. Now dogs and deer are gone. So wolves are very hungry. They can eat twenty-two pounds of meat in one feeding."

"Wolves don't eat humans."

"Tell that to the wolves."

Fisher kept his pistol pointed at Kestrel's heart but flicked his glance up to Yenin. He spoke quickly in Russian, "I can offer you help in exchange for information. I'm looking for Igor Kasperov and his daughter, Nadia. I know the SVR and Voron are looking for them, too. Do you know anything about their investigation? Maybe something they found? Anything? If you tell me, we'll let you go."

Yenin opened his mouth, but before he spoke, Kestrel raised his voice. "Don't tell him anything."

"He'll talk to me, Kestrel, otherwise I'll shoot you both in the legs and leave you here. Like you said, the wolves are hungry."

"You'll shoot me?" Kestrel asked. "You don't see me or my gun right here?"

Fisher sighed. "Briggs? Hit the bag."

The words had barely escaped Fisher's lips when the Nike bag was blasted off the table by a perfectly placed 7.62mm round. The bag fell to the ground with a nice hole in its side.

"Thank you, Briggs."

Kestrel, who'd ducked and whirled around with his pistol, searched all over the ceiling and found the entry hole in the wall.

"He never misses," Fisher added. Indeed, Briggs had vowed to step up his game, and step it up he had.

Fisher crossed toward Kestrel. "You run, I shoot you. You run, he shoots you. Simple."

Kestrel lifted his pistol. "How 'bout I put a bullet in your head?"

Fisher shrugged. "Then we're just two miserable men, dying in a radioactive shithole like this."

"Maybe that is for best."

"I have no more time for you, Kestrel." Fisher gestured to Yenin. "Maybe he wants to tell me something. Let him talk, then you get to walk, no questions asked."

"Bullshit, Fisher. I said no trust. No deal."

Fisher glanced up at Yenin. "Do you know anything about Kasperov? Do you know anything about the nuclear material stolen from Mayak?"

Yenin groaned and gasped, his eyes narrowed in agony, tears staining his stubbly cheeks. His breathing grew more labored, reaching a crescendo, then, finally, a word exploded from his lips: "Snegurochka."

"Shut up!" cried Kestrel.

"Briggs, on the count of three, you're going to shoot Kestrel in the head."

"Roger that. I'm on target."

"Okay, Briggs, one, two—"

"Wait!" cried Kestrel, eyes widening back on the wall where that first round had penetrated. "All right. Let the fool talk."

"Hold fire, Briggs."

"Roger that."

"Snegurochka," Yenin repeated.

"What the hell is he saying?" Fisher asked.

Kestrel made a face. "That word means Snow Maiden."

"Does that mean something to you?"

Kestrel's eyes grew wider. "Oh, yes, it does. Snow Maiden is the code name for Major Viktoria Kolosov of the GRU."

"Grim, you get that?"

"Got it. Running it now."

"Yenin, what about this woman? You tell me, and I'll get you down. It'll be over."

Yenin's face was beginning to twist in improbable angles as the pain really set in. His eyes barely focused on Fisher now, but then, after a few gasps, he said in broken English, "Big shoot-out in old metro tunnel. Nadia's bodyguards and two GRU agents killed. Girl captured. Snow Maiden ordered to hold her."

"Hold her where?" Fisher asked.

"Take me down, and I tell you," said Yenin.

Fisher glanced ironically at Kestrel. "I guess he learned his negotiation techniques from you." Fisher holstered his weapon, much to Kestrel's shock. "Okay, he doesn't want to talk, so he's all yours. Leave him here for the wolves, I don't care. We'll find the girl."

Fisher started for the door.

"Wait!" Yenin croaked. "They're holding girl in Sochi. She's in Sochi. They've got safe house there. Now take me down! Please!"

"Sam, Charlie here. Got the four-one-one on Sochi. Black Sea resort city. Lots of tourists . . ."

Fisher widened his gaze on Yenin. "Where in Sochi?" Fisher lifted his voice to a roar. "WHERE?"

Yenin closed his eyes, as though he had to think about it. "Hotel Olesska on Lenina Street. We use as safe house sometimes."

"I got it, Sam," said Charlie. "I'll start hacking into every cam within a ten-K radius."

"If you're lying . . ." Fisher warned the agent.

"I'm not," Yenin said.

"Do you know anything about Mayak?"

"No, nothing. Only rumors. No way could terrorists steal material. Must be inside job."

"No shit," Fisher said. He turned to Kestrel. "You'd better start answering my calls. Have a good night. Briggs? We don't need any more loose ends here."

"Roger that."

"Sam, what're you doing?" Grim asked.

"Mopping up."

As Fisher stepped out of the meat locker, a gunshot thumped into the room, and he didn't bother looking back. He knew Yenin had been taken out with a perfect headshot.

"Fisher!" Kestrel screamed.

"Don't come after me," Fisher cried. "I told you. He never misses."

—— *15* —————————————

THE girl was asleep again. Her left eye had swollen shut, and the Snow Maiden was contemplating whether to get her some ice or just let her suffer. The little princess had never known such pain. Stress for her was deciding between five-star restaurants and which charity balls to attend with her father. Physical pain involved nicking her legs while shaving. She'd never been interrogated and beaten down to the floor like a dog. She'd never been waterboarded or electrocuted, had her nails and teeth forcibly extracted, her toes removed one at a time. There was a whole new world of torture waiting for her, and she didn't even know it. All she'd known for the past few hours were the contours of the Snow Maiden's knuckles.

And all she could do was weep and deny that she knew anything about her father's whereabouts.

It was all perfunctory at best, with both of them dancing around each other until they really got down to business. Of course, it was important for the Snow Maiden to keep the girl alive, and she would; however, that didn't mean she couldn't work out a few issues and relieve some of her own stress.

The Snow Maiden glided across the plush red carpet to the window and pushed open the curtains. She stared out at the shimmering lights from the Black Sea coastline. The hotel was only a ten-minute walk from the water, and in addition to the incredible views, it offered a Finnish sauna and traditional Russian *banya* where she planned to relax later this evening.

Her trance was broken as the two men outside the hotel and the two next door began to check in, the Bluetooth receiver in her ear buzzing with their voices. She sighed and answered them.

Her superiors had foisted upon her four agents who deeply resented that she was in charge. The GRU had wanted her to turn over the girl to FSB agents because the investigation fell within their purview. This was an internal matter that did not belong in the hands of a foreign intelligence agent. But the Snow Maiden had implored her bosses, told them that she wanted to finish this job. Given her "excellent work" in the metro, they'd stood up for her and had convinced the FSB that they didn't need to waste a seasoned agent to oversee a babysitting job. Those administrators had finally given in and had allowed her to take Nadia to Sochi—but not without the FSB baggage coming along. No, the Snow Maiden wouldn't murder these men, although the thought had crossed her mind—four times to be precise. She'd already won the adulation she needed from her superiors, most notably Izotov himself, who'd bragged to his counterpart at the FSB that "no one but the Snow Maiden could have survived that gun battle, and she did!" That was glowing praise and would certainly contribute to her promotion; however, if she could get Nadia to talk, then that would be something. *Really* something. In her mind, this was not a babysitting job. This was an opportunity to single-handedly locate Igor Kasperov and bring him in.

She traced a finger along the glass. It was hard not to appreciate the irony unfurling before her eyes. Here she was, involved in the darker side of human nature, while outside the city of Sochi lay in all its grand and burgeoning splendor. Electricity was in the air as this place, known by many as the "Russian Riviera," prepared to host the 2014 Winter Olympic Games. Heavy construction was going on everywhere, even in the lot adjoining Hotel Olesska, where yet another hotel was being erected, one that would be crowded with media personnel once the games began. A ceaseless train of earth-moving dump trucks lumbered daily across Lenina Street, much to the chagrin of some guests—but not them. Their soundproofed room lay on the opposite side of the hotel, in its most private section, where intelligence agents often held political prisoners and others, keeping them far away from Moscow and from soiling the president's hands.

The FSB and GRU had developed a healthy relationship with the hotel's staff, and the facility itself, being only four stories and surrounded by large pine trees, made it easy to establish a defensive perimeter. Additionally, the hotel was only a five-minute drive from the train station and just ten minutes from Adler Airport. When agents like the Snow Maiden weren't attaching battery cables to the genitalia of prisoners, they could visit the nearby water park, sports and entertainment complexes, the Sochi Dolphinarium dolphin park, and the Discovery World Aquarium—not to mention the soaring skyline of the new Olympic park.

The Snow Maiden grinned darkly as she turned away from the window at the sound of Nadia stirring. "Are you hungry?"

Nadia lay across the bed, looking more like a corpse than a pampered rich man's daughter. They'd given her a change of clothes: a pair of jeans and a sweatshirt that made her appear a few years younger. She lifted her head, and finally, after a deep-throated cough, was able to sit up.

A flat-screen television sat atop a dresser behind them. "Would you like to watch TV?" the Snow Maiden asked.

"No."

"Would you like to tell me where your father is?"

Nadia widened her good eye on the Snow Maiden. "When this is over, I'm going to come back for you. My father has very powerful friends. He'll make it happen.

And when he does, I'm going to do ten times what you've done to me."

"Ten times? That's impressive. They taught you some math in that fancy college. So, do you think we're already done? Look at your beautiful fingernails . . . are those gels? And your nice teeth. You had them whitened? So beautiful . . ."

Nadia closed her eyes and sighed in frustration. "I told you. I was on my way to the airport. All I know is I was supposed to get on the plane. I have no idea where the plane was going."

"It was heading straight into the mountains, where it crashed."

"Whatever you say."

"I can get my computer and show you."

"I don't care."

The Snow Maiden dragged a chair over to the bed. She flipped it around and draped her arms over the back. "What's it like to be you?"

"What kind of question is that?"

"Tell me about your life."

"No."

The Snow Maiden glanced around the room. "There's nothing else to do."

Nadia set her teeth and began to nod. "I see what you're doing. Get me to talk. Get the whole Stockholm syndrome thing going. Get me comfortable, then I let something slip, huh? You think I'm stupid like the other scumbags you take here?"

"No, you're very intelligent. I read one of the research

papers you did for a class. I wish I knew as much about computers as you do."

"Yeah, then you wouldn't be stuck in some shitty government job . . ."

"So you're going to follow in your father's footsteps because he made sure you'd have that opportunity."

"That's right."

"Did you miss him?"

"What do you mean?"

"When you were growing up. I assume he was never around, always busy working on the computer viruses. Did he ever forget to pick you up? Did he ever forget a special occasion like your birthday?"

"Why do you care? You trying to work out your own issues by making me feel bad?"

"I'm just asking questions."

"He was a great father. But then my mother died."

"I'm sorry."

"No, you're not. You're trying to be my friend because you think I'll say something. You're so obvious. And pathetic. And what's with the crazy black hair and the boots?"

The Snow Maiden shrugged. "I like them."

Nadia took a deep breath and turned away. "There's something wrong with you. Something very wrong."

"What makes you say that?"

"How can you do this kind of work?"

"I enjoy it. I bet you would, too."

"Are you kidding me? You're just some government employee who had a terrible life. You're like some woman who wants to be a man with a big gun. That's all you are. You're nothing."

"You don't sound afraid anymore."

Nadia balled her hands into fists. "I'm not."

"The cuffs hurt. I'll leave them off if you're a good girl, but if you—"

Nadia launched herself off the bed and came at the Snow Maiden with her right fist held high above her head.

The Snow Maiden pushed back off the chair, even as Nadia's fist came down. The girl missed, and the Snow Maiden followed with a right hook to the girl's jaw and a left jab to her chest, knocking her squarely onto the bed.

In the next heartbeat, she straddled the girl, pinned her wrists to the bed and leaned in close to her ear and whispered, "Is this what you want? More pain?"

"Let me go."

"Where's your father?"

"He's right behind you."

The Snow Maiden grinned, then suddenly released the girl and tapped on Nadia's temple. "I think your father is right here, and he's driving you crazy."

"Why do you want him so badly?"

That woke the Snow Maiden's grin. "I wish I knew."

"Well, it's pretty clear he fucked over the government. He wouldn't tell me exactly how. He just said go to the airport. I begged him, pleaded with him. I never heard his voice sound like that."

"Like what?"

"Scared."

Neither of them spoke for a moment, but then the Snow Maiden blurted out, "I don't want to kill you."

Nadia flashed an ugly grin. "I'm okay with that."

"I'll confess: I hate you and people like you. And obviously, I can't kill you unless I'm sure you have nothing to give me."

"We're going around in circles here," Nadia said. "You don't believe me, so you'll keep asking the same questions over and over. And then I'll get so tired of hearing them that I'll begin telling you what you want to hear. But that's not the truth. I don't know where he is."

"Do you know where Joline is?"

Nadia's head drew back, and her mouth began to fall open in shock.

"I know where she is."

Suddenly, the door opened behind them and two of the Snow Maiden's men ushered in Joline Bossert, a twenty-one-year-old CSCS student with blond hair, narrow cheeks, and limbs seemingly too large for her fragile Swiss torso. She had earrings running up the sides of both ears, along with a pierced brow partially hidden behind her trendy blue glasses. She'd been stripped down to her beige bra and white panties.

She was Nadia's best friend from college. They were, according to Joline, inseparable.

The second Joline caught sight of Nadia. She spoke rapidly in Italian, since she was a native of Lugano: "Oh my God, Nadia, what's happening? Are you okay?

What're they doing to us? Why are we here? They . . . they . . . just grabbed me right out of the apartment!"

The Snow Maiden put her finger to Nadia's lips and sang, "I think you know where your father is . . ." She rose off the bed.

Behind her, Nadia bolted up and screamed, "You leave her alone!"

The Snow Maiden whirled and raised her voice: "First, before we begin this little reunion, I'd like to discuss a few details. This room has been modified just for us. It doesn't matter how loud you are. You could scream at the very top of your lungs and no one, not room service, not the old lady down the hall who is chain-smoking, not anyone will hear you . . . or her . . ." The Snow Maiden tipped her head toward Joline. "Now, she's going to die in front of you if you don't tell me where your father is. If you really don't know, well, I'm sorry, she's going to die anyway, then."

In the Snow Maiden's right pocket sat an assisted-opening folder, which she removed and thumbed open. The blade swung into place with enough spring action to catch Nadia's attention.

"I've cut a lot of people with this blade," the Snow Maiden said. "So it might be a little dull."

"I'm telling you, I don't know!"

The Snow Maiden shrugged and touched the Bluetooth headset at her ear. "Call the front desk," she ordered one of her men. "Tell them we'll be needing the third room in an hour or so. Tell them we're very sorry about the mess."

Nadia began screaming as the door opened and another man rushed to the bed and cuffed Nadia's wrists and ankles. Then he propped her up on the bed so she had a spectacular view of the show.

"You can close your eyes," the Snow Maiden told Nadia. "But sometimes that's worse, because as you listen to her scream, your imagination can conjure up something even more horrible than what I'm doing to her. Then again, you haven't seen the things I've seen, and I have a very vivid imagination. Now tell me . . . where's Daddy?"

"Nadia, please tell her!" cried Joline. "I don't want to die! Please . . ."

The Snow Maiden traced Joline's lips with the blade. "Are you listening to her, Nadia? I'm sure we don't need to discuss the rules of this game."

Nadia was already sobbing and barely able to speak. "I . . . I told you. I don't know where he is. He didn't tell me where he was going."

"And you have no ideas? No guesses?"

"He could be anywhere. Maybe one of the summer homes! Maybe he's gone to Florida with his girlfriend. I don't know!"

"I understand."

The Snow Maiden ran the knife along Joline's cheek, drawing a fine line of blood. Joline began wrenching violently against the agents holding her while Nadia wailed for the Snow Maiden to stop.

At the same time, one of the Snow Maiden's men was forced to pin Nadia back to the bed and hold her while the Snow Maiden chose her second incision on Nadia's opposite cheek.

It was hard to describe what she felt while working on the girl. There was something special as the incisions deepened and the blood began to pool. This was a young woman who had never been broken. She, like Nadia, had always been flawless, always sitting on shelves like pieces of pottery to be admired by passersby for their overt beauty—that was to say, beauty on the surface only.

But to the Snow Maiden, young ladies like this were more beautiful when they were damaged, more beautiful as they tried to piece themselves back together. The Japanese had a word for it: *kintsukuroi*—the art of repairing pottery with gold or silver lacquer and accepting that the piece is *more* beautiful for having been broken.

Joline would be sacrificed so that Nadia could be broken. Young Nadia would wear those golden scars, and she might finally glimpse the *real* world, a world unaltered by her father.

After a while the begging and gasping and pleading turned into a deep hum, and the Snow Maiden focused on her blade and the power she wielded with her mind. Each drop of blood came with a promise that when it was over, Nadia would be free of her father's grasp, free to become a real woman in a cruel and merciless world.

When the Snow Maiden was finished, her men hauled the body away, leaving her and Nadia alone once more. The Snow Maiden drifted back to the window, opened it, and took in a deep breath of the freezing air.

Nadia had pulled her knees into her chest and was still sobbing. The Snow Maiden returned to the bed. "All right, I believe you. You don't know where your father is."

"Why did you have to kill her?"

"To make you strong. To make you more like me."

Nadia glanced up and cried, "Oh my God. More like you? You're insane!"

After the barest of nods, the Snow Maiden rose and started toward the door. Before she grabbed the handle, she turned back and said, "While I'm gone, I want you to close your eyes and watch me cut her again. I want you to dream about it. I want you to let it get deep inside until it's beautiful. Will you do that for me?"

Nadia just looked at her incredulously.

The Snow Maiden averted her gaze and left. Two of her men entered the room after her as relief. She started across the hall to the next room, where she'd wash up, then head down to the sauna. As she reached out for the next doorknob, she realized her hand was trembling.

16

AS they lumbered into Paladin's control room, Fisher winced over Grim's heated gaze and crossed directly back to the armory with Briggs.

While Fisher stowed his weapons, Briggs took a seat and began to break down his rifle, preparing it to be cleaned. This was an important, meticulous, and quasi-religious task for operators such as themselves. Deposits like gunpowder residue and dust could clog the complex mechanisms of a rifle or handgun's action, trigger, and hammer so that they'd fail to perform their full motions as designed. Failures to load or eject a round could mean the difference between life and death. Consequently, Briggs began his work with well-practiced efficiency. Without looking up, he said, "You really bring out the best in Grim."

"She'll get over it."

"I could see her point."

"Look, Yenin worked for Tom Reed. He was locked out of Voron."

"Maybe he had more intel on Voron's operations."

"I doubt he knows more than Kestrel."

"And you thought it was more important to teach Kestrel a lesson."

"He's the more valuable asset."

Briggs made a face. "What criteria are you using to reach that conclusion?"

"Well, Mr. Prosecutor, I'm using the cold, hard facts."

"If you say so."

Fisher leaned toward the man. "You know, I was going to tell you what a great shot that was on the bag. Then the kill shot at the end—both of 'em right through the walls."

"You change your mind?"

Fisher hesitated. "No. Nice work."

Briggs glanced up from the table, his expression softening, if only a little. "Sam, I know in your eyes I've got a long way to go. You think I was born with a silver spoon in my mouth because I went to private schools and my father's a professor at Georgetown—"

"*And* you went to West Point."

"Yeah. But I worked for everything I have. And I don't take anything for granted. I hold myself to a higher standard."

"Well, you're here, aren't you?"

"Yeah. Point is, if I question one of your calls, it's because I'm doing my job. We need to play all the angles every time we go out there."

"I appreciate that. You keep me honest, but in the end, it's always my call."

"I understand."

"You know I can't do this forever."

Briggs feigned a shocked look. "But they told us we were going to live forever."

"They lied."

"Bastards."

"You could run this show one day."

"I don't know about that."

"We'll see."

A shuffle came from the hatch.

"Well, what do we got here? Two contaminated knuckleheads playing with guns."

Fisher glanced to the doorway where Kobin stood, sipping on a mug of something, probably coffee he wished were spiked with vodka.

"They left the cage open again?" Fisher asked.

"I picked the lock. But don't worry. I don't plan on running away 'cause the coffee's so fucking great here. So, I hear we might be going to Sochi?"

"That's classified."

"Okay, but if you never tasted *khachapuri*, then you can't leave without going to Natasha's. It's an outdoor café."

"What the hell is *khach*—whatever the heck you said?" asked Briggs.

Kobin's eyes lit up like a five-year-old watching a magic show. "It's this monster-sized pastry filled with melted cheese and butter, then they float an egg inside. It's a heart attack waiting to happen but so damned good."

Fisher snickered. "More valuable intelligence from the smuggler."

Briggs shook his head.

Kobin looked wounded. "Hey, you want intel? How 'bout this: You can't fly into Sochi. Not in this bird. And I know you guys like to go in heavy. So how you getting there? And more importantly, how you getting in there with all your gear? Sounds like you'll be needing me to arrange a delivery once you're on the ground. So laugh now, meatheads, but you'll come crawling back to me. They always do."

Kobin grinned crookedly and headed off.

"That's Russia," said Briggs. "Can't do an airdrop. CIA assets are too far away . . ."

"I'll talk to the prick. We'll set that up."

"And I'd like to get one of those pastries," said Briggs.

Fisher averted his gaze in shame. "Me, too."

They both looked up as Grim appeared in the hatchway. "Charlie's got footage of a group ushering Nadia into that hotel. Yenin's story checks out. That's actionable intel. Let's move."

THE fast ferry hydrofoil out of Trabzon, Turkey, made the trip directly north across the Black Sea to Sochi in just over four hours. There was no visa required to enter Russia for a seventy-two-hour stay, although tourists needed to remain aboard ship or book a room at one of the local hotels. The ferry ran three times per week from Trabzon and departed at about one P.M. local time, so the team was in luck. They made it back from Kiev to Incirlik in time to drive up and catch a ride aboard the *Hermes*. The ferry was a colorful red, white, and blue affair with massive foils lifting her hull from the water, along with a spaceship-like bow suggesting a futuristic prototype from another century.

While Charlie remained back on board Paladin to keep working on Kannonball's code, Grim joined them on the ferry and planned to coordinate from inside the hotel while Fisher and Briggs reconnoitered the place and planned their assault. Even though she'd done her best to conceal it, Fisher sensed that Grim was excited by the prospect of returning to the field.

They settled down into seats on the port side, and when Briggs excused himself for a moment, Fisher seized the opportunity to have a private word with Grim.

"We should talk about what happened in Vilcha."

"What's there to discuss?"

"I know you would've made a different call."

She opened her mouth to say something, bit it back, then finally spoke. "Sam, you need to take yourself out of the moment and think long-term."

"What do you mean?"

"You terminated Yenin. You let Kestrel walk with no way to track him . . ."

"Kestrel's not worth much anymore. And, yeah, maybe killing Yenin was a mistake, but I'm with Kestrel on this one: anyone who worked for Reed—"

"I worked for Reed."

"No, you worked for the POTUS."

"Sam, what I'm saying is, I would've appreciated a little consultation before you began shooting assets."

"Yenin wasn't an asset. He'd already been locked out, written off. Like Kestrel said, they would've anticipated his capture, his talking, so that anything he shared would've already been shifted, changed, covered up . . . he was yesterday's news. We got what we needed out of him."

"I'll say it again. I'd like to be consulted first."

"Duly noted."

Briggs returned and pointed out the window. "Nice view."

Fisher rolled his eyes. Grim ignored him.

"And we're all just one big happy family," Briggs said through a deep sigh.

After a minute or two to cool down, they were all taking in the coastline, with the silver walls of high-rise hotels framed by a brilliant green forest and the cocoa-colored mountains crowned with snow on the horizon. Fisher even spied dozens of palm trees sprouting from the city's broad, cobblestone quay. Sochi's climate was humid and subtropical, making it an odd choice for the winter games; however, once you headed up into the higher elevations, you understood why athletes from around the world would travel there. Now, during the winter months, the daytime temps hovered around fifty degrees Fahrenheit, still cold enough for jackets but hardly the biting temps they'd faced at the plane crash site.

For her part, Grim was carefully dressed for the weather in her black Aeroflot flight attendant's uniform and matching coat. She shouldered an expensive leather carry-on bag. She'd chosen not to wear the "cute little beret," as Charlie had put it, looking daggers at him after the remark.

Fisher and Briggs were unarmed and dressed business casual. They'd all had to pass through customs in Turkey, a long and unfortunate process, but their documentation was, of course, flawless. For the next few minutes, they brushed up on their Russian in order to help Grim, who admitted she was still a bit rusty. By the time they reached the port and were being guided in near the rows of yachts and other pleasure craft, Grim was joking with them like a native speaker.

They split up at the rental car office. She drove off in a small green Chevy sedan, heading south for about twenty kilometers to the hotel. Fisher and Briggs picked up a black Mercedes SUV and left for a meeting that, God help them, Kobin had arranged. Briggs was at the wheel while Fisher called up the GPS location with his smartphone.

SHE was a heavyset babushka, probably pushing seventy, and they met her about three kilometers outside the airport, beneath the rusting hulk of an old bridge that had been condemned by the local government. Her real name was Vera, but Kobin just called her "Bab" and instructed Fisher to do likewise. She climbed out of her brown minivan whose driver's side front tire was merely a donut spare. She waddled around to the rear doors, pushing back the yellow scarf covering her head to unloose a shock of gray hair as dense and matted as steel wool. She'd probably stopped wearing makeup decades ago, and her face was a relief map reflecting a long and exacting life.

"Do you have it?" she asked in English.

"The money?" Fisher asked.

"No, peanut butter."

Fisher hustled back to the SUV and produced two jars of extra crunchy that Kobin said they needed to seal the deal. He'd told Bab about Charlie's peanut butter addiction, and apparently she had one of her own.

"This is gold," she said, pressing one jar to her cheek. "Now, let me see money."

"We speak Russian," Fisher reminded her.

She chuckled under her breath. "No, you don't."

Briggs and Fisher exchanged a look, then Fisher handed over the money.

After tucking the jars under her arm and licking her thumb, she flicked through the rubles with thick, wizened fingers. "In nineteen sixties I work for CIA," she said with great pride. "Everyone knows Bab. You need something, come to Bab. Now, market is bullshit. People like Kobin ruin everything."

"So you don't like him, either," Fisher said with a grin.

She returned to the van, where she stowed her peanut butter, then turned back and threw up her hands in disgust.

Suddenly, the minivan's back door swung open and two young men in their twenties hopped out.

Briggs and Fisher responded by ducking to either side of the van, but Bab was hollering, "Oh, my grandsons, don't worry! They carry boxes for me."

"Be nice for a little heads-up," Briggs told her.

The taller kid was wearing a faded AC/DC T-shirt and jeans, while the shorter, heavier one wore a hockey jersey, a replica of those worn by the Russian men's national team. After some obligatory handshakes that revealed their shyness, the two men opened several anvil cases to display more than a dozen handguns—Berettas, SIGs, Glocks, and a few others that even Fisher did not recognize. Longer cases held six rifles, one of them a Dragunov sniper rifle. They unzipped some oversized nylon bags to reveal several tactical vests along with holsters and heavy leather gun belts.

Briggs reached forward, but Bab slapped away his arm. "First, we make promise."

"What?" asked Fisher.

"First we make promise that you don't die using my guns. Second, money is for rental. Not keep. Ammo is yours. No return if you don't use it all, but guns and pistols come back to me. Understand?"

"We'll make all the arrangements," Fisher said.

"Do you have any frangible rounds?" Briggs asked. "Such as the Reduced Ricochet, Limited Penetration round?"

Bab frowned and looked at Fisher. "Where you find him?"

"He's okay," said Fisher. "Whatever you have will be fine."

"Yes, I have good bullets for you. And oh, yes, here, Kobin was very specific." She crossed to the front of the van, opened the passenger's side door, then produced two pairs of trifocals, older multivision models without sonar to be sure, but classified trifocals nonetheless. Along with them, she had a pair of OPSATs—again, dated ones, but lo and behold, OPSATs.

"Where the hell did you get those?"

"Old Third Echelon dead drop in Grozny."

"How do you know about Third Echelon?"

She waved him off, as though the question bored her. "Do you want fancy watch and binocular or not?"

"Yes, ma'am," said Briggs, collecting the gear.

"So, we have deal?" she asked, proffering her hand to Fisher.

"Okay."

Fisher took her hand. She squeezed his tightly and jerked him down toward her face. "Come on, just one kiss." She puckered up and pulled him closer.

Fisher tugged back, and she smacked him across the face before he could pull free. He turned away, his cheek smarting, as she and her grandsons broke into a fit of laughter. "Just kidding!" she said. "Pick pistols and rifles you want. Do you need explosives? I have some."

Maybe she had more than that, Fisher thought. "If you have access to a dead drop, then maybe you've got more of our old gear? Sticky cams? EMP grenades?"

"No, sorry, already sold."

"Sold?" Briggs asked, his jaw going slack.

"It's no worry. Most clients use spy gear to catch cheating wives."

The two grandsons nodded over that.

"All right, let's see what you've got," said Fisher, his eyes riveted on a .40-caliber SIG P226 tac ops edition not unlike his SEAL pistol. He placed the gun in one of his own bags, then picked up a Glock 19 for his secondary. Briggs chose a Beretta 92FS and a Smith & Wesson M&P Shield as his backup. The world-famous Dragunov was, of course, also coming along for the ride. Selections made, Fisher and Briggs collected magazines and ammunition.

Briggs took one look at the ammo and whispered to Fisher, "Are you serious?"

"Just take it," Fisher ordered.

Their ammo had come unboxed, stored in plastic bags, and was the cheap reloaded crap most discerning marksmen would avoid.

The entire exchange took no more than another three minutes, and when they were finished, Fisher returned to Bab and said, "I'll give you a kiss on the cheek if you really want one."

She blushed. He'd called her bluff. She shouted for her grandsons to get back in the van. They did.

Drawing in a deep breath, she closed her eyes and presented her cheek. He gave her the customary three kisses on alternate cheeks, then said, "*Bolshoe spasibo.*"

"You're welcome," she said, opening her eyes. "You seem like good man. Do good things with my guns, not bad ones."

"Okay."

"And thank you for peanut butter. At my age, not many things make me excited. American peanut butter is one."

"Glad we could help."

Back in the SUV, Briggs brought their OPSATs online, and Grim, who had already booked her room in the hotel, received a rather surprising call from Fisher, who told her to boot up her computer, that he and Briggs were checking in.

"Where did you get those OPSATs?" she asked, her voice coming through their subdermals.

"At the Russian Flea Market," answered Briggs.

"And let's just say closing down 3E was a better idea than we thought," said Fisher. "It seems some of our dead drops have been compromised."

"That's impossible."

"Tell that to the babushka we just met."

"Wow."

"So, we're armed and ready to move in once the sun goes down. Got anything else?"

Grim spoke quickly: "I walked the entire hotel. I haven't pinpointed their room or rooms yet. Video showed what appeared to be five people in all with

Nadia, but that's not to say they don't have more posted here."

"Hey, Sam, it's Charlie. I've got eyes on their security cameras. Thing is, they've only got cameras in the lobby, main entrance, and parking lot. Just two more on the exterior of the building. Nothing in the hallways, rooms, or elevators—so we're blind there."

"We need to mark one of the guards and tail him back to their rooms."

"I'm ready when you are, Sam," said Grim.

"On our way."

17

JUST after midnight, when the last guest had retreated from the hotel's brick paver terrace, Fisher and Briggs ascended into the pine trees growing beside and over-shadowing the building. The hotel reminded him of one he'd stayed at while visiting the Grand Canyon as a kid, nestled in the forest and with balconies that afforded the place a motel/alpine ski resort facade. A row of steeply pitched dormers covered in bright green shingles crowned the roofline, their windows glowing.

From this vantage point they had an excellent view of three sides of the building. Charlie covered their blind spot via the security cameras, but what made the job more challenging was the lack of a rooftop entrance.

Charlie, however, had already keyed his way into the

hotel's registration system. They'd run all the names of the guests through the SMI, not expecting to encounter red flags since the FSB and SVR had assumedly taken care of all that, their rooms permanently booked. A map of the hotel appeared in Fisher and Briggs's OPSATs. The highlighted vacant rooms were clearly marked on every floor. They were close enough to descend and cross from their trees directly onto the roof. From there, they could reach a balcony, pick the lock or cut the glass, and get inside.

However, this would be anything but a routine rescue. They had unfamiliar weapons, no Kevlar protection, and outdated trifocals and OPSATs whose custom batteries said they had approximately 51 percent worth of charge, but you never knew. And Briggs had twice reminded Fisher about their questionable ammo, which had probably been reloaded by a couple of dedicated Russian college students in their basement shop and sold for extra money.

Shoving his trifocals down over his eyes, Fisher zoomed in on a man who'd just left the main entrance. He came down the short flight of steps, slowed as he reached the terrace, then reached into his suit pocket to fish out a cigarette. No, it wasn't a real cigarette but one of those electronic versions: he was trying to quit. The Bluetooth receiver in his ear caught Fisher's attention. Fisher and Briggs were wearing their subvocal transceiver patches on their throats—the SVT patches were easily smuggled past customs in Turkey as "Band-Aids"—and thus Fisher immediately called in this guy.

"I have him, too, Sam," said Briggs.

"Could be just some assclown playing on his cell phone and smoking," said Charlie. "But if I can get a better look at his face, we'll run him through facial recognition."

"Patch into my trifocals," Fisher ordered him.

"Gotcha, Sam, okay, zoom in some more."

"Zooming."

"Tell him to say cheese."

Fisher did. Only in Russian. Charlie liked that, said he'd captured an image, and began running it.

"Grim, come down to the lobby," Fisher ordered.

"I'm already here but can't talk."

"Okay. Stay put. Let's see where he goes."

"Hey, Sam, Charlie here. There's a fat old Russian bastard trying to hit on Grim."

Fisher stifled a laugh. "Keep an eye on her."

"Will do. And there we go, got him," said Charlie. "Dude's name is Travkin, FSB. Shot, scored! He's got to be one of our men."

"Nice work, Charlie."

"I'm not after the fame and fortune—"

"Just the Swiss baristas," Fisher finished.

"She hasn't called me back."

"Wonder why." Fisher took a long breath. "All right, let's get ready. He's heading back inside."

"Have a look, Sam . . ."

Charlie sent the security camera imagery directly to their OPSATs. Fisher watched as Travkin strode into the lobby. The reception desk seemed antiquated and straight out of an old Soviet Union newsroom, complete with nine wall clocks showing the Coordinated Universal Time, or UTC, zones across Russia. A presidential proclamation cutting Russia's times zones from eleven to nine explained two dark circles where the paint hadn't faded. Travkin steered himself toward the elevators. Grim dropped in behind him, and Fisher tried to ignore the way her flight attendant's uniform clung to her hips.

But then Fisher's heart rose into his throat as he thought about Grim getting inside that elevator, alone with the agent.

However, that didn't happen. The heavyset man Charlie had mentioned came into view and joined the trio. They vanished into the lift.

"It's Grim's show now," said Charlie.

"I'm not liking this," Fisher said. "She should've stayed back there with you."

"You don't think she can handle herself?" asked Charlie.

"Armed, yes. But right now—"

"And there we go, she's opened a line," Charlie reported.

Fisher listened to the conversation in Russian. Grim had both men enthralled with a story of a "crazy" passenger aboard one of her flights. The elevator chime sounded, and then . . . silence.

"We're on the third floor," she whispered. "Front of the building. There it is . . . all the way at the end, room 301. He's turning, key-carding the door. I'm heading back to my room now. Stand by."

Fisher pulled up the hotel's blueprints and zoomed in on the room in question. Another box showed that the room was booked in the name of Jacques T. Laurent of Quebec, Canada, a fake identity to be sure. Here was a moment when he missed the new sonar, but hell, he wouldn't trade his years of tactical experience for any single piece of gear. He'd cleared hundreds of rooms in his day and knew how to reach forward with all of his senses to detect even the slightest shift of weight from someone behind a door.

But that still didn't rule out using what he had.

"Briggs, I'm going onto the roof to get in tight for a clean IR scan. I want to know how many inside."

"Roger that."

"Sam, I'm back in my room, and we've got a problem."

He gritted his teeth. "What's wrong? Room service ran out of champagne?"

"I'm serious. Charlie, tell him," answered Grim.

"All right, Sam, I've picked up some Bluetooth signals not linked to any phone receiver. These guys are wearing BioHarness watches that measure heart rate and heart rate variability. They give you a heart electrocardiogram, and they also monitor breathing, skin temperature, motion—including speed, distance, even posture—"

"I know where this is going."

"Yeah, if any one of them takes off his watch or dies, a base station alarm gets tripped. The base station's in that room."

"Well, if this was easy, they would've called the CIA," quipped Fisher.

"Hey, now," said Briggs.

Charlie continued: "Good news is we can wrap up the recon right now. I can tell you exactly how many guys have been fitted, and exactly where they are. There's one in the lot behind you, one in the blind spot now. Two more up in the room, including Travkin, but a fifth is down in the restaurant."

"And that's it?"

"Party of five. That's it. Plus the girl. Don't think she's wearing one. That's not to say they don't have an overwatch team up in the mountains or at the airport, but that's all I have for now."

"Sam, before you hit the room, we need to take out as many of them as possible," said Grim.

"You don't need to remind me."

"Then I'll remind you that you can't kill them. Less-than-lethal measures only, otherwise we trip the bio alarm."

"You gotta love technology," Charlie chipped in.

Fisher swore under his breath. "Back in the good old days you could kill a guy, take his uniform, and no one was the wiser. Now everyone's plugged in. All right, Briggs, you take the guy in the lot. I'll get the one out back. Are we good to go?"

"Wait a minute, so I need to take this guy out silently but not kill him?" asked Briggs.

"Is that too old-school for you?" Fisher asked.

"No, not at all. But after that, I assume we'll be moving quickly, because they won't be checking in."

"Exactly. Keeping them alive is only buying us a little time."

"Sam, I'll get back to the third floor and see if I can get one of those maid's carts to block the door. If you gain entry through the balcony, we'll slow their exit. One of you takes the balcony, the other the hall."

"Perfect."

"Uh, are you forgetting something?" asked Charlie.

Fisher frowned. "What's that?"

"You guys are going into a hot room. What's to stop them from just shooting Nadia?"

"She's their bargaining chip with Kasperov," said Fisher. "They'll do anything to keep her alive."

"I hope you're right. And don't underestimate that Snow Maiden. I did a little digging on her, and she's already got a major rep with the GRU."

"I don't care who she is. They need the girl alive. That's their weakness, and now we exploit it. Enough talk. Briggs? Move out."

BY the time Fisher reached the terrace, his gloves were sticky with pine sap, so he removed them and fought back the desire to draw his pistol. There were a few silent ways to kill men, some said as many as eight, but the number of ways you could incapacitate a man without killing him and without relying on drugs, well . . . that was another story. Only a true artist could take a man to the edge of the abyss without sending him over, and in that regard, Fisher was a veritable Michelangelo.

He skulked his way around the back of the hotel. The cool night air blowing in off the sea had a salty tang that was at once welcoming and sent a chill down his spine.

His prey stood across a small driveway where taxis would pick up their fares during the day. He, like his comrade Travkin, was enthralled by his phone, and Fisher found it ironic how the general public despised those who were distracted by technology while he promoted it—promoted it because it made his job easier. During his early years, guards, lookouts, spotters, and other assorted thugs would, for the most part, actually pay a decent amount of attention if they weren't playing cards or looking at dog-eared copies of porno mags; nowadays, these young bastards were all immediately drawn like addicts to the hallucinogenic glow of their screens when they were supposed to be observers. The only thing this guy would observe now was the void of unconsciousness.

"Sam, Charlie here. Another guy coming out on your end, shit, hold position."

Fisher was crouched behind some shrubs near a maintenance door. The second agent appeared from the door and shouted something to the other one across the street. Fisher couldn't quite hear their conversation, but the men were arguing. He pricked up his ears and caught a few snippets: something about one man having to dispose of the body. Damn, they had better not be talking about Nadia.

"Sam, Briggs here. My guy's out. Gagged and tied. Clock's ticking now."

"Roger that. Get up to the balcony outside 301. Plan your entry."

"On my way."

By the time Fisher glanced up again, the agent who'd come out to join his comrade was returning to the hotel. The second he passed inside, Fisher darted across the street, ducked behind several parked cars, then glided soundlessly along them, coming up behind the first agent, who was a second away from returning his gaze to his smartphone.

The unsuspecting FSB man had no idea that he was about to take a nap the hard way.

Fisher began by looping his right arm around the man's neck, making sure the crook of his elbow was beneath the agent's chin. Next, he placed the hand of that arm on his opposite bicep and then applied his left palm forcefully to the back of the agent's head, pushing the man's head and neck into the crook of his flexed arm.

Fisher's attack didn't stop there. He applied additional pressure by pinioning the man's lower body. He did this by swinging his legs to lock around the agent's and arching his back, just as the man dropped his phone and, as expected, reached up toward Fisher's head.

The "blood choke" was a strangulation technique that compressed the carotid arteries without compressing the airway. The goal was to create cerebral ischemia and a temporary hypoxic condition in the brain.

A well-applied blood choke should render an

opponent unconscious in a matter of seconds. Ironically, the blood choke required little physical strength to perform correctly and was a favorite of those operators who lacked the upper body conditioning for a more traditional stranglehold.

The agent struggled a few seconds more, then went limp in Fisher's arm. He wouldn't be unconscious for long.

Fisher got to work, dragging him into the forest behind the cars. He set the man down and checked for a carotid pulse. Good, still there. He bound the man's wrists behind his back with one of the agent's bootlaces, then improvised a gag with one of the man's socks and his belt. He removed the man's pistol, emptied the chamber, then took the magazine and the two spares the man was carrying and hurled them away, into the woods.

"Third guy's come back outside, Sam," said Charlie with an audible tremor in his voice.

"What's his problem?"

"Don't know. But he's looking around for his buddy, shit . . ."

"Sam, you'd better get him before he gets back in the hotel."

Fisher burst from the forest and went running straight at the man.

As the agent reached into his jacket to draw his not-so-expertly-concealed pistol, Fisher seized the man and tripped him flat onto his back, knocking the wind out of him.

Before the agent had a chance to regain his senses,

Fisher spun him around, jerked the man's arm behind his back and broke it. *Snap!*

Grimacing over the man's scream, Fisher put him in a blood choke and had him unconscious in exactly eleven seconds. He dragged the agent behind the parked cars, then checked for a pulse. Perfect.

Once more, he used the agent's bootlace, belt, and sock to immobilize and gag him. He disarmed the man and shoved his pistol and magazines behind the wheel of the nearest car. His pulse now raging, Fisher charged into the hotel.

"Briggs! I'm heading up the stairwell to the third floor. When I tell you, just shoot out that sliding glass door and move in. I'll be coming in through the main door."

"Roger that, but I've got IR on the room and something's wrong," said Briggs.

"Yeah, he's right," cried Charlie. "We got big problems. The BioHarness watches? Two of them have gone dead. Alarm's been tripped."

Fisher snorted. "No way, my two guys were good."

"So was mine," said Briggs.

"Grim, where are you?" cried Fisher. "Grim?"

Her silence sent him bounding up the stairwell. He reached the third-floor hallway where, at the end, he spotted a maid's cart knocked aside just outside room 301.

As he ran, Grim finally answered, "Sam, I'm here, back in my room. I've been trying to figure out how they got tipped off."

"Shit! Hotel security cams just went down—like they pulled the plug," said Charlie. "No power to the system."

"I'm heading inside the room," Fisher said. He shot past the maid's cart and found the door to room 301 hanging half open. He drew his SIG and tensed.

He swept his pistol from corner to corner, searching, assessing, taking inventory.

Faint trace of perfume in the air. TV. Double bed. Footprints on the rug. Many sets. Small electronic unit on the dresser: the BioHarness station. Bathroom. Small suitcases still lying open, clothes inside.

"Room's clear." He drew the curtain covering the balcony, then threw the lock and slid open the glass door. Briggs was crouched down and waiting for him.

"What the hell, Sam? How'd we lose them?"

The sound of screeching tires from below stole their attention.

A brown Skoda Yeti with driver and passenger in the front seat came bouncing out of the adjacent lot, turned onto the hotel's driveway, then roared toward the exit.

"That's them," cried Fisher before he vaulted over the railing and plunged toward the SUV.

— *18* —

IT was just Fisher's luck that Bab had sold the EMP grenades she'd stolen from the old dead drop. A carefully tossed grenade would've rendered the Skoda's engine useless. Game over. There was no way the Snow Maiden and her partner could've escaped with Nadia on foot.

Additionally, Fisher could've put Briggs to work with his sniper's rifle in an attempt to take out a rear tire or two, but the rifle was slung around his back and he doubted Briggs could get it on target in time. They had their sidearms, but taking wild potshots would've been much too dangerous with Nadia inside the SUV—and they had to assume she was.

These were, admittedly, all afterthoughts that struck

Fisher while he was in the air, realizing that, holy shit, landing on top of the SUV was going to hurt.

Knowing how to move through the impact was half the battle won. They taught you that in jumper school— how to land without breaking your legs. Your feet struck first, then you threw yourself sideways to distribute the shock along five points of contact: the balls of your feet, the calf, the thigh, the hip, and the side of your back.

Still, the years had not been kind to Fisher's knees, and he was not prepared for another operation on a torn ACL, no. He could take the pain; hell, he embraced the pain, but an impact that might send him rolling off the top of the Skoda to crash to the asphalt had quickly become a very real and breath-robbing possibility.

His boots made impact first, creating a sizable dent in the roof, and then, as the SUV's momentum threatened to send him flying backward, he threw himself forward, onto his chest, reaching out for the roof racks on either side. His right hand latched on first, and that was good, since the driver cut the wheel hard left, leaving the hotel's driveway for Lenina Street. Fisher was wrenched sideways before hooking his boot onto the rack and pulling himself back up.

The first gunshot blasted through the rooftop about two inches away from his arm. In fact, as he shifted away, his jacket sleeve got caught on the ragged edge of the bullet hole.

Incredible. The shot had been fired from the passenger, and judging from the size of the hole, it was probably from a .40-caliber handgun. That someone had been reckless enough to discharge a weapon inside a closed vehicle with the windows rolled up was nearly as insane as what he was doing. Between the deafening crack and the heavy firing gases and smoke, not to mention the lead and traces of mercury in the air from the primer, the occupants inside would soon choke on their own foolishness.

But that didn't stop them. Two more rounds punched through, and at the same time, voices sounded in the subdermal:

"I've got an idea to cut them off," cried Briggs.

"What's going on?" cried Charlie. "I'm black over here."

"Charlie, get into the cams along Lenina Street," Grim said. "I'm heading after them."

Fisher sensed the next few rounds were coming before they did, so he dove for the left side, latching onto the rack with both hands, then slid himself to the side as the roof came alive with more gunfire, the lunatic inside firing one, two, three more shots.

The driver's side window came down, and smoke began pouring out as the man at the wheel was screaming that he couldn't hear anything now and that he couldn't see and that she was insane and "don't fire that weapon in closed quarters!" The rear windows opened, and more smoke began to trail.

Without warning and before Fisher could even look up to brace himself, they plowed right into a white sedan in front of them, the other driver reflexively hitting his brakes and slowing them down, his horn wailing.

Fisher released one hand and tried to reach into his holster to grab his SIG.

But just then, the driver rolled the wheel hard, trying to get around the other car and nearly throwing Fisher off the roof. He was forced to hang on with both hands now—no chance to reach for the pistol. The sedan with its shattered bumper hanging half off finally drifted away to the side, the driver, a homely woman wearing a hotel maid's uniform, waving her fist and screaming at them.

Up ahead, the Y-shaped streetlights stretched away for miles along the coast. The road itself was divided by a tall stone median lined with shrubs or fencing, and it blurred by at a dizzying rate.

A thought took hold.

Fisher pulled himself up toward the driver's side door, preparing to make another quick reach for his pistol with his slightly weaker hand. He planned to thrust his hand down through the driver's side window to shoot the man.

However, he sensed a vibration from the right side of the car, thought it might be the window lowering. As he turned, he spotted a woman coming up from the passenger's side, bringing a pistol to bear on him. She was striking, with soft, pale skin and haunting eyes. Her long hair whipped like shimmering black flames, and for just a half second they locked gazes—

Before Fisher swung himself around and booted the pistol away as she fired, the round going high.

So this was Major Viktoria Kolosov of the GRU, the infamous Snow Maiden.

Black leather jacket. Full-sized handgun. Teeth bared.

As her hand came back down, Fisher reached into his holster and drew the SIG, but in that second he already knew he was too late. She had the advantage.

Her face would be the last thing he saw in this world, not his daughter, not a memory of something beautiful like her birth or something drawn from the early years of his marriage. No, it'd be this bitch whose lips protruded in a smirk.

But then the Snow Maiden was slipping backward away from the roof rack, her grip ripped free—

Because the driver had cut the wheel hard left to get around a slower-moving taxi ahead.

Fisher now clung to the rack for dear life himself, his body swinging around as, for just a second, he caught a glimpse of the Snow Maiden over the side. She'd reached up and snatched the windowsill at the last second and now struggled to pull herself up with one hand, her back now parallel with the road.

"Sam, Charlie here. Got you on the cams. Those two are Travkin and the Snow Maiden. Can't see anyone else inside, which makes me think this car could be a diversion and they're moving the girl out with another team."

Bullshit. That couldn't be the case. Fisher needed to know—and he needed to know now.

He pulled himself up and leaned over the side to catch a glimpse of the SUV's rear seat and cargo hold. There she was, young Nadia, bound and gagged and lying across the backseat. "The package is here, Charlie," he grunted into his SVT. "I'm looking right at her."

The thundering roar of a diesel engine came from

behind, and as the road curved slightly to the right, brilliant headlights appeared.

Shots cracked from within that glare, and the rounds pinged off the passenger's side door, forcing the Snow Maiden back inside. Fisher was ready to reach around once more to shoot Travkin, but those headlights and the wailing racket enveloped him. He glanced over his shoulder.

A huge tri-axle dump truck from the construction site next door to the hotel raced by them in the right lane, and though his eyes were tearing from the wind in his face, Fisher still caught sight of the driver: Briggs.

That he'd commandeered the truck was an impressive display of quick thinking. That he could actually drive one and was prying every bit of speed out of the engine was an even more welcome surprise.

The dump truck raced by, billowing thick smoke from twin exhaust pipes rising from either side of the cab. Piles of broken concrete and dirt jutted from the open-box bed, with sand and pebbles whipping across the SUV.

Briggs cut in front of them, heading straight toward an intersection where the light had just turned red.

Charlie screamed.

Car horns wailed.

Briggs plowed right into the intersection, driving a taxi and a pickup truck off to the side of the road, one truck missing a T-bone with his cab by barely a meter.

Travkin had no choice but to follow Briggs's line through the gauntlet as two more cars approached.

Up ahead now, the dump truck's hydraulic lift system slowly raised the bed, and the rear door flipped open.

Now Fisher grinned as hundreds of pounds of concrete and dirt began splaying across both lanes of the road, dust clouds rising, the cacophony of cracking and booming cement sounding like artillery fire in the night.

Travkin didn't react in time. He drove straight toward a chunk of concrete as wide as the SUV itself, turning only at the last second. The Skoda took flight.

And Fisher was no longer smiling.

They came crashing down, with Fisher's arms straining against the bumps as his entire body was lifted twice from the roof. Was it over? No, they kept on, only to rumble across several more pieces of stone.

It was all Fisher could do to maintain his grip, and then, after another hard blow to the front wheels, the SUV was once more in the air, floating hopelessly like a bloated, wingless bird.

Fisher glanced up.

And lost his breath.

They were heading straight for the concrete median, the wall standing at least two meters, the gray bricks speeding up at them. A head-on collision was inevitable, impact in two seconds . . .

Fisher released his grip on the rack, allowing himself to slide off the roof. He struck the grass and dirt with his shoulder and hip. The dreaded crunch of a broken collarbone never came as he followed through with a roll to further dissipate the shock.

Before he could look up at the SUV, it hit the wall with an explosive boom echoed quickly by the higher pitched tinkling of flying glass and the hissing of spewing steam and fluids. Two more pops resounded—the air bags deploying.

The sea breeze whipped the dust clouds over the Skoda, shielding it from view for a moment as Fisher scrambled to his feet.

Out ahead, Briggs had pulled the dump truck to the side of the road and was leaping down from the cab.

"Sam, it's Grim. I'm two minutes away!"

"Hold back," Fisher cried, just as gunfire sent him crashing back down into the dirt and rolling toward the wall for cover.

"Sam, local police are on the way," reported Charlie.

"How long?"

"It's Russia. Don't know. Maybe an extra minute?"

"Great. Briggs, hold fire now. Nadia's still in there!"

"Roger, but she's firing at me!"

"Keep her busy. I'm moving up."

With his SIG in one hand, Fisher burst from cover and fired two rounds at the wall beside the SUV.

The pistol was a double action/single action, so the first trigger pull was tougher, ten pounds to be precise, while the second and all subsequent pulls was less than half that and with a much shorter reset.

His third and fourth shots forced Travkin back toward the SUV, where he opened up the rear door and sought cover behind it. Fisher saw that the agent's head was cut, his nose bleeding. He was probably still fatigued, too. Good.

Travkin peered out and squeezed off at least four more shots, two hitting the wall near Fisher, the others striking the dirt behind him.

Fisher squeezed his trigger in reply, but the round failed to feed, damn it. That cheap ammo was coming back to haunt them, as Briggs had predicted. Fisher dropped to his gut, ejected the mag, and wrenched back the slide, tipping the pistol to allow the jammed round to fall out.

At the same time a hailstorm of fire came in from the other side of the SUV, this probably from the Snow Maiden, who seemed hell-bent on emptying her magazines, the salvos coming thick and fast.

Fisher slammed home his own magazine, then racked the slide, chambering a fresh round.

Back on his feet, crouched over and advancing along the wall, he fired two more shots before the next one jammed again. Garbage ammo and shit aftermarket magazine!

He holstered the pistol and reached for his backup—but it was gone, slipped free while he'd been fighting to hang on to the SUV.

"Briggs, put some fire along the wall to your right, just above the car."

"Gotcha."

As the bricks came alive, the sparks flickering and dancing, Travkin couldn't help but turn back to engage Briggs, as did the Snow Maiden, still out of sight on the other side of the SUV.

Holding his breath, Fisher made his move, vaulting toward the Skoda and reaching the man just as he swung around. Fisher drove himself into the rear door, knocking Travkin onto his back and then, before the agent could sit up, Fisher dragged him by the ankles beneath the door, stopping halfway before coming around behind him.

Reflexively, Travkin tried to sit up but found the door inches from his neck. At the same time, Fisher was already ripping the pistol from the agent's grip and turning it on him.

The decision to kill never came lightly but when it did, there was never any hesitation. A single headshot point-blank finished Travkin as the police sirens wailed in the distance.

Fisher ducked down to see if he could shoot the Snow Maiden right through the SUV's cabin—but she was gone.

Two more rounds chewed into the wall.

"Briggs, hold fire," Fisher stage-whispered. He quietly ejected the agent's magazine, which felt painfully light. He checked it. Empty. He searched the man for another magazine. Nothing. Damn, he'd killed Travkin with his final round. Fisher dumped the gun and drew his SIG once more, racking the slide and clearing the jammed round.

"Sam, she's tucked in tight near the front of the car, where the radiator's hissing," said Briggs. "I saw her toss away two magazines, and she didn't reload. She might be out of ammo. Wait, she's moving now. Lost her. I think she's heading your way."

For the span of exactly three heartbeats the road fell eerily quiet, save for that hissing radiator and the drumming of Fisher's pulse.

Even those klaxons from the police cars seemed muted, and the traffic in the distance began moving more slowly, as though his instincts had automatically switched off all interference so he could focus on the slightest crunch of pebble, the barest whisper of breath escaping from the Snow Maiden's lips.

Then, abruptly, it all hit him again—the sirens growing louder, the stench of leaking gasoline, the wind beginning to turn icy as he circled around the truck.

His right ankle came out from under him before he realized that the Snow Maiden was beneath the SUV. He hit the ground, tried to roll to get the pistol aimed at her, but she was on him so fast that he thought for a second he was being attacked by a mountain lion or a jaguar.

She struck a roundhouse to his jaw while reaching up to clutch his wrist, nails digging in to trap his pistol over his head. With a groan, he sat up, trying to force the pistol forward toward her head.

And then, in a move that was as acrobatic as it was confusing, she locked both hands around the pistol and used it like a gymnast's horse, launching herself away, both legs high in the air, her boots arcing in a black leather rainbow as she drew on her full body weight and momentum to free the pistol from his sweaty grasp. He spun back, now unarmed.

She hit the ground, rolled, and came up with the business end of the SIG. Her idea of doing business was, of course, to point the gun at his forehead. "Who are you?" she demanded in Russian.

"Briggs?" Fisher muttered. "Now would be a good time to shoot her."

"I don't have a bead. I'm moving up for a better shot," Briggs answered. "The sights are off on this piece of crap rental pistol."

"Sam, the police will be there any minute," said Grim. "I need to move in now!"

"I said, who are you?" the Snow Maiden screamed.

19

FISHER'S gaze averted from the Snow Maiden's fiery eyes to her trigger finger. The gun was slightly too large for her, and the pad of her index finger barely reached over the trigger, meaning if she fired, her shots would tend to go left. Too small of a gun and too much pad over the trigger would send them to the right. This was all academic, of course, because she had Fisher point-blank in her sights. It was just a matter of whether she'd hit him perfectly center mass or a few inches in either direction.

"You're looking for Kasperov," Fisher began, trying to distract her. "We know where he is."

The Snow Maiden opened her mouth, but something on the periphery caught her attention, Briggs perhaps.

As she flicked her gaze to the left, Fisher started toward her—

She backed away and pulled the trigger.

The shot rang out with an ear-piercing explosion that sent Fisher stumbling back and falling onto his rump.

But the only pain was in his ears, and when he glanced up, he spotted the Snow Maiden staring down in shock at the smoking pistol in her hands, the slide blown clean off.

One of those cheap rounds had prematurely exploded inside the weapon, possibly firing out of battery.

Fisher bolted to his feet, crying, "Briggs, get Nadia! Grim, get over here!"

The Snow Maiden threw down the pistol and lifted her arms in a defensive block as Fisher lunged at her.

While he outweighed the woman by at least sixty, maybe even eighty pounds, he once more marveled at her agility. Even as he tried to seize her wrists and straddle her, she was already writhing out of his grip and sliding between his legs, only to roll back and hook her ankles around his neck, forcing him back into a blood choke conducted with her legs.

Whether she'd learned these unconventional techniques with the Russian circus or had invented them herself was beside the point; she was the most asymmetric combatant he'd ever faced, twisting and turning like an oily snake.

She even growled now through her exertion, as though every sinew in her body had a voice. With each pound of pressure she applied to his neck, it seemed as though she cast out another demon. He'd just met her, but she fought like it was personal.

A chill of panic struck as he realized he couldn't pry

free her legs. The world darkened along the edges, like ink bleeding into his field of view.

A gunshot boomed.

And suddenly the pressure was gone. He could breathe. He wrenched himself up. Turned. She was gone.

Briggs was hauling him to his feet.

"I think I hit her, but she took off over the wall. Want me to go?"

Grim came to a squealing halt in her rental. "Come on!"

Fisher blinked hard as the blood rushed back into his head. He looked at Briggs, at Grim, then finally said, "Help me get Nadia into the car."

Still dizzy, Fisher turned back to the SUV, where Nadia was lying, her lips taped shut, her eyes wide. They'd fastened her wrists and ankles with zipper cuffs that they ignored for now, lifting the girl and rushing back to Grim's car.

After getting Nadia into the backseat, Briggs crossed to the passenger's seat while Fisher remained in back. As they took off for the next intersection, Fisher gently removed the tape on Nadia's lips. She took a few tentative breaths. Fisher saw now that her eye was red and bruised and had probably been much more swollen. She looked at him for a few seconds, her brain seemingly unable to function until she finally asked in Russian, "Who are you? Did my father send you?"

Fisher glanced at Grim, who pursed her lips then said, "No use lying to her."

Fisher softened his tone. "We're Americans."

"So I'm being kidnapped again?"

"No, we're trying to help your father. We know he's

on the run. We're offering him—and you—asylum. Do you know where he is?"

She shook her head. "How did you find me?"

"It wasn't easy."

"She killed my friend."

"Who? The Snow Maiden?"

"Is that what they call her? She's . . . she's . . ." Nadia began to break down.

Fisher placed a hand on her shoulder. "It's all right. We're taking you to our air force base in Turkey. She can't touch you anymore."

"Sam, it's Charlie again. Police on the scene now. They've recovered a few of the weapons. I tracked the Snow Maiden on security cams for a few blocks, but then I lost her. She was favoring one of her arms, so Briggs might've shot her. Interesting that she doesn't want any contact with the local authorities."

"She's not supposed to blow her cover."

"Well, she lost Nadia."

"No, she didn't," Fisher corrected. "Not yet."

"What do you mean?"

"We'll get to that later."

Charlie sighed. "All right, but I bet she's on the shit list in Moscow . . ."

"I doubt that scares her."

"Right. Anyway, glad you're still with the living."

"Me, too."

Fisher glanced once more at Nadia, so frail and pathetic, looking as though she had nothing.

Instead of everything.

20

THEIR exfiltration route had involved chartering a boat out into the Black Sea and rendezvousing with a Black Hawk chopper whose crew would haul each of them up and into the hovering bird. However, Kobin had arranged for a much more pleasant yet equally clandestine exit. The crew of a private yacht owned by one of his gunrunning associates met them in Bichvinta, a city about thirty miles south of the hotel. They boarded the yacht and were ferried across the Black Sea and back to Trabzon. There, they met the crew of a CIA charter jet and were whisked back to Incirlik, some 360 miles southwest of Trabzon.

In order to maintain operational security, Nadia would stay aboard Paladin, where she would be examined by a doctor before being transferred to another jet for a flight back to the States. The 39th Medical Group's commander sent them a general practitioner named Evren from the Deployed Flightline Clinic. The doctor was blindfolded and taken aboard the aircraft, where he was guided by Briggs to the infirmary.

"Sorry about all the secrecy," Fisher said, removing the man's blindfold.

Evren's gaze panned across the room and toward the hatch beyond. "C-17?" he asked.

"Something like that. Gets us from point A to point B." Fisher glanced over at the cot near the far wall, where Nadia was resting, covered by a blanket and with an arm draped over her forehead. "The doctor's here to examine you," Fisher said in Russian.

"I'm fine," she said.

"I insist."

Fisher muttered in the doctor's ear, "I want you to check her from head to toe. I want you to look for recent incisions, small ones. We think she might have a tracking chip, and we need to get it out."

"All right. And of course, I was never here, never saw you, her, or this plane."

"My diagnosis for you is sudden, acute amnesia."

Evren snickered. "Why don't you leave the diagnoses to me. If we could have a moment of privacy?"

Fisher grinned and gestured to Briggs. They left the infirmary and returned to the control center, where Charlie spun around in his chair and said, "She talk yet?"

Fisher shook his head. "We need to take this slowly."

"She knows where her father is," said Charlie.

"Maybe not," said Briggs. "He's figured out now that they've got her, or at least had her, so he's trying to anticipate what she might say."

Fisher sighed. "And right now she's not saying much, trying to protect him."

"She said they killed her friend in front of her. What makes you think we'll get her to talk?" asked Briggs.

Fisher considered that. "We need to earn her trust."

Grim, who'd been conferring with Ollie, came back over to Fisher. She was holding Nadia's diary. "There's nothing in here to suggest a location—just a lot of rantings about teachers, school, books, and how ugly the boys are in her classes. Actually, pretty depressing stuff for a little rich girl."

"Hey, Sam, you get a chance to try the *khachapuri*?"

Fisher glanced at Kobin, then returned his gaze to Grim. "Does he need to be here?"

"Hey, spy boy, who got you home from Sochi? And by the way, Bab is pissed about her guns."

Fisher snorted. "We'll pay her back with peanut butter."

"Yeah, the old hag would love that."

"And tell her the ammo sucked!" cried Briggs. "She's probably had her grandsons reloading it."

Fisher wasn't complaining. The ammo sucked, all right, but it had also saved his life.

"So you got the girl," said Kobin. "Now you call Daddy and wave the bait in his face."

"And you think it's that easy?" asked Grim.

"It is—if you know the right players."

"And you do?"

"Look, if you want, I'll put the word out to my contacts that we have her," said Kobin. "See if any of them can pass it on. Maybe it'll reach Kasperov. He's got personal security, and a lot of those guys, well, let's just say they've worked the black markets. You never know. If he realizes the Americans have his daughter, maybe he'll come running to you."

"No way. We're not advertising that we have her," said Fisher. "If that gets back to the Kremlin it'll really stir the pot. We'll take it from here."

"And where are you taking it?" asked Kobin.

Fisher glared at Kobin, who threw up his hands.

"Look, I just want to help," Kobin said.

Charlie turned back from one of his monitors. "Sam, the doctor's calling for you."

Fisher returned to the infirmary, where Evren frowned and kept his voice low. "There *is* a small incision near her lower back. I felt a capsule-shaped mass embedded beneath the skin."

"That's it. I need you to take it out right now."

"What about her consent?"

"I'm telling you to take it out. That's an order!"

"You have that authority?"

"Trust me, doc. I do."

"I'll need at least a local anesthetic and something to keep her calm."

"We've got everything you need."

"What would you like me to say to her?"

Fisher considered that. "You prep. I'll get her ready." He crossed back to Nadia's cot and leaned over, softening his expression. "I know you've been through a lot. Do you remember if they sedated you? Maybe stuck a needle in your back?"

"They told me I fell and passed out and hurt my back. They told me I cut it and needed stitches."

"They put a tracking device in your back. We're going to remove it now. You won't feel anything."

Nadia bolted up and reached around to feel the wound. "You're right. I can feel it in there."

"Let us get it out."

"Okay, yes, get it out of me."

"First, did your father say anything to you about why he needed to run?"

"Not exactly. But he was always talking about all the pressure the government put on him. This is about them. I know it is."

"Do you know if they were asking him to do anything for them? Maybe something he didn't want to do?"

"I don't know. He didn't like to talk about work. He said it made him feel guilty. He always talked about vacations. Where are we going now?"

"There's another plane on its way that'll take you back to the United States."

"I want to see my father."

"Then help us find him. You sure you don't know anything?"

She closed her eyes. "I keep telling everyone, I have no idea where he is."

"You understand that if he broke the law or failed to obey them in some way, you'll never see him again."

"I know that!"

"Was there any secret way you spoke to your father, maybe through a third party or what we call a 'cutout'?"

"No."

"Are you sure?"

"When I went away to school, he set up some kind of e-mail thing for family members, some kind of security thing, but I never used it and I don't even know the address or the passwords or anything."

"Do you know what this is?" Grim asked, standing behind them now.

Nadia frowned at the necklace and pendant dangling from Grim's hand. "You were in my apartment? You stole my things?"

"No," said Fisher. "Everything we borrowed will be returned to you."

"So how did you get this?" asked Grim.

Nadia rolled her eyes. "It's just an ugly piece of jewelry my father gave me."

"Where'd he get it?"

"On one of his trips somewhere. He's always bringing me back stuff I don't even want."

Grim turned to Fisher and said, "Ollie finished his analysis. There's clay with traces of gold ore and mercury inside the pendant. The sample is Andean in origin."

"The Andes. South America," said Fisher.

"Correct. And there's only one gold mining

operation in the world where rampant mercury refining is still practiced by local miners. The place is called La Rinconada, and it's in Peru. It's known as the highest city in the world."

Nadia's eyes widened in recognition. "That's right. My father's been there several times. He was setting up a headquarters in Lima. And he was talking about the charity work he wants to do up there at the mining town. He was saying there's terrible pollution and awful schools. He wanted to help the kids and clean up the environment."

"Why there? The world is full of slums and misery," Fisher said.

"I don't know, but some of our ancestors were Donbass miners in Russia. Some went to Pennsylvania to work in the coal mines. My father liked to tell stories about them."

"He's a philanthropist. He's got an attachment to miners. What else do you need?" asked Charlie, who was eavesdropping on the conversation from the hallway.

Fisher glanced back to the doctor. "Take out her chip. Please don't damage it. Call us when you're finished."

Evren nodded.

Fisher gestured that they all return to the control center, where he said, "I think Kasperov's up there in La Rinconada."

Grim squinted in thought. "Why would one of the richest men in the world go there?"

"Because it's not on the GRU's radar. They'll check out all the obvious places like we did and assume he's a man of creature comforts and wouldn't give them up. We might've blown off this place if it weren't for the pendant."

"So your gut tells you he's there," said Grim.

Fisher made a face. It was always his gut versus her facts. "Look, he probably doesn't plan to stay long. He'll wait it out until the Russians have to pull back most of their field assets. But for now, I say he's lying low. Why not there? It's hard to reach and a real shithole."

"So he probably flew in to the nearest airport by jet, maybe took a chopper up to the city," said Grim. "Charlie, get on it. Maybe you can find a charter company that ferries people up there, get into their records, get us anything."

"You got it."

"I'll assist on that," said Briggs.

"Kobin, you got any contacts in Peru?" Fisher asked.

"There was a guy in Lima who used to transport some stuff for me. I know he had some ties to a cartel that bought a lot of gold. Couldn't hurt contacting him."

"Do it," said Fisher.

"Hey, guys," Charlie called from his station. "Looks like the nearest airport is in Juliaca. It's about seventy miles southwest. It's a real hub for contraband. I've already got the list of charter companies operating out of there. Working on getting into their records now."

Grim and Fisher crossed to the SMI table, where Grim brought up a map of Peru and zoomed in on Juliaca. "Population a quarter million, and it's the capital of the Puno Region. They call it 'The Windy City' just like Chicago."

"That airstrip long enough for us?" Fisher asked.

"Most of the military airstrips we use are at least four-teen thousand feet. Checking . . ." Grim zoomed in on the airport and keyed in a request for statistics. "Well, there we go. Runway length 13,780 feet."

"Should be enough?" Fisher asked.

"A C-17 like this once landed at a civilian airport in Tampa with a runway no longer than 3,400 feet. That pilot must've hit the brakes pretty hard and that's cutting it as close as it gets."

"No kidding."

The big screens behind them lit up with a video call from President Caldwell. She looked exhausted but managed to lift her voice: "Checking in again, Sam. The CIA charter to pick up Nadia will arrive in less than thirty minutes. How's she doing? I want to speak with her."

"Right now we're having a tracker removed from her back, but after that, I'm sure she'll be able to talk."

"Good. We'll be transporting her to a safe house near Langley. I want you to assure her that she's in good hands and that we're doing everything we can to assist her and her family."

"Of course. And now we have some actionable intel on Kasperov, all pointing to Peru." Fisher gave her a cap-sule summary of what they'd found.

"If you find him," said Caldwell, "I want you to offer him more than just asylum. Impress upon him that we'll help rebuild and restructure his company. He's dedi-cated his entire professional life to Internet security and probably thinks his career has ended. Well, it hasn't. Tell him America can keep his dream alive—no matter how complicated he thinks that'll be. And we'll clear his name of all these preposterous allegations the Kremlin is leveling at him."

"What allegations?" Fisher asked.

"They're saying he embezzled funds, that officers of his company accepted bribes to disclose top secret documents, and the list goes on and on."

"Wow, all right. We'll take care of it," Fisher assured her.

"We'll be in touch."

The screen went blank, and Charlie once more said that the doctor was calling.

Fisher and Grim met him outside the infirmary, where he handed Fisher a small plastic bag containing the translucent capsule/tracker, one Fisher had seen before used by the SVR and FSB.

"Simple operation. Four stitches. She's sleeping now."

"Excellent," Fisher said.

"Well, other than some blunt trauma to her face, she seems to be doing okay," said the doctor. "She'll need to have the new stitches removed in a week or so. If there's nothing else, I guess I'm ready for my blindfold."

"We appreciate your cooperation," Fisher said.

Grim called to one of the analysts to escort the doctor out. As she strode away toward the control center, Fisher drifted back into the infirmary, where Nadia had just rolled over to face him.

"Is it over?" she asked.

"Yes, we removed the chip. Your plane should be here very soon. I'm sorry about the wait."

"Are you really going to help my father?"

"I work for the President of the United States, and she tells me that we'll be doing everything we can. That means something. Those words come from the most powerful woman on the planet. Do you understand?"

She nodded. "Thank you."

"The president wants to speak to you, when you're ready."

"All right. I just realized I don't even know your name."

"It's Sam. And to be honest, you remind me of my own daughter."

"Really?"

He nodded.

A shadow passed over them.

"Hey, Sam, my guy in Lima just called back," said Kobin. "Oh, sorry to interrupt. But hey, don't you think she's a little young for . . ."

Fisher closed his eyes, trying to contain the explosion forming at the back of his throat.

"Sorry, yeah, well, anyway," Kobin stammered, "My guy in Lima's got intel that'll blow your mind."

21

"THAT'S him," said Briggs.

Fisher zoomed in with his trifocals on the man entering the Corporación Minera Ananea's tin-roofed office lying in the shadows of the towering, snowcapped peaks of La Rinconada.

"You get a shot of his face?" Fisher asked.

"Got it," Briggs answered. "And uploaded."

"Charlie, transfer that photo back to the safe house in Virginia," Fisher ordered. "See if Nadia can ID this guy."

"Already done. You want fries with that?"

"Nice. Get me confirmation ASAP."

Fisher eased back along the mountainside, slipping behind the ice-covered boulders along the cliff that overlooked the mining headquarters, which was no more than four double-wide trailers lying in the cowl of the glacier. The buildings were identified by a small sign bearing the company's tiny blue logo. Seven dust-covered SUVs were parked near one trailer, their off-road tires pinpricked with chips of stone.

Fisher and Briggs were perched at more than eighteen thousand feet in the Peruvian Andes, the wind like knives across their cheeks, the night washing away into a saffron haze to the east.

The past sixteen hours had felt like only two, and ironically, Kobin—once the selfish, self-absorbed, ego-maniacal crackhead smuggler—had come through for them in spades.

"Follow the money, find the man," he'd said.

Trouble was, Igor Kasperov was too damned shrewd to make mistakes. Kobin believed that he'd rely upon favors, stashes of cash, or other such underground or even illegal means to procure both transport and living quarters, and to pay off those who needed to remain quiet regarding his whereabouts. Sure, he'd attempt to limit his contacts as much as possible, but he couldn't do everything alone.

And he couldn't pay off everyone.

That's where Kobin came in. He always boasted that he was the go-to man with a direct line into the seedy exploits of smugglers, cartels, mercenaries, and guerilla-backed incursions across the globe. Sometimes the hype outweighed the facts, but not this time.

"Okay, teammates, prepare to be schooled," he'd told

them, holding court in the control center as though he owned the plane.

"Teammates?" Briggs asked, as though the word had gone sour on his lips.

"Shuddup, Action Jackson. So . . . I'll put it to you this way. La Rinconada's gold mining operation is a money-laundering wet dream for the cartels. Here's how it works. The cartel-backed banks use American dollars to buy the gold from the mining company at one hundred and ten percent over current gold spot prices—that's the standard fee for money laundering. The cartels have a team of gold and silver bullion traders, and these greedy little fuckers sell the gold in the open market, and you know with the volatility we have today, they usually recoup more than their premium fee. So my guy in Lima has run guns, drugs, and even gold for these guys, meaning he's tapped into what's going on up there. His contact at the mining company office says that somebody's been drafting checks drawn against some Swiss and offshore accounts to buy untraceable U.S. dollars, ten percent over face value, which is the fee for what we call remote and discrete ATM services." Kobin began to gesticulate wildly, a half-crazed glimmer flooding his eyes. "Boys and girls, think about it. Who the hell but a rich man would be drafting off of Swiss and offshore accounts? Sam's right. Kasperov is up there, and he's no dummy. He's doing more than just lying low. That fucking Russian is picking up some serious cash so he's untraceable and good to go for his next trip."

Fisher drew back his head. "Holy shit, Kobin. Nice work."

"I plan to verify all this," said Grim.

"Be my guest," said Kobin. "I keep telling you fuckers how valuable I am. When are you dumbasses gonna learn? Schooled? Oh, that would be you people."

"I don't think so," said Briggs.

Kobin ignored him and faced Fisher. "You see? You never want to turn me over to Kestrel. I'm way too valuable."

Grim stepped between them and said, "I hate 'im. But he's earned his keep—for now."

"Agreed," Fisher said. "Let's get the hell out of here."

After transferring Nadia to the CIA charter, they had taken off. The flight from Incirlik to Juliaca, Peru, was over 7,300 miles, meaning they had about 2,700 miles between each midair refueling. With a cruising speed of about 515 miles per hour, the flight had taken more than fourteen hours, giving them ample time to sleep and prep.

In the meantime, Grim had coordinated with the Special Activities Division. They sent a paramilitary ops officer to Juliaca to reconnoiter the airport, searching for any spotters Kasperov might have planted there.

Grim had also pointed out that Paladin's arrival might raise a few suspicions, so they'd planned to land at about 0200 local time and have the plane met by refueling services to make it appear as though this was only a brief layover.

Presently, they displayed bogus tail numbers along

with the letters "AETC" and additional markings for the 97th Air Mobility Wing out of Altus AFB, Oklahoma. Altus AFB was the Air Education and Training Command, or AETC, for C-17s and KC-135s. Mission permitting, Paladin's tail markings were changed every ninety days, and it was imperative that the transport always displayed them, lest they be immediately pegged as a spec ops unit.

Their CIA contact in Juliaca had reported no signs of spotters at the airport or its environs; however, there was still no way to tell if Kasperov had someone on the inside who worked at the airport and who'd been overlooked.

Charlie's research on helicopter charters up to the mountain was inconclusive because several companies operated daily, ferrying, he assumed, mining executives, engineers, and reps from equipment manufacturers. None of those records indicated anything more than the numbers of passengers, not descriptions, names, IDs, or anything else useful. Some of the companies might've kept hard-copy files of that data in their offices, but Charlie found none available electronically. This was, after all, Peru.

Once they'd landed, Fisher and Briggs had rented an old 2003 Toyota Tacoma crew cab pickup. They headed up for the seventy-five-mile drive to the city along a road notorious for bandits who preyed upon miners returning with their pockets stuffed with cash.

Adjusting to the altitude had been a significant challenge, more so because they parked their rental about a mile outside the city and hiked in on foot, arriving in the early-morning hours, their weapons and goggles concealed under heavy parkas purchased at the airport.

Fighting for breath, they'd worked their way along the perimeter hills to avoid being spotted, then had descended to overlook the city, a shantytown of tin huts built at precarious angles and glittering like a hellish oasis.

Perhaps that was an understatement.

This was a slum more garbage-laden, more foul-smelling, and more . . . *sad* . . . than any Fisher had ever encountered—despite his world travels. According to the team's intel, as many as fifty thousand people braved the stiflingly thin air and bitter cold to work in the deep tunnels and pick along the mountainsides. There was no sewage system, no running water, no paved roads, no sanitation of any kind. The gold found here was, as Grim had earlier mentioned, processed with mercury, one of the planet's most toxic elements, and it had found its way into everything. The only reason why electrical wires spanned the huts like the circuit board of an old operator's system was because the mining company had brought in that convenience to power their drilling machinery and recharge their shuttles that rumbled through the maze of mine shafts.

Up on the side of a mountain the locals ironically called "Sleeping Beauty," bulldozers were already plowing deep gashes into the earth, with whole families wading out into the icy pools of contaminated mud, fishing for gold. Women in broad skirts were struggling up the cliffs of loose shale, heaving bags of ore, believing they could find some gold flecks hidden among the waste. Even more disturbing were the children stumbling behind them, shouldering bags of their own.

Farther up, inside the mines, men toiled in shafts sometimes flooded with lethal amounts of carbon monoxide and reinforced with timbers already threatening to collapse. Every year miners died from faulty fuses on dynamite cables, while others got trapped by the shifting glacier. They worked for thirty days without payment under the *cachorreo* system. On the thirty-first day they were allowed to take with them as much ore as they could carry on their shoulders. While the system seemed unfair, many of the multigenerational miners appreciated it and did quite well; however, like an Old West boomtown, there weren't many places to spend their money, save for the local bars where they satisfied their alcohol addictions. The vicious cycle continued: work, eat, get drunk, sleep. Life here could not be much harsher, and Fisher could see why Kasperov wanted to help these people.

"I can't even bear to look," said Briggs.

Fisher shook his head. "I know."

Less then thirty minutes later, they were in position to reconnoiter the mining office, and within another thirty minutes they had marked their target.

"Sam, I just got word back from Nadia," Charlie said breathlessly. "That guy is definitely one of her father's bodyguards. His name's Anatoly."

"Grim, you hear that?"

"I heard it."

"Then you agree, he's here," said Fisher. "So, Charlie, I hope you followed up with a threat assessment."

"Hell, yeah, I did. She said he usually travels with four or five bodyguards, plus we can assume he's got his girlfriend with him. Don't think she'll be an issue unless she's a martial artist, a gun expert, and a supermodel."

"Just like me," Fisher quipped.

Charlie went on: "I asked if she knew any way we could contact this Anatoly guy, and she said they took her cell phone, she doesn't know the numbers, and that they probably wouldn't answer their phones anyway."

"That's okay. We'll talk to him ourselves. We're moving in."

Fisher gave a hand signal to Briggs. They crouched down and left their cover, shifting gingerly along the mountain, following a ridge whose edges were piled high with snow. His gut tightened at the sound of his footfalls, and he tried to ease his boots onto the next length of ice-encrusted snow.

His hackles rising, Fisher called for a halt and scanned the mountainside behind them. Nothing but blue-and-white ice and a jagged seam where the sunlight met the deep shadows. He hesitated a moment more.

"What?" Briggs asked.

"Thought I heard something up there. Ah, probably nothing."

"I'll do a sonar scan."

Suddenly, down below, a trailer door swung open, and their target appeared. Anatoly was a barrel-chested man, well over six feet, and currently zipping up a parka that barely fit him. He'd obviously sold Kasperov on his sheer size and intimidation factor. Many of these apes knew how to bulk up, but their cardiovascular fitness was often lacking.

Unfortunately, Anatoly was about to prove Fisher wrong, even in this high altitude.

A small section of rock and gray ice went tumbling down into the parking lot.

"Wasn't me," stage-whispered Briggs.

"Came from above," said Fisher.

They *were* being followed.

Anatoly glanced up, beyond Fisher and Briggs, then his gaze lowered and focused on them before they could duck.

He bolted. *Shit!*

They needed to stop him before his thumb reached his smartphone. One call would trip all the alarms and send Kasperov running.

Fisher was already analyzing the distance to the target and factoring in his equipment load.

Thirty meters.

Anatoly not only ran, but he knew exactly what to do, seeking cover first behind one of the parked cars, then drawing his pistol and firing four rounds into the ice just below.

Weapons drawn, Fisher and Briggs darted across the hill toward the next shoulder of rock jutting out about a meter and offering scant cover.

Anatoly was buying time to make that call.

Fisher held his breath. If they couldn't stop the man,

they could render the phone useless. He let fly one of his EMP grenades, the cylinder tumbling end over end like a dagger.

To be technical, the grenade was a flux compression generator bomb, and as it hit the ice, rolling within a meter of Anatoly's boots, a fuse ignited the explosive material within. That explosion traveled up through the middle of the cylinder to create a moving short circuit. That short circuit compressed a magnetic field and unleashed an intense nonnuclear electromagnetic pulse. Fisher had set the target radius tight—just two meters.

After the buzz and pop, a hissing not unlike static from a broken television resounded for two seconds.

Anatoly's phone was now dead.

But his legs worked just fine.

He broke from the cars and thundered around the back of the double-wide trailers, picking his way between mats of shiny ice. He headed up a road leading toward an irregular-shaped maw carved into the mountainside, with bright yellow warning placards posted to the right and left.

22

"WHY'S he going in there?" cried Briggs.

Fisher's gaze swept to the left, to another pair of tunnel entrances about a hundred meters off, in the distance. "Must come out on the other side! Shortcut back to town."

"Sam, what's going on?" asked Grim.

"We've got a tail. And our guy's on the move, heading into a tunnel. Might lose contact with you. Stand by."

"Charlie, you got a map of these tunnels?" Briggs asked.

"No way. From what I read they're constantly digging new ones while the others cave in. Be safe in there!"

The gunfire had brought the mining company bosses out of their trailers, and Fisher tossed a look back at those men before he and Briggs passed into the cold darkness, their boots crunching loudly across the thick gravel bed.

They tugged down their trifocals and activated their night vision. Fisher's loadout for this operation included an assortment of less-than-lethal weapons, most notably a tactical crossbow he'd been fielding, along with a quiver of sticky shocker darts. The darts were, in effect, cordless Tasers that delivered enough current to stun an opponent. He chose to bring them now because it'd be less than polite to kill Kasperov's bodyguards—especially when they were trying to persuade the man to come home with them.

For his part Anatoly had no intention of being shocked and had lengthened his lead. He was already out of sight, having run straight down the first shaft for about ten meters, then he'd made a sharp left turn and was gone. He'd knocked over one miner who was coming outside and stolen the helmet of another because he needed the man's light to navigate his way through the otherwise dark maze.

The tunnel was barely two meters high, about three wide, sans any reinforcements near the entrance. The miners' battery-powered carts and shuttles had worn deep grooves in the floor, and Fisher dropped into one of those ruts, leading Briggs down the first shaft toward the connecting tunnel.

With the shadows peeled back by their night vision, and their breaths trailing thick over their shoulders, Fisher picked up the pace, with Briggs repeatedly checking their six o'clock for that tail.

A muted roll of explosions from somewhere on the other side of the mountain sent a wavering bass note up through their legs, followed by clouds of dust swirling down from the ceiling. The musky scent near the entrance had given way to something colder, dryer, like the air inside that old meat locker in Vilcha.

With a start, Fisher slowed as a golf-cart-like shuttle came humming around a corner, straight toward them. The miner at the wheel was already waving his fist and hollering in Spanish about no one being in the tunnels, but Fisher and Briggs hit the wall and raced past him. The shaft grew a bit more narrow, the support beams brushing their shoulders before the tunnel emptied into a much wider chamber at least ten meters across where blasting had left ragged scars across the rock.

They had the span of two seconds to take in the view before a wink of muzzle fire lit near the far exit, followed a millisecond later by the pistol's report, the cracks echoing so loudly that Fisher's ears stung as he hit the ground.

Grim's voice crackled in his subdermal, the words garbled, no comm operation down here, as he suspected. Not much to tell her, though. *We're pinned down, about to die. As usual.*

Fisher propped up on his elbows and steadied the crossbow, but by the time he'd lined up the shot, Anatoly had already vanished down the next shaft.

This time Briggs was on his feet first and Fisher pulled up the rear, dropping in behind the young man, fighting to keep up. They swept through the chamber and descended into the next passageway at a sudden and nerve-racking thirty-degree angle, their boots threaten-ing to give way. This was not part of the main shaft but some kind of a detour burrow that had been constructed around a tunnel to their right that had caved in.

For a second Fisher thought he heard rocks tumbling behind them. He swung around, then glanced up to the top of the tunnel. Shadows shifted on the ceiling.

"Sam, come on!" shouted Briggs. "I see him!"

Fisher turned back and charged in behind Briggs as the floor finally grew more level. Once more, concussive booms shook through the tunnel, these much more fierce, and Fisher realized that the tunnels had been evacuated for blasting, which would explain why they'd encountered so few miners. Despite the heavy wooden girders spanning the ceiling above, Fisher felt the walls shaking and closing in. Briggs began to slow and called back. "Not liking this, Sam."

"Me, neither, but there he is!"

Anatoly appeared in a section of tunnel running per-fectly straight for more than ten meters, his helmet light flickering like lightning.

He stopped short and turned back, with Briggs div-ing onto his chest and Fisher lunging ahead as the gun-fire ricocheted off the walls and ceiling.

"Hold your fire!" Fisher screamed at the man in Rus-sian. "We're with you!"

The bodyguard wasn't falling for a gambit that simple. He answered with another round that echoed away.

Fisher managed to roll and come up with the

crossbow, cutting loose with a bolt that arced straight down the tunnel and collided with the wall not a second after Anatoly rolled away. Briggs was there first, scooping up the bolt and tossing it back to Fisher even as they rounded the next corner.

Barely three breaths later, they came into an oval-shaped antechamber broadening toward a brightly lit cavern, the largest subterranean area they'd encountered thus far, the ceiling soaring some six meters, the place at least twice as wide. Electrical cables snaked along the walls to power the bright lights festooned across the ceiling, and below, along the far wall, lay piles of rock and gravel that rose above their heads, blown free in the days prior and waiting for the miners' picks, axes, and shovels.

Another explosion rattled the overhead lights, and Fisher was reminded of a saying the miners had from the intel docs: *"Al labor me voy, no sé si volveré,"* which translated to "Off to work I go, I don't know if I'll make it back." He certainly shared that sentiment.

Briggs led him through the chamber, keeping tight to the piles of rock—

But before they could reach the next exit with its steel-reinforced crossbeams and girders, the crack of Anatoly's pistol resounded from ahead . . . followed immediately by some lower-pitched rifle fire from behind.

"What the hell?" cried Briggs, ducking behind two boulders that had split like arrowheads. Fisher peered out from behind the rock, magnified the view, and saw two mining company security guards dropping to cover on the opposite side of the chamber.

He shared that news with Briggs, then gave another hand signal, indicating they should head around the piles of rock and advance on the exit from the left flank.

Footfalls behind sent Fisher whirling around.

Both guards had broken from cover and were high-tailing it straight for them.

Fisher had the crossbow up and his first bolt in the air before he could take another breath.

Even as that bolt struck the lead guard squarely in the chest, Fisher was already reloading the weapon.

As guard number one wailed in agony, dropped to his knees, then tried to reach up and pry free the shocker from his body, Fisher cut loose the second bolt, dodging from the incoming fire as the sticky shocker thumped on number two's chest, a bit lower but still a good hit almost center mass.

Their cursing in Spanish and wailing sounded strangely medieval and cued Briggs to take off, with Fisher tight on his heels, repressing a grin over his counterattack. Even suppressed weapons made a significant and audible clicking, especially as you moved into the larger calibers, but the crossbow's string was whisper quiet. Old guys rule and old-school wins again.

By the time they reached the exit, they could hear shouting, muddled at first, then growing louder behind them. They raced into the next shaft and aimed for a faint glow bobbing on the dusty air like a channel marker.

"This bastard can run," said Briggs.

"They've been up here longer than us. They're used to the altitude," said Fisher, stealing his next breath.

Two more shots rang out, but they originated ahead and weren't directed at Fisher and Briggs. Had Anatoly just engaged more security men? Fisher hoped so. That'd slow him down.

The tunnel began jogging lazily to the left, and then, off to their right, they spotted another mining shuttle.

They slowed, and Briggs cursed as they took in Anatoly's handiwork:

One man was slumped over the wheel, the other lay beside his shovel with a gunshot wound in his neck. He clutched the wound and reached out toward them, then began pointing at an open cardboard box beside their cart. The box was labeled DINAMITA EXPLOSIVO with triangular warning symbols. Several bundles remained, but the man was trying to indicate something else that dawned on Fisher.

He opened his mouth to curse.

But he never finished.

The explosion ahead thundered so loudly and the concussion came so powerfully that Fisher and Briggs were blown flat onto their backs, the ground quaking, sharp-edged debris blasting through the tunnel.

There might've been a roar of flames, he wasn't sure, but a heat wave passed over him, followed by clouds of choking black smoke that had him tucking his face into his parka.

"Keep down," he told Briggs, who was right beside him, writhing and offering up more strings of epithets.

Fisher's ears rang as the hailstorm of rock rained down on them, his pulse quickening over thoughts that at any second the entire tunnel would collapse.

Still covering his mouth and nose, he forced his head up and hazarded a look through his trifocals. Bad idea. His worst fears were coming true.

The side wall about five meters away began to collapse, splintering apart as though a demon were kicking his way through from the other side. The ceiling buckled and finally succumbed to all the force, the tunnel filling up with massive pieces of shale haloed in gravel and swelling dust.

"Get up!" he cried to Briggs. "We'll be cut off!"

Briggs rose beside Fisher, coughing, and they pushed through the billowing dust, their goggles penetrating the veils until they reached the pile of rubble.

While Fisher expected the worst, he mounted the first pile of rubble, picking his way carefully across it as the timbers above creaked and more dust swirled down, making him feel as though he were shifting through an hourglass.

With a shudder of hope, he found an opening barely wide enough to squeeze through. He handed his cross-bow and quiver to Briggs, pulled himself about two meters through it, then reached back and accepted the weapons. Briggs pulled himself through, and Fisher helped him down. Small miracle. They'd bridged the tunnel collapse.

Yet they both coughed even more now, and the air seemed much thinner.

"I'm getting a headache," said Briggs.

"Let's go," Fisher urged him, feeling his own head rage with drummers and cymbal crashers.

Briggs took a few steps forward, then thrust out his hand for balance, barely finding the wall before he fell. "Dizzy, too."

Intel on the mine said that symptoms of carbon monoxide poisoning included headache, dizziness, weakness, nausea, vomiting, chest pain, and confusion—all from an odorless, colorless gas, a silent and elusive killer, the chemical version of one Sam Fisher.

"We need to get out of here," he cried. "Come on, run!"

They started forward, but not five steps later the ground quaked again.

Gasping, Fisher turned his gaze up to the ceiling, where a crack had opened and began splintering into more cracks, the webs threatening to pry apart the crossbars and buckle the supporting girders to their left and right.

The first explosion must've weakened the tunnel in this section. Fisher was no engineer, no seasoned miner, but he determined that if they didn't reach the far end of the tunnel in the next few breaths, their deaths, wakes, funerals, and burials would occur with drive-thru expediency. At least Grim would save a few bucks on the flowers.

Briggs picked up the pace as shards of rock began plummeting behind them. The ceiling began to give way in a timpani roll of thunder that Fisher imagined would consume them whole.

236 TOM CLANCY'S SPLINTER CELL

Helmet lights were flashing at the far end, and Fisher picked up the pace, struggling up beside Briggs, who was beginning to falter.

"Almost there," he urged the man, his voice strangely thin and unrecognizable.

With a terrific boom the rest of the ceiling collapsed, spitting forward a huge dust cloud that knocked both of them down onto their hands and knees.

The ground shook again, and Fisher tucked his face back into his parka for a few breaths.

When he glanced over at Briggs, the man was lying flat on his belly and unconscious. He tried to scream, but nothing came out. His cheeks caved in.

There were few feelings in the world that Fisher despised more than helplessness. Being in control gave him a sense of peace and security, a sense of place and purpose.

But damn it, they couldn't fight if they couldn't breathe. He fell forward, smiting a fist on the ground.

No, this couldn't be it. Not here, not now, not like this.

He thought he would vomit, but the darkness came first.

"*WHAT are you afraid of?*"

Fisher wasn't sure who was asking the question, but the voice sounded strangely like his own.

"*I'm afraid that everything I've done with my life will*

mean nothing. I'm afraid of losing my daughter again. I'm afraid of being a terrible father."

"What else?"

"Nothing."

"What about death?"

"No. I'm only afraid for my friends . . . for Sarah."

The sun was in his eyes, and he was no longer pinned against a mantle of stars. The world spun chaotically for a moment, and his head throbbed.

He gasped and bolted upright, his senses failing him at first. Then . . . the nausea returned.

Opening his eyes to slits, he stared at the woman floating over him, her face out of focus then slowly, inevitably, growing distinct. Wild black hair. Chapped lips.

The Snow Maiden.

23

MAJOR Viktoria Kolosov smirked at the two Americans she'd been tracking since they'd escaped from Sochi.

She'd been unable to find anything on the taller, older one, but there was some intel on the black man who'd shot her in the arm, a former CIA paramilitary spec ops officer, surname Briggs, thus it was no stretch to assume that the other operator was a spy as well.

Judging from the looks on their faces, they'd thought she'd given up. What did they know about her resolve? Her tenacity?

Very little back then. Very much right now.

She'd used Nadia's chip to track them from Sochi to Bichvinta to Trabzon, and then back to Incirlik Air Base, where the signal from the chip had been cut off. It was there that she'd called upon an SVR agent operating within the base. He reported the transfer of a young woman from a C-17 to a private charter jet. That would be Nadia, whisked off to the United States, the chip removed from her back. She was a total loss now; however, the agents who'd captured her were, she believed, still on Kasperov's trail, and she needed to follow them. That Nadia had been taken to the C-17 first instead of the base intrigued the Snow Maiden, and so she followed up on that aircraft.

Where was it headed next? She needed to review the flight plan, and yes its pilots would file one. No matter how clandestine the plane or its mission, clearances needed to be granted so that the aircraft wasn't mistaken for a hostile and engaged by antiaircraft guns or attacked by fighter jets. The Americans could lie all they wanted about the plane's true identity but not its course, especially if it planned to fly through other governments' airspace.

The government of Turkey required a flight plan six hours prior to takeoff, although special permissions were granted for some military and diplomatic aircraft, allowing them to file just an hour or two prior, or even just after takeoff.

Using the C-17's tail numbers, her contact at Incirlik had learned that a Diplomatic Overflight Permit had been issued to the C-17 by the government of Brazil. He'd also discovered that a similar permit had been issued to the same aircraft by the government of Peru. In fact, Peru required a Non-scheduled Overflight Permit and a Non-scheduled Landing Permit. That landing permit disclosed the plane's ultimate destination: Juliaca.

The GRU was not without its own assets, and the Snow Maiden was able to catch a flight aboard a GRU owned and operated Gulfstream G650 out of nearby Adana Şakirpaşa Airport. While en route, she received help treating her gunshot wound from the attendant (clean entry and exit, no major complications). She arrived in Juliaca nearly two hours before the C-17 without refueling and flying literally on fumes. Following the agents up to La Rinconada had not been difficult. She'd hitched a ride aboard a mining truck that had left only a few minutes after the two men had departed in their pickup truck. She'd bought a Bible at the airport and clutched it as though she were a Christian missionary, a missionary with 9mm and .40-caliber pistols tucked under her arms and more than one thousand dollars in American greenbacks jammed in her pockets.

Her reports back to Izotov were fragmented. New lead, leaving Sochi. Following up. What about the girl, he'd asked. No reply . . .

If she reported Nadia's loss, they'd come for her. Izotov's assistants were already trying to reach her regarding the deaths of the FSB agents.

It was better now to overlook the losses and keep focused on Kasperov. If she brought him back, losing the girl would mean nothing.

She was close now. Closer than ever.

* * *

"SAM, we've got a corporate chopper taking off, heading up to the mine," said Charlie. "Just the pilot and copilot on board."

While the kid's voice buzzed through his subdermal, the words seemed unintelligible at first as Fisher focused once more on the Snow Maiden, who was now holding a suppressed pistol to his head. He glanced over at Briggs, who was lying on his side. His eyelids fluttered open.

Fisher sat up and blinked hard. They were outside another mining entrance. It appeared that she'd dragged them out with the help of several ruddy-faced young men who where standing behind her, counting U.S. banknotes—tens and twenties. There were no security men, no bosses, just this small group and the Snow Maiden, and they, too, were all hidden from view by a line of parked bulldozers to their immediate left. His pistol, crossbow, trifocals, and OPSAT were gone. He wasn't sure about his karambit, but he wasn't reaching back for it. Not yet.

"What's your name?" she asked, her English heavily accented but discernable.

Fisher averted his gaze and muttered, "Grim, if you can hear me, we might be needing a little help."

Suddenly, the Snow Maiden hunkered down and ripped the SVT patch from his throat. "What's your name?"

"My name's Sam," he said in Russian.

She switched to Russian. "Who was the man you were chasing?"

"My daddy."

"Answer me!"

Fisher widened his eyes. "You want to find Kasperov, right?"

"You know where he is?"

"That guy we were chasing . . . did he get away?"

She nodded.

"Then there's no time. We need to go!"

She snorted. "*We* need to go? I don't think so." She pressed the suppressor against his forehead. "Where is Kasperov?"

Fisher narrowed his gaze. "I know who you are, Snegurochka. I've heard all about you."

"Then you know this conversation will not end well."

"Not for you."

She leaned in closer and brought a hand up to his chin. "You look tired. You look . . . broken. You've been doing this too long."

"Or not long enough."

"Where is Kasperov? You tell me now, otherwise I'll cut you slow, the way I cut Nadia's friend." In her other hand she now gripped his karambit. Well that answered the question regarding his knife.

"Are you alone?" he asked.

"You mean besides my new friends here?" She gestured back to the miners.

"Yeah."

"If you know all about me, then you know I brought an army."

"That's not what I heard."

"I have comrades posted throughout the entire city, with another twenty people back in Juliaca. Not only will we capture Kasperov, but I'll be bringing you two back with me. Three prizes in one day. And, of course, I'll be interrogating you myself." She ran the tip of the karambit across Fisher's cheek, not deep enough to cut him but with a promise that she would.

"That sounds like a date. Can we go now?"

"You really are in a hurry."

"We need to go."

"How many bodyguards does he have?"

Fisher cursed. "Look, we've got no time. He's on the run right now."

Briggs sat up now, glanced back to the miners, and spoke rapidly in Spanish: "She's a Russian spy. We'll double what she gave you. Think about it."

"Show me the money," said one of the miners.

Briggs grimaced and said, "I got five hundred bucks in my pocket. He's got even more."

"They're lying," cried the Snow Maiden.

"I promise we have the money," said Briggs.

"Hey," Fisher cried, regaining the Snow Maiden's attention. He steeled his voice. "Coming after us was your first mistake."

"Oh, really?"

"Letting us live was your second."

She chuckled under her breath.

"Trying to hold two weapons on me at once? Well, that was your third."

As he was speaking, Fisher was already visualizing his maneuver the way great athletes visualized their victories before even competing.

His arms came up in the sweeping, poetic movements of an Olympic swimmer, seizing the Snow Maiden's pistol with one hand and forcing it away from his head while he grabbed the wrist of her knife hand and drove it back. That must've been the arm where she'd been shot, as her struggle was much weaker on that side.

Briggs needed no cue, no orders. He was already rushing behind the Snow Maiden to put her in one of their now well-practiced blood chokes.

Her reflexes took over, her hand involuntarily flexing, and she fired a round into the air while Briggs applied more pressure.

To Fisher's surprise, one of the miners, the tallest, rushed over and dug fingers into the Snow Maiden's grip, prying free the karambit, which tumbled to the slush-covered ground. Seeing this, Fisher placed both of his hands on her pistol and began wrestling it free. He managed to squeeze his fingers up, above hers, and pressed the magazine release button. The magazine tumbled from the handle. She still clutched the gun, but now she only had one round in the chamber.

With a guttural hiss, the Snow Maiden reached up and tried to claw Briggs's face, even as Fisher tore the pistol from her grip, the force nearly knocking him onto his rump.

The Snow Maiden slipped her legs behind Briggs's ankles and suddenly tripped him back, onto the ground, the impact breaking his hold on her.

Even as Fisher brought the pistol around, the Snow Maiden was rolling backward, launching herself into a reverse somersault and landing on her boots.

She gasped, her face and neck flushed, a weird grin splitting her lips. "Pull the trigger," she urged him. "And don't worry, the round won't explode in the chamber."

Fisher glanced at the pistol and the red LED light just beneath the hammer. Damn, it was electronically keyed only to her.

"Maybe the knife?" she suggested, glancing toward the blade half covered in mud.

Fisher looked to the miners. "Double what she paid you," he said in Spanish.

The tall one nodded.

And at once, Fisher, Briggs, and all four miners surrounded and pounced on the Snow Maiden.

It took two miners to hold down each of her wrists, with Briggs fighting to maintain his grip on her ankles while Fisher produced several sets of zipper cuffs from his parka's inner pocket and quickly bound her wrists and ankles. She fought against them as if they were priests trying to perform an exorcism, screaming and cursing in Russian.

"Charlie says the chopper's five minutes out," said Briggs. "Gotta be for Kasperov."

"I need a car," Fisher told the tallest miner in Spanish.

"I have one," the man said in English.

"And our gear? Pistols, a crossbow? Some night-vision goggles and big watches?"

"She put them in a bag over there."

"I need them back."

"Okay. You're Americans, yes?"

"Yeah."

"CIA?"

Fisher shook his head. "Your English is good. Can we get moving?"

"Sorry. Come with me."

Fisher turned back and hollered, "Briggs, search her! See if she's got our phones."

"Already did, here!" He tossed Fisher his smartphone. "Weird thing is, she only had our phones. Nothing else. No way to contact her people."

Fisher shrugged. "Okay, get her down to the helipad. I'll meet you there."

He took off running after the miner.

24

AFTER collecting their gear, Fisher followed the man down along a steep dirt path to a narrow service road lacing its way up the mountain. A broken string of cars was parked along the embankment, some owned by the workers, others by the supervisors and machine operators, the miner explained. He was lucky enough to afford a small four-cylinder sedan because before coming up to La Rinconada he'd been an attorney in Arequipa, but his practice had suffered greatly after a corruption scandal involving one of his partners. Fisher couldn't believe that a man with his education would resort to the crapshoot of the mines, but he assured Fisher that many of the workers had once been professionals in the cities before they'd fallen on hard times. The temptation of quick money was too great to resist.

He said his name was Hector and admitted that he'd heard a rumor about the rich Russian who'd returned to the city. They said he was beginning work on his humanitarian project. They hadn't seen him yet, but they had followed his bodyguards, wondering if any of them would be robbed. Hector did not know where Kasperov was, but he did know the swiftest route to the helipad located just outside the city, lying on a small plateau.

Fisher paid him a hundred dollars for his help—a meager amount that would go a long way in Peru—and the man surprised him by saying that he would've helped without the money but that yes, he would accept it. His two sons had moved to the Salinas Valley in California, and he had a place in his heart for all Americans, whom he had said had shown his sons the love and support they needed. In barely five minutes Fisher knew this miner's life story, and he couldn't help but be moved.

Now, as they neared the helipad, a speck appeared in the sky, and as they slowed, Fisher thrust his head out the window and shielded his face from the glare.

The chopper was a twin-engine AgustaWestland AW139 with four windows on each side of the fuselage and seating for a dozen or more, Fisher estimated. This helo wasn't the over-the-top rich man's transport and was painted in a rather subdued white and gray, but neither was it a flying rust bucket.

A dust cloud appeared in the car's side-view mirror, where Fisher watched the approach of two mining company SUVs, which turned to reveal company logos on the doors. It seemed Kasperov was receiving a well-protected send-off from the mining bosses who'd scored some easy money from the oligarch.

Fisher told Hector to pull off the road about thirty meters from the helipad. He thought a moment, then cursed and removed his pistols, leaving them and the crossbow on the floor before he got out.

"No matter what happens, you just sit here, okay?" he asked Hector.

"Okay."

Fisher stepped away from the car and faced the oncoming vehicles. He waved with both hands as the rotor wash whipped over him and tugged at his parka.

At least six men burst out of the SUVs with pistols drawn. They screamed in Russian and Spanish for him to get down on his knees and place his hands behind his head.

He took a deep breath and complied.

As big Anatoly approached, Fisher shouted in Russian, "I'm an American. I have an offer from President Caldwell. Tell Kasperov we've rescued his daughter from the GRU!"

"Oh, really, you're an American?" Anatoly asked. "Then to hell with you, American! I saw you back in the mine!" He kicked Fisher in the stomach, knocking him onto his side.

Boots were everywhere now as Kasperov's men surrounded him, one cuffing his right wrist and fighting to cuff the left as he fought to pull away.

More shouting erupted from the lead SUV.

Fisher glanced up—

And there he was, the man himself, Igor Kasperov, removing the black fur *ushanka* from his head and allowing his long, sandy hair to flutter free in the wind. His expensive black parka was fitted with military-style Velcro and zippered pockets, suggesting he was some general come down from the mountain to inspect his troops. He scratched at the pearl-colored stubble on his cheeks and squinted toward the helipad.

Watching him emerge from the SUV was, for a moment, like seeing the bronze statue of some legend come to life. For a moment, even Fisher felt a little starstruck, since he had reviewed hours of interviews and had scrolled through hundreds of photos that suggested the software genius was some media-created persona and not a real human being.

"I want to talk to him!" Kasperov cried. "Bring him here! Now!"

Anatoly hauled Fisher to his feet. They searched him, and Anatoly confiscated his phone before ushering Fisher back toward the SUV. The handcuffs were on tight now, the blood cut off to Fisher's hands, which were already growing numb.

Two of the other guards were hauling Hector the miner out of car, and Fisher yelled, "Don't hurt him! He's just my ride!"

Kasperov had climbed back into the SUV, out of the wind and cold. One of the other guards held open a back door, and Fisher was shoved inside, falling into a seat beside Kasperov and his supermodel girlfriend, her perfect face encircled by her parka's white fur trim.

"Who are you?" demanded Kasperov.

Fisher took a few seconds to compose himself, then spoke rapidly in Russian. "Sir, I'm here with an offer from President Caldwell. She'll offer you political asylum, but more than that she'll help rebuild your company."

"Everyone wants a piece of me now."

"We're just here to help."

"How can I trust you?"

"You gave your daughter a pendant with some gold inside, some gold from the mines here."

Kasperov looked startled. "How do you know that?"

"Because she told us. She helped us find you."

The man grabbed Fisher by his parka's collar and spoke through his teeth: "Where is she?"

"The GRU was holding her in Sochi. My team got her out. We flew her back to the U.S. She's in a safe house near Langley. If you want, you can talk to her right now."

"Bullshit! You're holding her prisoner!"

"Anatoly took my phone. Let me have it. We'll call Nadia. I'll prove it to you."

"You're stalling for some reason. You're a Russian agent, aren't you?"

"We just captured the agent who's been after you. They call her Snegurochka, the Snow Maiden. I think she's working alone, but we can't be sure."

Kasperov drew back his head. "*Snegurochka*? I know her."

"Are you kidding me?"

"We worked on a case together."

"Then you know what a hard time we've had. Please, let me have my phone. Let's call your daughter. It'll just take a minute."

Kasperov glanced to his girlfriend, who whispered something to him. He faced Fisher and said, "All right." He motioned to Anatoly outside, who opened the door. "Take off his cuffs. Give me his phone."

"Are you sure, sir?"

"Take off his cuffs!"

Anatoly reluctantly complied, freeing Fisher and returning the smartphone. Fisher rubbed his wrists, thanked Kasperov, then quickly called Charlie back at the plane. "I'm sitting here with Mr. Kasperov."

"Whoa, really?"

"Calm down. I need you to patch me through to the safe house. He needs to speak with Nadia right now. Tell Grim to get the POTUS on the line and have her standing by."

"Gotcha. Just give me a second."

A commotion outside sent the other bodyguards jogging by, and Fisher craned his head to spot another car, a dilapidated sedan missing its front bumper and bouncing on worn-out shocks toward the helipad.

"That's my partner," Fisher told Kasperov. "And he's got the Snow Maiden with him. Can you tell your men to back off?"

Kasperov fished out his own smartphone and made a call, barking orders to Anatoly.

"Sam, I've got her on the line."

"Nadia, it's Sam again. I'm here with your father. Can you hear me?"

"Yes, please, let me talk to him."

Before handing the phone over to Kasperov, Fisher glanced empathically at the man. "Like I said, all we want to do is help. You have to believe that." He handed over the phone.

Kasperov scrutinized Fisher before tentatively accepting the phone.

"Nadia? Is that you?"

While Fisher could not hear what Nadia was saying, Kasperov broke down almost immediately, backhanding away the tears and telling her how sorry he was and how much he loved her. He asked if she was safe, and Fisher suspected that she told him more than enough to help their case.

He returned the phone to Fisher, who spoke once more with Charlie: "Is the president standing by?"

"I have her now."

"Good. Madame President, Mr. Kasperov is here." Fisher widened his gaze. "You just spoke to your daughter. Now I'm giving you the President of the United States. If, after this, you still think I'm a Russian agent, then you're not the genius they say you are."

Kasperov's eyes had grown pink. He stared at Fisher for a moment, his gaze much softer now as he lifted the phone to his ear and spoke in English: "This is Igor Kasperov . . ."

He didn't say much at first, probably because Caldwell

was selling him hard on coming to the United States. In Fisher's humble opinion they had a viable and convincing offer: They would reunite the man with his daughter, provide him with protection against the wrath of the Russian government, *and* help him rebuild his business empire. No amount of cash could buy those outcomes now.

"I can't say why I fled Russia. Not here, not now," said Kasperov. "But, okay, I go to Juliaca. I board your plane, but I want your guarantees in writing. All right, then. Good-bye, Madame President."

He handed over the phone, and Fisher reassured him that they'd videoconference with Nadia once they returned to the plane, and they'd provide any other proof he needed.

Kasperov resumed his native tongue. "So you really are an American agent. Do you have a name?"

Fisher grinned wearily. "You heard it. I'm Sam."

Kasperov glanced away and began to laugh.

"I'm sorry?" Fisher asked, wondering if Kasperov would let him in on the joke.

"I want to know your whole name. Your *real* name."

"I could tell you anything I want, and it could still be a lie."

"But you won't, because we're going to trust each other now." Kasperov reached over and proffered his hand.

Fisher took the man's hand and shook it firmly. "Very well, then, sir. My name is Sam Fisher."

25

BEFORE they boarded the chopper, Kasperov wanted to take a moment to speak with the Snow Maiden, and Fisher indulged him, escorting the man back to Briggs's car, where the Russian agent sat, brooding, her gaze burning through the open window. "Igor, you got fatter," she said with a crooked grin.

"They told me you were holding my daughter in Sochi."

"We had fun. We got ice cream."

"I'd like to kill you right now, but I'm going to do worse . . . much worse. I'm going to hand you over to the Americans."

She threw back her head and cackled.

"I'm thrilled that amuses you."

"Igor, that's no threat. You think they'll torture me? There's no extraordinary rendition or black sites. They've lost the stomach for it. The Americans are weak now, controlled by a liberal media, a Congress at war with itself, and a president too concerned with appearances. I'll be going on vacation."

Fisher shouldered up beside Kasperov to face the Snow Maiden. "You won't be interrogated by the government. At least not at first. You'll be interrogated by me. And I have the freedom to get what I need through any means possible. You don't have to believe me now, but I'll prove it to you, and the experience will be anything but a vacation."

"You're a comedian," she told Fisher. "Do you have more good jokes to entertain me?"

Fisher gritted his teeth. "When we get back to my plane, you'll understand." Fisher turned to Briggs. "Let's go."

As they headed toward the chopper with the Snow Maiden clutched by two of Kasperov's men, Fisher thanked Hector once more, along with the other miners.

"Your sons would be proud of what you did today," Fisher told the man.

"Thank you."

They boarded the chopper, with the Snow Maiden in the back row, seated between Anatoly and Briggs.

"Grim, it's me. We're taking off with Kasperov. Should be there shortly. Tell the flight crew to get prepped for takeoff."

"You got it, Sam. Nice work."

He smiled inwardly. Compliments from Grim were rare gems indeed. "See you in a few."

The chopper pitched forward and began to rise, the force throwing Fisher back into his seat.

As the pilot wheeled around, taking them across the snow-covered slopes and continuing to lift off, Briggs cursed, then cried, "What the hell?"

Fisher craned his neck—

Just as the Snow Maiden bolted up from her seat a second before Anatoly was finished with her seat belt.

Hunched over in the tight cabin, she made two carefully placed hops, then turned, slamming her back against the side door and getting her hands on the latch.

Fisher's mouth fell open.

She had timed it perfectly.

While they'd been filing somewhat victoriously into the cabin, their guards down, she'd been working.

She'd studied the door handle, the angles and forces involved, the push-button lock. She'd judged the distance from her seat to the door. She'd guessed about how much maneuverability she'd have and knew she'd need to make her break before Anatoly buckled her in.

As Briggs lunged for her, the side door slid open behind her, the cold air whooshing into the cabin and beginning to howl. She wriggled her brows at Fisher before letting herself fall backward—

Into the air.

Fisher threw off his buckles and came in behind Briggs, the wind nearly blinding now.

"Shut the door!" cried the copilot.

They watched as the Snow Maiden plunged ten, maybe fifteen meters, slamming hard into the snow and plunging at least another meter through the ice crust and into the softer powder beneath.

"Circle back!" shouted Fisher.

As Briggs rolled shut the door and locked it, the pilot banked hard, taking them back toward the Snow Maiden, a mere dot against a sheet of pale white.

They swooped down, and Fisher riveted his gaze on her, searching for any signs of movement.

"That fall must've killed her," said Briggs. "Probably snapped her neck."

"Yes, she would rather kill herself than be taken prisoner," said Kasperov. "They're trained to do that. If there's no way to escape, then they'll try everything they can to commit suicide. I guess the days of the poisoned tooth are over, otherwise this could've been avoided."

"I don't think she was trying to kill herself," said Fisher. "And I don't think she's dead. Just unconscious. We need to go back."

"Nowhere to land down there," said the pilot. "That means it's the helipad or nothing, and you'll need to hike back up there on foot to get her."

"And carry her back down," said Briggs, staring out the window. "She looks dead. She wasn't the target. But if we need to confirm, then let's do it."

"Grim, we've got a complication," Fisher said.

"What, exactly?"

Fisher struggled for the words. "The Snow Maiden accidentally fell out of the chopper."

Briggs looked at him and winced.

"What?" cried Grim.

"Point is, we're going to be late."

"No, no way."

"Maybe an hour. It's nothing."

"Sam, listen to me. We've got two jets inbound and they'll be on the tarmac within an hour. They're both owned by MCS Charter out of Moscow, a known front company for the GRU. Same company that owns that Gulfstream G650 that I'm thinking must've dropped off the Snow Maiden."

"Shit, maybe she blew an alarm."

"Or maybe they're tracking her and she didn't know it. Either way, we need to get the hell out of here. Now."

Fisher stared hard at the Snow Maiden's motionless form as the helo continued to circle overhead. They had nothing, not even the agent's cell phone to bring back. She had to be operating rogue to head up to La Rinconada with no comm.

Fisher looked at Briggs, then at Kasperov and his girlfriend. He bit back a curse and lifted his voice, "All right, pilot. Just get us back to Juliaca. Top speed."

THE Snow Maiden waited until the sound of the helicopter grew faint.

Then she sat up, scowling over the deep aches in her back and shoulders. Was anything broken? She wasn't sure but she didn't think so. She blinked hard, and then it finally dawned on her—what she had just done. She began to chuckle so hard that she nearly choked.

Down below, near the helipad, some of the miners who'd been watching the helo lift off began hiking up the slope, toward her.

GRIM and Charlie were waiting for them as they rushed up Paladin's rear loading ramp. Kasperov came forward, ringed by his bodyguards, his girlfriend clinging to his arm.

"And who are they?" he asked Fisher.

"The rest of my team."

Fisher made the requisite introductions, with Charlie shaking Kasperov's hand and stammering like a groupie. Then, as the loading ramp groaned up behind them, Grim lifted her voice and said, "Mr. Kasperov. We can't tell you exactly who we are, and we're going to ask that you and your party forget everything you see here, but nevertheless, I want to welcome you aboard Paladin."

Kasperov crossed quickly to the SMI table, throwing up his hands, his eyes growing wide and bright. "This . . . is this what I think it is?"

"No," Grim said with a smile. "And you never saw it." She tapped a few screens, and abruptly they had a live stream to Nadia's room back at the safe house. She was watching TV, then turned at the light turning green near the computer monitor.

"Oh my God, Dad?" She moved to the video camera,

her pale face filling the screen, her bruises beginning to turn purple and yellow.

"Yes, I'm here! What happened to your eye? Did she hit you?"

"Don't worry about it. I'm okay."

"Are you sure?"

"Dad, please, we have to stay with the Americans now. We can trust them. Okay? Listen to me for once."

"I already have," said Kasperov. "And I'm so sorry, Nadia. I did this to you."

"Shut up. You're always so dramatic. And maybe what happened to us is not such a bad thing. Now you don't have to complain about the government anymore. You're free of them, yes?"

"Yes, you're right. I love you."

"And I love you."

Grim lifted her chin. "Nadia, we have to say good-bye for now. We'll have your father call you when we land in Virginia."

"All right, thank you."

Kasperov nodded his thanks and blinked back the tears welling in his eyes.

Grim faced the group. "We've got jump seats on the wall toward the back. Everybody needs to buckle in for takeoff."

Charlie came over to Fisher and slapped him on the shoulder. "Great job, Sam. You and Briggs rock-starred the shit out of this operation."

Fisher ignored the praise, his thoughts still locked on

the slopes outside the mine. "Can you get me a satellite on the mountain where we lost the Snow Maiden?"

"Not sure we got anything within range right now, but we can try." Charlie rushed over to his station and, as was his wont, banged on his keyboard in a fury that sounded as though the keys might snap off. Screens and access codes flashed by so quickly that Fisher got dizzy. Charlie patched into a satellite that snapped an image of the mountainside.

"Shit, I knew it," said Fisher.

"Knew what? I don't see anything."

"That's what I mean. She was right there. Now she's gone. She wasn't dead."

"So what? We're so gone now she'll never catch us."

"You tell me how she found us here?"

"I don't know."

"You tell me how she survived the fall?"

"Well, that's easier. Depends on the drop and how deep and hard the snow is. Hell, during World War II the Russians ran out of parachutes and used to put soldiers inside bales of hay and throw 'em out of airplanes so they'd land in the snow."

"Where'd you read that?"

"In high school. Was the only cool part in the whole book."

Fisher exhaled in disgust.

"No worries now, Sam. Screw her. We got Kasperov. The Kremlin will take care of her for us."

"Unless she's gone rogue. Then anything's possible." Fisher swore and shook his head. "I hate loose ends."

* * *

ONCE they'd left the airport and reached their cruising speed and altitude of Mach 0.74 and thirty-four thousand feet, respectively, Kasperov asked that he and his girlfriend be allowed to rest. They'd barely slept since fleeing Moscow, and while he'd agreed to another conversation with the president, for the time being he needed a meal and a few hours to close his eyes without that constant twitch of fear in the back of his mind.

Fisher and Grim agreed to Kasperov's request, allowing the man and his girlfriend to sleep in the infirmary. His bodyguards remained outside, where Kobin found a new hobby in harassing them.

While Charlie and Grim continued their intel gathering and assessment, Briggs worked in the armory, cleaning and prepping weapons.

Fisher took a moment to drag Kobin away from his new bestest buddies. "You still in touch with your guy in Lima?"

"He's looking for payment now. Maybe you can help me grease his palm?"

"Electronic transfer okay?" asked Fisher.

"I'm sure it is."

"Tell him he's still on our tab. Got a Russian agent, probably heading out through Juliaca. Need confirmation that she left. Maybe he can help track her."

"This the Snow Maiden Charlie's been talking about?"

"Yeah."

"I heard she's a real ball breaker."

"That's right."

"I'll see what I can do."

"And Kobin?"

"Yeah?"

"I'm glad you're still alive."

"Wow, Fisher. You're gonna make me cry."

"Yeah, in pain, if you don't shut up. Call your guy. Get me what I need."

THE trip back from Peru to Virginia would take over eight hours, and Kasperov did not rise from his slumber for nearly six. Once he was rested and ready, he asked his girlfriend to leave the infirmary so that he, Fisher, and Grim could have a private conversation with the president, whose face glowed from a nearby monitor.

"All right, Mr. Kasperov. I'll be blunt," Caldwell began. "A hundred pounds of weapons-grade uranium is stolen from Mayak. Not long after, you suddenly flee your country. Is there a connection? What're you running from?"

"I need assurances, guarantees that you'll keep me and my family safe—because what I will tell you *will* get me killed."

"You have my word. And behind me is the greatest military machine the world has ever known. What else do you need?"

"Trust. And can you put price on that?"

"No. But you can let us earn yours. What do you have for us?"

"It's not Treskayev," Kasperov answered quickly. "I know him. He's good man, supported by you and your government. But they've put gun to his head."

"Who?" asked Caldwell.

"Men . . . men like me. I have only opinion, no proof, so no actionable intel as you say. But I know who they are. Perov, the arms manufacturer; Yanayev, the aerospace mogul; and Kargin, the investment banker. Mostly ex-KGB, Yeltsin's drinking buddies back in '93. When he busted up state financial apparatus, they got special consideration. Now they buy American sports teams, hunt for American wives, and put big pressure on Treskayev. There are more, but these three are troika that lead all others."

"What do they want?" Fisher asked.

Kasperov snorted. "What all men want: money . . . power. They've secretly won sympathy of prime minister, and he's recruited many of deputy prime ministers, and they in turn have won over federal ministers. Right now, America stands in their way. Their plan is to weaken your government and undermine your economy, and they would do so in three stages. I was to be first stage."

"Let me guess: a computer virus attack against the United States," Grim concluded.

Kasperov nodded slowly. "We call it 'Calamity Jane.'"

"And it attacks our banking system," said Caldwell.

"Much more than that. It renders GPS systems useless by exploiting systemic problem with cryptographic keying scheme."

"That's impossible," said Grim. "The GPS control segment is encrypted and uses top secret algorithms. It's managed from five redundant, high-security, and very hard to reach ground stations all over the world. The master control station is in Colorado Springs, with a backup at Vandenberg. You guys can't get into their systems. No way."

"Calamity Jane takes all of that into account. It brings down banking system. It exploits vulnerabilities in military computer systems, and it interferes with GPS. Even Chinese have nothing like it. And more you try to kill it, more powerful it becomes."

President Caldwell closed her eyes, bracing for impact. "How much time do we have?"

"You've misunderstood," said Kasperov. "I refused to release it. That's why I ran. They asked me to construct it, assured me it would be nothing more than deterrent, and I even convinced myself that creating it would help me to write best software to combat such virus. Keep your enemies close, right?"

"Yeah, but you had to suspect something," said Fisher. "You had to know that one day, they'd ask you to use it."

Kasperov pursed his lips and shook the hair out of his eyes. "Maybe in more limited way and on much smaller scale. I always assumed that ruining America's economy would ruin Russia's. Conventional wisdom no longer true for oligarchs. They will take risk and break world's dependence on your economy. They say clean break is only way."

"So they came to you, gave you the orders to throw the switch, and you told them to screw off and bolted," said Fisher. "But why the loud exit?"

"I wanted to go quietly, but I knew my people would suffer. I wanted to give them time for escape. I couldn't just leave them with nothing."

"Can the Kremlin gain access to the virus?" Grim asked emphatically.

"No," said Kasperov. "There is no way."

"Are you willing to turn it over to us?" asked Caldwell.

"Absolutely not. Men should not wield such power."

"Maybe you should've thought of that before you started banging in your code," said Fisher.

"Maybe so."

"You said their plan has three stages. If you're out, can they still go through with the other two?" asked Grim.

"I would think so."

Grim's tone grew more demanding. "And what are they?"

"First, some important background. One of my company's more recent projects involves hardening thorium reactor control computers against cyber attack."

"Thorium . . . is that a nuclear material?" asked Fisher.

Grim had already pulled it up on her tablet computer and read from the screen. "It's a fissile material that can be used for nuclear fuel. They call thorium reactors the 'clean reactors.' The stuff is a lot safer to work with than uranium or plutonium but pretty toxic nonetheless, especially if you get it into your lungs."

"That's right," said Kasperov. "Well, we received pressure from government to limit scope of our research—for political reasons, of course. There's a lot of money at stake here, so I began small investigation, trying to understand why Kremlin wasn't supporting my work."

"And what did you find?" Fisher asked.

"It was quite simple. Once hundreds of thorium reactors in Europe go online, Europeans will eventually become fossil fuel independent—and this will destroy Russia customer base. I had no idea my work would help undermine Russian economy."

Grim frowned. "But how does that involve us?"

"I'll tell you how," Caldwell interjected. "We just struck a deal to sell our current stockpiles of thorium to Europe, along with moving out some material belonging to France and India. The buyers were lining up."

"Yes, I know all about that," said Kasperov. "And I know that oligarchs are not happy about sale."

"Exactly how *unhappy* are they?" asked Fisher, sensing where this was going.

Kasperov hesitated. "Unhappy enough to make sure your thorium never reaches destination."

Grim's tone grew urgent. "Madame President, you said we just struck a deal. What's the status of the thorium?"

"Final approval on the sales occurred last week. I assume it's being prepared for shipment."

Grim bolted out of her chair and went charging across the room, toward the hatch.

Fisher glanced to Kasperov. "Come with me!"

26

CHARLIE was calling out to Grim as Fisher and Kasperov arrived in the control center:

"Just got a huge hit on our old friend Rahmani from Bolivia."

"It has to wait, Charlie!"

"All right, but—"

"Listen, right now we need to get into hazmat transport out of Yucca Mountain, Nevada. Ghost truck fleet. We need direct access to their command center in Albuquerque. I need to know if they're currently shipping any thorium."

"Did you say thorium?" Charlie looked at her for a moment, letting that sink in.

"Charlie!"

"Yeah, yeah, I'm on it!"

"I'll help him get access," said President Caldwell, her image coming up on one of the control center's big screens.

"I'll assist," said Briggs, rushing into the room and dropping into a computer station.

In the meantime, Grim stared determinedly at the SMI's screen. She brought up a 378-page Oak Ridge National Lab report on the thorium stockpile in Nevada, and Fisher scanned a bar graph over her shoulder.

There were 3,500 tons of thorium stored in 21,585 metal drums. Each drum weighed an average of 330 pounds. The United States owned 18,924 drums of monolithic material, India had 760 of granulated pebbles, and France had 1,901 of dry powder all stored at the same site, buried in the side of a mountain.

Not a second after reading that, Grim typed in a request, and a wireframe representation of a tractor trailer began rotating on the screen, with data scrolling beside it:

A twenty-foot-long truck could hold approximately 120 drums. This was assuming no pallets, the drums packed into shipping containers. A tri-axel slider chassis could carry up to 44,000 pounds on U.S. roads. The 120 drums would have a total weight of approximately 40,000 pounds.

Over 800,000 hazmat shipments hit the roads every day, and all were highly regulated by the government. There were even classified routes across the United States for the transfer of such materials, with attempts made to keep them away from large population centers, but that was often impossible. The most recent map glowed beside Grim's truck; however, when the government wanted to ship something highly classified such as nuclear materials, weapons, or other such top secret military technology, there was no map to be found, no record of the shipment. They'd call upon a "black" or "ghost fleet" of trucks whose drivers would not answer to their civilian employers but be directed by the government operators themselves. No other entities save for the government could track them or communicate with them. The dispatchers at their respective companies would be aware that drivers were on the road and transporting "something," but no other information would be available.

Ghost fleet cabs were fitted with custom composite armor and lightweight armored glass, as well as redundant communications systems with dashboard panic buttons. The comms were part of a Qualcomm-like fleet management computer wired directly into the truck's data bus. The command centers could monitor and track a vehicle's GPS coordinates, get readings from the dashboard instrumentation, and engage in encrypted communications directly with the driver via an in-cab keyboard. Drivers or command center managers had the ability to disable the truck via traditional means such as shutting off the fuel supply and by the recent adoption of flux compression generators so the vehicle could not be moved or opened, its electronics permanently disabled by a localized electromagnetic pulse wave. Drivers had nicknamed that switch the "PON-R," pronounced "pone-ar" and meaning "point of no return," a familiar term also used by aviators to reference a point where their fuel level would no longer allow them to return to the airfield.

In addition to the sophisticated kill switches, the trucks were designed to defend themselves with conceal- able Metal Storm robotic 40mm guns that could quickly deliver massive barrages of suppressing fire over a large area.

From the outside, though, you'd never know they were anything but your run-of-the-mill haulers, with standard diamond-shaped warning placards and labels, and painted with their company logos. Even the small comm domes atop their cabs were a common sight on such tractors.

And as expected, sensitive materials were not left in the hands of apprentices. Ghost fleet drivers comprised some of the most experienced haulers on the road, many with over two million miles of hazmat transports under their belts.

The data Fisher continued scanning was merely a refresher course. It was his business to know about the ghost fleet and their operations since hazmat materials were likely targets for terrorist attacks.

"Okay, got it," said Charlie. "TSMT's in charge of the shipment. President Caldwell just got me access to the ghost fleet's network."

Tri-State Motor Transit was one of a handful of com- panies that specialized in moving hazardous materials for both civilian clients and government contractors. They had a reputation for having some of the most adept and skillful drivers in the industry—but if their shipments had been compromised, then all the safety training and experience in the world could still fail them.

"Okay, patching through," Charlie said.

The SMI flashed as a map of the United States blossomed to life, outlines of states glowing in brilliant green with an overlay of cargo routes shimmering in red.

Grim began pointing to the flashing blue dots on the major highways. "Here they are. I count eight, Charlie."

"Confirm. Eight trucks. They've left Nevada and are en route to the Port of Jacksonville, Florida. They've scattered the loads, though. Each truck is about eight hours behind the one in front of it, with a few of them taking a more northern route you can see there."

"Do these trucks have escorts?" Kasperov asked from behind them. "Department of Homeland Security teams or something?"

"No, they don't travel with escorts," said Fisher. "Draws too much attention."

"Mr. Kasperov, you said the oligarchs might attack these shipments," Grim began. "Do you have anything more specific?"

Kasperov flinched and could not meet Grim's gaze.

"If they want to take out the entire shipment, they'll wait until all the trucks reach the port," said Charlie. "They could blow the cargo ship or even launch an air attack from the shipping yard. Hell, they could already have the shipping yard rigged to blow."

Grim raised her voice, her tone twice as emphatic. "Mr. Kasperov? Do you know something? If you do, you have to tell us. You realize what's at stake here, don't you?"

Fisher stepped over to the man. "We rescued your daughter. You do this for her. You *talk*."

Kasperov nodded. "As I said, their plan has three stages. I was to be first. They never told me about other stages. One of my best employees spied on one of them, hacked his computers, and told me about it."

"Are you talking about Kannonball?" Charlie asked.

"Yes, Patrik Ruggov, Kannonball. He learned about shadow war oligarchs have against your nation. The president was trying to put an end, but they kept on. He learned about teams of Iranians they hired who were smuggled into United States across Mexican border and purchases of large quantities of C-4 explosives from cartels. He told me about many trips to Nevada. He learned that stage two of attack was to be terror and contamination. But again, I never thought they would go through with it. Always a deterrent, a way to threaten Treskayev, manipulate him."

"Where's the lead truck now?" asked Fisher.

Grim pointed to the map. "Topeka, Kansas. Looks like it's nearing exit 361B just south of the North Kansas Avenue Bridge, rolling at sixty-eight miles per hour."

"So we've got some time before all the trucks reach Jacksonville," said Fisher.

"Maybe not," said Grim. "I'll have the SMI generate a blast scenario—because if you think about it, multiple hits on multiple trucks would spread the most terror and contamination. That's what they're after."

"So you think the C-4's already on board the trucks?" asked Fisher. "They won't blow them all in Jacksonville?"

"Not enough bang for their buck. I think the shipping containers were rigged before the drums were ever loaded. An inside job with security at the site. Launching an attack along the route requires them to know the route beforehand. Rigging the bombs on a simple timer or via remote detonation's a lot easier."

"Jesus, I hope you're wrong," said Fisher.

"Me, too," said Grim. "Because look at this."

The SMI had generated a flashing blip with concentric circles to illustrate the explosion of the lead truck on the I-70 off-ramp at Exit 361B near the bridge.

The shipping containers enclosing the barrels of thorium could withstand external temperatures as high as 1,400 degrees, but they were never designed to contain the overpressure and the chemically generated heat produced by an internal detonation of an estimated two hundred pounds of C-4 needed to fully destroy the shipment.

Windows of data opened up alongside the neighborhood map of ground zero. These boxes detailed the devastation in the immediacy of present tense:

Twenty-seven vehicles are demolished, their occupants killed outright. I-70's overpass collapses onto N. Kansas Avenue directly below,

producing an additional thirty-eight traffic
fatalities.

While there is no actual nuclear yield, there is
widespread window, roof, and negligible struc-
tural blast damage in residential West Meade,
north across the Kansas River to Veteran's
Park. There are shattered high-rise windows as
far south as SE Sixth Avenue in downtown
Topeka, and all the way out to Ripley Park in the
east. Flash fires erupt seemingly everywhere,
initiated by falling white-hot debris.

"In powder form thorium nitrate acts as an accelerant
in the presence of heat or explosive devices when deto-
nated," Grim said. "The same way secondary explosions
of accumulated dust in air vents spread fire through ships
and buildings. Check it out. It's those secondary explosions that extend the blast area to nearly three miles in
diameter."

Fisher's mouth began to fall open as he continued
reading the data.

Topeka's first responders are initially over-
whelmed, and it will be hours before significant
outside assistance can reach the city.

"What about the contamination?" he asked.

"I mentioned this earlier, but here are the technical
facts: Thorium nitrate emits radioactive particles that

can be breathed in or swallowed or can penetrate the skin. Most of the initial responders won't be aware that they're being exposed to ash and dust from a highly toxic chemical." Grim checked another data window. "If the stuff's ingested it can reduce the ability of the bone marrow to make blood cells and, in bone, it has a biological half-life of twenty-two years. In all other organs and tissue the biological half-life is about two years. While it's not as bad as plutonium, it'll kill you just the same."

Fisher continued scanning the medical report near the edge of the screen: Acute potential health effects included irritated skin causing a rash or a burning feeling on contact. Ingestion caused nausea, vomiting, dizziness, abdominal cramps, ulceration, and bleeding from the small intestine, as well as bloody diarrhea, weakness, general depression, headache, and mental impairment. Prolonged exposure could affect the liver, kidneys, lungs, and bone marrow, as Grim had mentioned. The stuff was a recognized cancer hazard and could damage the male reproductive glands.

And yet another window illustrated through a powdery white overlay how the blast would spread a fine layer of radioactive particles and debris onto exposed individuals, homes, vehicles, plants, animals, sidewalks, and highways, while a significant amount would fall into the nearby Kansas River, whose waters flowed eastward.

Fisher realized that such a blast near any river system could cause a catastrophe for future cleanup crews. In this case it'd be a civil nightmare for Lawrence and

Kansas City, both downstream of the blast. The terrorists would be contaminating the air *and* the water.

But there was more . . .

According to the SMI, at the time of the blast the
prevailing winds would be out of the south, meaning
the contamination would not just be confined to a rough
circle with a three-mile diameter. That was the initial
zone.

In the minutes following the detonation, an ever-
expanding radioactive dust cloud more than two thousand feet high would be depositing psychological terror
and physical illness along a twenty-mile swath, five miles
wide.

In all, 97,000 of Topeka's 250,000 citizens would be
contaminated in varying degrees.

Many would die in a city that President Caldwell
called her hometown.

"Madame President, all eight of those trucks need to
be stopped immediately," said Grim.

"I concur," said Fisher. "If they're rigged to blow,
EMP's the only way to take them out."

"You need to be sure of this," Caldwell said.

Fisher turned to Kasperov, his voice never more steely.
"Are we sure?"

The man nodded nervously. "Stop those trucks."

27

FISHER caught himself holding his breath as Charlie brought up the I-70 traffic cams from Topeka. They watched as the lead thorium truck was directed off the highway and toward a dirt lot behind a row of warehouses. From there, Charlie switched to the ghost truck's dash cam, where the driver tapped a command into his keyboard, hit the panic button, then hopped out of the cab.

The SMI next lit up with similar traffic cam footage from the other trucks scattered across the United States, all seven being directed to areas away from the highway to disable their vehicles. Fisher watched one driver in Chattanooga, Tennessee, and the SMI noted that a detonation there would have effectively closed the I-24,

I-75, and I-59 interchange, where three hazmat trucking routes converged. Chattanooga's 180,000 citizens would've been thrust into a radioactive hell, even as the Tennessee River carried contamination southwest into Alabama and Mississippi. He could barely imagine what would happen if all eight had gone up simultaneously.

"Madame President, we need a thorough investigation into the Yucca Mountain site security," said Grim. "Hazmat and EOD teams need to search every one of the trucks. The thorium needs to be removed and transferred to secondary trailers."

"We'll be on that immediately," said Caldwell. "And, Mr. Kasperov, if we do find explosives aboard any of those trucks, then you realize that what you did today saved thousand of lives."

"Thank you, Madame President. But you must understand that oligarchs have little tolerance for failure."

"What do you mean?"

Kasperov frowned, glanced at the team, then spoke evenly, "I mean it's not over. I believe they sent one man to oversee operation, triggerman if you will. He would locate one or more of trucks using spotters along route. He would wait until best moment to destroy them."

"What're you saying?"

"I'm saying I know this man, and right now, he's calling his bosses in Moscow for instructions."

"What instructions?"

Kasperov's expression turned grave. "Mr. Fisher, there is always plan B."

Fisher lost his breath. "We need to find this guy—right now!"

"The NSA's got tabs on all the big players in Russia," said Grim. She faced Kasperov. "I need to pursue those names you gave us."

Kasperov closed his eyes. "Some of these men were once my friends."

"Not anymore," said Fisher.

"Can I borrow a computer?" he asked resignedly. "I will help you."

Briggs rose from his station and escorted Kasperov to his chair, where the man sat and began typing in the names he'd given them: Perov, the arms manufacturer; Yanayev, the aerospace mogul; and Kargin, the investment banker. Charlie and Grim were already patched into his screen, and Grim directed the SMI to access the NSA's databases and began searching the phone records of those three men, keying in on calls placed within the hour between Moscow and anywhere in the United States. Charlie was monitoring the same feed.

"Got something," he said. "Gotta be it. It's the only one. Call coming in to a dacha outside Moscow, one of Kargin's lines. Well, this is strange. Call was placed from the Omni Houston Hotel at Westside. But it's not a smartphone. Long distance using the room phone."

"Why the hell would he do that?" asked Grim.

"Maybe he thinks he's been compromised already," said Fisher. "Didn't want to use his own phone. Maybe that phone was the trigger."

"Either way we would've traced him, so it doesn't matter," said Charlie. "I'm already in the hotel, bringing up the security cameras."

"Flight deck, change course. Get us to Houston," said Fisher.

"Roger that," said the pilot. "Any plans to land or just recon?"

"I'll let you know. What's our ETA?"

"We're already in the gulf with a significant tailwind. You want me to crank it up, I'll get you there in less than twenty minutes."

"Roger that. Top speed." Fisher swung around to regard Grim. "Any of the trucks near Houston?"

"No. Not sure why he picked that location. Just random, maybe. Wouldn't matter where he was if he planned to remote detonate via cell or satellite phone."

"Check this out, guys," said Charlie, transferring the hotel's security camera footage to the overhead screens.

A group of three men were hurrying down a hallway. They were dressed in designer suits and were led by a fourth, an older man, at least sixty, with a gray widow's peak and carrying a briefcase.

Charlie froze the image and zoomed in on their faces.

"That's him," said Kasperov, pointing out the gray-haired man. "I know him only by his nickname, 'Chern.'"

"Facial recognition in progress," said Charlie as the image was immediately cut and lifted out of the footage to run against hundreds of thousands of others captured within the Russian Federation.

"Wow, this guy's really underground," said Charlie. "Usually get a hit within seconds."

"He's supposed to be member of SBP, Presidential Security Service, but he serves unofficially as President Treskayev's courier. I suppose even this is not true anymore. He's left to work for oligarchs."

"And to be honest, sir, I don't think he ever worked for the SBP," said Charlie. "We've got good records of that organization, and if he's been there a long time, trust me, we'd have his face."

Charlie switched to the exterior views from the hotel, and they watched Chern and his men climb into a slate blue Infiniti G37 luxury sedan. Charlie ordered the camera to zoom in and got the tag number. "Rental car out of the airport. Got the record here. Bogus ID and credit card."

"Charlie, we can't lose him," said Fisher.

"We could have local authorities pick him up," said Briggs.

"He's already spooked, and he's too important to trust with some local yokels. Plus we've got operational security to consider. Let's see if we can get to him first."

"I agree," said Grim. "We'll keep Houston police and the local feds on standby."

"They're on I-10," said Charlie. "Just got him on the traffic camera. But they're heading west, away from the airport."

Grim zoomed in on the SMI's map. "The executive airport's about eighteen miles west of the hotel."

"Flight plans of everything coming in and out of there," said Grim.

"I'll pull those," said Briggs.

Kasperov rose from his chair and, still staring at the monitors, drifted over to Fisher and muttered in Russian, "This is quite a team you have."

Fisher nodded. "If you would've told me last year I'd be working with them, I would've laughed at you."

"And why is that?"

"Being a team player's not exactly my MO."

"I understand. I spent most of my life alone, behind a computer—and now I'm beginning to regret it. But I guess it's not too late . . . for either of us."

"No, it's not."

"Hey, Grim, there's a private charter on the ground that's fueling up right now," said Briggs. "Flight plan shows it's heading to Denver."

"And from there they fly up to Anchorage and on to Russia," said Grim.

"Flight deck, get us to the Houston Executive Airport," said Fisher. "Briggs, get ahold of that charter pilot. Tell him I want to speak to him."

"You got it."

"Sounds like you have a plan," said Grim with a gleam in her eyes.

28

TEN minutes later, as twilight washed a pale crimson across the western sky, Fisher and Briggs leapt from Paladin and plunged into the cold air over Houston. After a brief free fall, they popped chutes and floated soundlessly toward the pair of hangars on the airport's northeast side.

Houston Executive Airport covered an area of about 1,980 acres split by a single asphalt runway designated 18/36 and measuring more than 6,000 feet by 100 feet. The runway ran north–south, and on its west side lay a pair of taxiways joining in a Y shape to form a single road leading to the main hangar/service center and its fuel farm. This, according to the broad placard hanging over the hangar, was Henriksen Jet Center, named after the airport's founder and owner, local pilot Ron Henriksen.

Fisher took note of the targets below as the pilot's voice buzzed through his subdermal: "Standing by. Final approach on your mark."

"Roger that," answered Fisher.

"Sam, Charlie here. Just spoke with the charter company's owner. He says the Russians are really pissed off. Pilot says he's not sure he can stall them any longer. Turns out one of the Russians is an airplane mechanic himself and they're having a hard time bullshitting him about the engine malfunction."

"Just need another five minutes. Grim, we need to time this perfectly."

"Understood."

"Briggs, how're you feeling today?"

"Feeling pretty dangerous."

"Good. Just remember. We keep the old man alive."

"No lead poisoning for grandpa. Gotcha."

Fisher steered himself behind the hangar and came to a gentle landing fifteen seconds ahead of Briggs.

Leaving nothing to chance, they'd donned their tac-suits and goggles and had brought along both their primary and secondary pistols as well as SIG516 rifles slung over their backs. The rifles had 10.5 inch barrels and were fitted with thirty round magazines of 5.56mm ammo. Better yet, those rounds were factory fresh, not reloaded by Russians whose fingers were covered in peanut butter. The rifles were also fitted with grenade launchers, but said grenades had been replaced by the less-than-lethal sticky shockers like the ones Fisher had used with his crossbow.

They stored their chutes and vanished into the lengthening shadows behind the facility. The pungent scent of jet fuel hung heavy in the air, reminding Fisher of the Kasperov jet's crash.

Pistols drawn and with Fisher on point, they darted along the hangar walls, moving across the building to the corner, where Fisher hunkered down, signaling Briggs to halt.

Goggles over his eyes now, Fisher zoomed in on the charter jet, a Citation CJ2 that had been fueled and moved to just outside the hangar. A maintenance panel had been opened on one of the engines, and a mechanic in coveralls stood on a rolling ladder, speaking with one of the suited men Fisher had seen in the hotel camera video. Charlie confirmed that he was one of Chern's accomplices.

Fisher raised his hand and made a circular motion in the air.

Briggs understood and set free one of the micro UAVs, the tri-rotor humming away above the hangar, then slowly passing it as Fisher activated the drone's camera, patching the image into his OPSAT.

The building's rolling metal door was wide open, and inside were Chern; a man dressed business casual who Fisher assumed was the pilot; two other of Chern's associates; and another man, a heavyset guy wearing Levi's, gator-skin boots, and a Stetson cowboy hat—probably the charter company's owner.

"Okay, Sam, I see them," said Grim.

"Call the owner, tell him we're good to go," said Fisher.

"Calling."

"Pilot, you're clear," said Fisher.

"Roger that," answered the pilot. "Coming in."

The grumbling of Paladin's engines grew more distinct, drawing the attention of the mechanic on the ladder and Chern's associate.

Removing his cowboy hat, the fat man took a phone call, then glanced up and waddled out of the hangar, across the tarmac and toward the ladder. He began waving his hand at the mechanic.

Fisher gave Briggs another hand signal: get ready.

Just as the mechanic and Chern's man began descending the ladder, Fisher glanced to Briggs and nodded.

They took off running along the side wall, reached the next corner, then crouched down again, the hangar door just around the corner to their right. They could hear the men now, lifting their voices over the Paladin's rumble. A glance at his OPSAT showed the group leaving the hangar, peering up, one pointing at the bewinged behemoth on its final approach toward the runway.

"That's a military craft," cried one of the men in Russian.

"Do you get military landings here?" Chern asked the cowboy.

"Sure, yeah, all the time. Routine."

"Bullshit! This is private executive airport," cried Chern.

At that, all three of Chern's men drew pistols from concealed holsters. They held the mechanic, the pilot, and the cowboy at gunpoint.

"Okay, we got their attention," said Charlie.

"Sam, you ready?" asked Grim.

"Yeah," Fisher answered. "Three hostages, four bad guys, one plane . . . no problem."

"Come on!" shouted Chern. "We're taking off!"

Briggs came up beside Fisher, shoved up his trifocals, and said, "Got my targets marked."

Fisher nodded. "Let's roll."

29

AS Paladin's tires hit the tarmac with puffs of burning rubber and the plane's hydraulic landing gear boomed as it worked to suppress the massive forces of impact, Fisher and Briggs slipped around the hangar and ducked inside, behind the doorway, keeping to the shadows.

"We're all going for a ride now," shouted Chern. He gestured to his men that they take the pilot, mechanic, and cowboy owner into the plane.

Briggs lifted his rifle.

As did Fisher.

Freeing the hostages would require three perfectly timed and placed shots. Even the slightest miscalculation might allow one of Chern's men to reflexively pull his trigger and kill his hostage.

Fisher hoped that any lingering doubts Briggs might've had were already put to bed—because he was taking two shots while Fisher took one, focusing all of his attention on the dark-haired Russian clutching the cowboy.

Meanwhile, Paladin's pilot was steering the C-17 toward the taxiway with the intent of parking the plane between the two exits, creating a 585,000-pound roadblock.

If for some reason, Paladin had been late or the operation on the ground had gone south and the Russians had managed to get near their jet, Fisher had a pair of EMP grenades tucked into one of his belt pouches. Destroying the electronics of an expensive jet was hardly a consideration when it came to matters of national security, but if they could save the taxpayers a hefty repayment to the cowboy they would. Besides, having the C-17 on the ground would allow them to make a hasty exit with their high-value target. Fisher couldn't wait to see the look on Chern's face when he was reunited with Kasperov. They would all need glasses of vodka for that conversation.

Judging from Paladin's current position on the runway and the men now moving toward the jet, Fisher assumed that the charter pilot couldn't get his plane moving in time. The C-17 was coming, and nothing could stop it.

Chern's party began storming across the tarmac, their gazes still distracted by the Paladin's approach.

"Come on, Sam, I got a bead," said Briggs.

"On three," answered Fisher. He counted down while

staring through his night-vision scope, the reticle centered over the Russian's head as the man walked toward the plane.

Fisher took a deep breath.

Exhaled halfway.

And slowly squeezed the trigger. The hammer strike was, indeed, a surprise, and before the round even left his muzzle, he could tell this was a good shot.

The round struck the Russian's head, knocking him forward, onto his stomach.

Briggs's rifle cracked a nanosecond after Fisher's, and another of Chern's men took a round just left of his ear and tumbled sideways, away from the mechanic he'd been escorting.

Then, with remarkable precision, Briggs got on his second target as the man was attempting to hit the deck. Chern's last associate was a handsome blond man with the trendy hairstyle of a Calvin Klein model. Briggs's round removed a section of the man's head before he reached the ground.

The old man Chern whirled and seized the pilot, grabbing him in a choke hold and using him to shield himself against Fisher and Briggs.

Chern stole a glance over his shoulder as Paladin's nose came up behind the tiny charter jet like a white shark casting its massive shadow over the tarmac.

Fisher burst from the gloom with Briggs at his side. They charged toward Chern, who shuffled in retreat, nearing the open door and fold-out stairs.

Briggs shouted for the cowboy and mechanic to get

back to the hangar, and they weren't arguing. Fisher had never seen a man that large run that fast.

Fisher locked his gaze on Chern and shouted in Russian, "Sorry, this flight's been cancelled!"

"You think glib remarks can save you now?" Chern cried.

Charlie, who now had control of the drone, brought the UAV in tight over Fisher and Chern.

Meanwhile, Briggs had his rifle raised at the Russian, keeping the man's head in his sights.

The charter pilot was a clean-cut guy in his thirties, probably a young father who looked tense but was smart enough to keep still and offer no resistance, giving Briggs a cleaner line. Still, a sticky shocker to the head was not a good thing, especially for an old man like Chern. Better to free the hostage and target his center of mass with that shocker.

"Stand down," Fisher ordered as he lifted his hand toward Paladin. "You're done."

Chern took a step back toward the jet. "You're a little man with a big job. And this job is too big for you."

"Listen to me," Fisher cried even louder now, his patience gone, his anger working its way into his hands and the vice-like grip he kept on the rifle.

Chern shook his head. "There are no more words!"

Fisher lowered his rifle and took a step closer. "We know who you are. We know what you've done. Don't waste any more of my time with this standoff—because my partner *will* blow your brains out."

"He'll do nothing! You want me for information!"

Fisher smiled. "I don't need shit from you. Your plan has three stages. We know all about them. We know who your bosses are, and right now President Treskayev is having them all arrested. It's over!"

Chern muttered something under his breath, his hair beginning to rage in the engine wash, his piercing blue eyes widening with what Fisher assumed would be a sense of defeat but strangely, something else was there. Something unnerving. His gaze was now borderline maniacal, and whatever he had in that briefcase must've been hugely important, because he'd taken the pilot with one hand but had never let go of the case.

Abruptly, he shoved the pilot aside, and the man took off running toward the hangar.

"You made the right decision," Fisher shouted.

Chern clutched the briefcase to his chest and began shaking his head. "We must all make our sacrifices for the motherland."

Fisher's mouth fell open.

There was no computer with satellite link inside that briefcase.

No documents associated with the oligarchs' plan.

No innocent travel arrangements or pornographic magazines or personal hygiene items.

There was, Fisher concluded in that second, only one thing:

A way for Chern to ensure that he was not captured by the enemy and turned for information.

Chern had been prepared all along for that contingency, and his associates had probably had no idea that inside his simple briefcase were blocks of C-4 rigged to a detonator built into the case's handle.

Chern's thumb slammed down on a button at the base of that handle.

Fisher turned to Briggs and cried, "Run!"

Grim and Charlie were shouting in their ears, but it was all white noise as Fisher wondered how many steps he could take before the explosion went off.

An even more troubling thought jabbed like a needle: What if Chern wasn't just committing suicide?

What if he had something much more powerful than C-4 inside that case?

"There is always plan B," Kasperov had said.

— *30*

THAT Fisher had run past Chern, beneath the charter
jet's nose, and toward Paladin One was a decision born
of experience and not an instinctual reaction to fear. An
untrained man would've unconsciously retreated to the
rear, as nature had intended. You back away from danger,
not run toward it.

But Fisher knew that sprinting across the tarmac and
back toward the hangar would've left them unprotected
and that the detonation would've first shredded them,
then set ablaze what was left of their bodies. Having his
remains positively identified by an FBI forensics team
was not exactly on his bucket list.

As he and Briggs passed beneath the jet, Chern did,
indeed, make his sacrifice to the motherland.

The explosion shook the asphalt and kicked the charter jet back toward Paladin One in the first second.

Next came the concussion that swept Fisher and Briggs off their feet and launched them into the air, even as their ears began to ring.

Strangely enough, as Fisher's boots left the ground, his thoughts focused not on the impending doom and promise of physical pain but on identifying the nature of the explosion. And he sure as hell knew the sound of C-4 detonating versus other types of explosions. So there was a moment of relief—a sigh that lasted all of a second in knowing that this was a conventional explosion. This was not one of the famed or, rather, infamous RA-115s, aka "suitcase nukes" identified years ago by GRU defector Stanislav Lunev.

Better still, because the charter plane was taking the brunt of the explosion *and* they were wearing their Kevlar-weave tac-suits, Fisher thought maybe, just maybe, they might actually survive the blast.

They flew nearly twenty feet before crashing and rolling to the tarmac, the fireballs lifting behind them, the fully fueled charter plane engulfed in the flames.

Lying there, just a few meters away from Paladin One's forward landing gear, Fisher wanted to stand and signal the pilot to get the hell out—

But there was no need. As if on cue, the plane began backing away from the fires, the engines spinning up as Fisher stole a look back, the world still spinning from his fall, the roaring just a muted bass note behind the high-pitched ringing.

The charter jet had been cut in half just behind the wings, its cockpit blown onto its side, the tail assembly lying askew and licked by orange fires spreading rapidly across the tarmac, fed by severed fuel lines. Puddles of pale yellow fluid swelled around the plane and whooshed into flames.

In the distance, a larger group of charter company personnel stood in the shade of the hangar, gaping at the devastation, a heat haze billowing toward them.

Fisher's OPSAT was flashing with a message from Grim:

911 called. Feds and fire service on the way! Get back to the plane!

"Briggs!" Fisher could barely hear his own voice.

Briggs said something as he scraped himself off the asphalt. He turned back and proffered a hand to Fisher, who groaned and rose.

Just as he caught his balance, the flames roared more fiercely behind them, and Briggs's lips moved in a shout that might've been, "Plane's gonna blow!" but all Fisher heard was that steady and deafening hum.

They hauled ass out of there, with first responders' flashing lights now out on the service road and the on-site fire crew rolling forward in their yellow trucks.

With another hollow burst, the rest of the fuel went up, tearing apart the wings with more tremors and sending sharp-edged pieces of the jet boomeranging in all directions.

Fisher charged toward the C-17's aft, where the loading ramp was beginning to descend.

Something struck him hard in the back, knocking him flat onto his stomach.

He turned his head, saw a section of one seat lying on the ground beside him. He felt something wet on his right hand. More fuel. He shot up, and seeing Briggs race ahead, he dragged himself forward, stumbling in behind the man.

The pilot was wheeling the plane around, and it was Kobin who, with a line and harness attached to his waist, descended the ramp, ready to haul them aboard.

Looking like a bad actor in a poorly dubbed foreign film, Kobin screamed, cursed, and waved them aboard, a few of his words penetrating the hum in Fisher's ears.

The smuggler seized Briggs, who turned back and took Fisher's hand, and they bolted up the ramp, dropping to their knees inside the bay.

Fisher's hearing was beginning to return, if only a little, and he looked at Kobin, whose mouth was still running a mile a minute. Fisher waved his hand then pointed to his ear. *Can't hear you!*

A short stop suddenly knocked them to the right, then the plane began to turn once more. Emergency liftoff time.

Fisher and Briggs stumbled their way out of the bay and collapsed into chairs inside the infirmary.

For a moment, a wave of pins and needles passed through Fisher's shoulders, working up into his head, and he thought, *Well, maybe I'm going to pass out.*

He didn't, and when the light returned to his eyes,

Charlie and Grim were there, with Kasperov standing behind them.

"I got it all on video," said Charlie. "Especially the part where you told him we knew who he was and how Treskayev is going after the oligarchs now."

"President Caldwell has the video, Sam," Grim said. "And she's sending it to Treskayev as more proof."

Fisher nodded, then glanced over at Briggs, whose lip and nose were bleeding. "You all right?"

Briggs looked at him oddly for a second, then nodded, "Yeah, yeah, okay. Still can't hear very well."

"Good." He faced Grim. "I thought Chern might've been their plan B."

"No, they had a van full of C-4 following the lead truck," Grim said. They tried to get into the zone after the tractor pulled over, but the FBI picked them up. Don't have anything definitive yet, but rumor is they might be Iranians."

"They find the explosives on the trucks?"

"Yeah, but only three of the eight were wired. Still, that would've been enough." Grim faced Kasperov. "The president was right. You saved a lot of people today."

"And so did he," Kasperov said, lifting his head toward Fisher.

Fisher rubbed the corners of his eyes. "All right, no more messing with Texas. Let's get the hell out of here."

"Too bad we didn't get Chern," Charlie said. "But at least nobody else got hurt, right?"

Fisher rose and slapped a palm on the young man's shoulder. "You're right, Charlie. You're damned right."

WITHIN the next hour, the blunt trauma to Fisher's body began to reveal itself in a patchwork of bruises accompanied by deep aches and pains that had him wincing as he sat down in the control center with Charlie and Grim. Briggs took up a chair behind them; Kasperov had returned to the infirmary.

"I wish I could say it's over, but it's not," Grim began. "That hit Charlie got on Rahmani? It's good."

Charlie rapped a knuckle on one of his computer screens, where pictures of cylindrical devices with phone-sized or boom box–sized instruments attached to them were accompanied by cross-section drawings, labels, and text. Caps on the tubes' ends bore stickers displaying the international radiation symbol. "Remember how Kasperov told us about his work hardening thorium reactor control computers against cyber attack? Well, he does a lot of work with a whole lot of energy companies, especially those who do oil and gas drilling. Obviously they need highly secure networks, and a lot of them geared up big-time after Stuxnet."

Fisher was familiar with the computer worm known as "Stuxnet," discovered in June 2010 by VirusBlokAda, an antivirus software vendor headquartered in Belarus. The word *stuxnet* in Russian meant "will spoil" or "will be extinguished," but the worm's name might've also come from key file names hidden in the code. The worm penetrated the air-gapped Iranian nuclear processing facility computer network in Natanz via infected thumb drives. Once inside, Stuxnet took command of the Siemens S7 industrial control system. The affected S7 sent false "normal" data to monitors while ordering the uranium-enriching centrifuges to spin at speeds outside their tolerances. Hundreds of centrifuges had been destroyed. Whether or not the United States and Israel had partnered to sabotage Iran's uranium enrichment program with the worm was, for some, still a point of contention; however, Fisher would neither confirm nor deny any information regarding U.S. involvement. Suffice it to say that Iran's nuclear efforts in the past decade would have been fast-tracked had their facilities been protected by the kind of software that Kasperov Labs produced.

"Here's what we're thinking," Charlie continued. "And I ran this by Kasperov and he agrees. The oligarchs might've gotten an idea from something based on Kasperov's work."

"What idea?" asked Fisher.

"One of his clients is a company called NGP. They're the world's supplier of neutron generators for what these guys call neutron porosity oil well logging." Charlie regarded his computer screen. "That's what I've been looking at here—pics of those generators."

"What exactly do they do?" asked Briggs.

"Basically, engineers use these suckers to record the composition of the ground around oil wells. And that information is usually classified."

Fisher nodded. "So how's our boy Rahmani fit into all this?"

"Six weeks ago NGP shipped a generator to Iran. That's pretty routine since Iranian engineers are always scouting out new oil fields. It's the name on the customer's invoice that blew my mind: Abu Jafar Harawi."

"One of Rahmani's known aliases," Grim added.

"That's right," said Fisher. "Unless it's another guy with the same name?"

"We don't think so. The Special Activities Division has a contact in Iran, a MOIS agent who flipped. This guy ID'd Rahmani in Iran, and he confirmed that he saw Rahmani two days prior to that shipment. Rahmani was there and he took possession."

"They've got a hundred pounds of enriched uranium, along with a neutron generator," Fisher began, thinking aloud. "Are they using that generator to help build a bomb?"

Charlie shook his head. "Not help build it, but use it to act as a booster agent."

"Back up," said Grim. "I put out a BOLO to all our allies on that NGP shipping crate, and one of Israel's Mossad agents played a hunch. He took a trip over to Natanz, which you'll recall is Iran's premier nuclear enrichment facility."

"Oh, man," Briggs said. "This sounds bad."

"No kidding," said Charlie.

"The shipping crate should've been found at an oil field distribution depot, but yeah, it wound up in Natanz," Grim said. "So let me posit this: Our Russian

oligarchs helped the Iranians obtain the neutron generator because they're building a simple uranium target-
ring type bomb using the stolen material from Mayak.
It's definitely not a newer plutonium implosion device
because the facility at Natanz doesn't have an airtight lab
or room. Plutonium's a bitch to machine and work with.
Just ask the Russians at Chernobyl all about that."

Fisher exchanged a look with Briggs as Charlie picked
up where Grim left off:

"So they'll use this off-the-shelf neutron generator to
pump in a stream of slow-moving neutrons to boost the
bomb's nuclear yield. If they've done their homework
and surrounded the uranium with a good tungsten car-
bide tamper to act as a neutron reflector as well as delay
the explosion of the reacting material, then they've got a
cheap, Walmart-style version of a working nuke."

"Is the generator still there?" asked Briggs.

"We think so," said Grim.

"And here's another theory," added Charlie. "The
Iranians could use the generator, so they can list it within
a larger shipment—"

"Which would help disguise the bomb," Fisher
concluded.

Charlie shrugged. "It might, but we don't have a clue
what they're using for a trigger—meaning we don't
know what the finished bomb will look like."

Fisher nodded then turned to Grim. "Potential
targets?"

"Historically, the Iranians don't directly engage in
terrorism; they use proxies like Hamas and Hezbollah,"

she said. "A bulky gun-type nuke warhead won't fit on the tip of an aerodynamic missile, so Israel's not the target. But, consider this: The market value of Iranian oil is inversely proportional to the flow of Arabian oil, and that Arabian oil is sitting just across the Strait of Hormuz."

"So you're thinking an oil well," Fisher said.

"Or at least some place that would routinely receive neutron generators as part of a larger shipment. The Iranians do the oligarchs' dirty work and both parties score big."

"All right, I follow you so far," Fisher said. "But now this has me thinking—we confirmed that the Iranians were *not* involved with the Blacklist Engineers. So what makes the Russians better partners?"

"I'm not sure, but I bet the oligarchs have been working with the Iranians on this for a lot longer than we realize. The Iranians stood by and watched Sadiq and his Blacklist Engineers initiate their plan, and they observed us and targeted our weaknesses," Grim said. "And maybe they found in the oligarchs a better-connected and -financed ally who could pull off a theft like the one at Mayak. Maybe there were political or ideological differences between Sadiq's people and the Iranians, and the outcomes may not have benefited Iran."

"Maybe they thought Sadiq was an asshole," said Charlie.

Fisher repressed a grin and nodded.

Ollie called from his station. "POTUS on the line."

They turned their heads to the overhead screen, where President Caldwell offered a curt greeting. "I've been on the phone with President Treskayev all afternoon. We just showed him the video you took."

Fisher narrowed his gaze on her. "Did you ask him if he had any suspicions about this man Chern?"

"I did. And he wouldn't talk about that. He's says the oligarchs on our list must've been tipped off and fled, but all the intel assets in Asia and Europe have been alerted. When I informed him about the neutron generator and Natanz, he flatly denied that any Russian citizens would be involved. I told him that for a veteran politician he was acting rather naïve."

"I agree," said Grim.

"Honestly, though, he's not my biggest problem right now. Israel's Knesset is debating a preemptive air strike on the Natanz facility, and the country's air force has already slipped into our equivalent of DEFCON One. Now this whole thing could turn into a Middle East powder keg."

"Sounds like we're going to Iran," said Fisher.

Caldwell sighed in frustration, then finally nodded. "If I recall, you know your way around there, at least Quds Force headquarters, anyway. You'll have my help."

Grim was at the SMI table. "If we fly into Baghdad, we're still looking at an eleven-hour road trip."

"HALO jump?" Fisher asked.

Grim shook her head. "They've got some serious antiaircraft guns. There's just no good way to get there. It's smack in the middle of the desert."

"We'll work it out," Fisher assured the president.

But they were wasting their time—

Because not six hours later, as they cruised over the Atlantic, Grim heard back from one of the Mossad ground agents assigned to be their eyes and ears on Natanz.

He breathlessly reported that one of his colleagues had been in a struggle with a perimeter guard and that both men had died. Just before his death, the agent had photographed traffic coming in and out of the facility—government cars, military vehicles, and various delivery trucks.

Even more importantly, he'd moved in close to a loading dock and had captured something large and draped in tarpaulins being transferred into a tractor trailer. The agent died before he could transmit those images, which were found stored on his camera.

"That has to be it," Grim said. "They couldn't attach the neutron generator in the field."

"So they've built their bomb," said Fisher.

Grim nodded. "And now it's gone."

31

FISHER balled his hands into fists as he scanned the data passing across the SMI's display.

"I'm doing everything I can," Grim said, clutching the edge of the table. "It's just the photos weren't very clear. We got no markings off the trailer. I talked to NCS, and they're willing to send in a drone, but it might be too late. Satellite was out of range but it's back up now. We're still backtracking everything that came out of Natanz. We've got eyes on all shipping out of Iranian ports, we've alerted field ops on the ground there to provide HUMINT. I've just queried the SMI for primary targets, calling up those sites that've already used neutron generators—"

"Which is pretty much every oil well in the entire Middle East," Fisher said.

"Not all of them," said Grim. "But it's a long list. The SMI predicts that they're transporting the weapon south, toward Kuwait and Saudi Arabia."

"All right, let's go with what Charlie said—biggest bang for the buck. What oil well target would have the most repercussions on the American economy—because that's what this is about, right? The oligarchs are trying to weaken us through a virus, a dirty bomb attack, and by taking out an oil target to jack up the price of their own crude and destabilize the entire market."

"Sorry to interrupt," Charlie said. "But we've finally received permission to land in Dubai. That should put us within range of potential targets. I've notified the flight deck."

"What's our ETA?"

"About twelve hours."

"Damn, it'll take them barely five hours to reach the coast," said Fisher.

"And we're not sure exactly when the tractor left Natanz, so it could be there already," said Grim. "One among hundreds of tractor trailers moving in and out."

"Flight deck," Fisher called. "I need you to fly so fast the wings melt off. Do you read me?"

"Roger that, Sam. Best possible speed until the wings melt off."

Fisher nodded and glanced to Grim. "Be right back."

He headed to the infirmary, where he pulled

Kasperov aside and spoke in Russian. "We *were* going to drop you off at Dulles, but time's against us. We're making a detour."

"That's all right. I assume I'm very safe here."

"I guarantee that."

"So it's good we remain—but not for much longer. I do want to see my daughter. For now let me know if I can help with anything else."

"I will."

"Mr. Fisher, I'm sorry it's come to this. The oligarchs do not represent the Russian people, only a tiny minority, like your so-called one percent."

"I know. And the irony is, you and the rest of them, you got your money after the Soviet Union collapsed, so you were free to pursue greed at any cost."

"Just like America?" Kasperov asked. "As if to say your Congress isn't controlled by big businessmen?"

Fisher hesitated. "They'd never resort to this."

"You don't know that. Some men will do anything."

"But not us, right? Not you. You did the right thing— and in my line of work, I don't run into many people who have a conscience."

ELEVEN hours and fifty-eight minutes later they landed at Dubai International Airport.

Fisher had barely slept, and Grim had refused to leave the SMI table, even as dark circles had formed under her eyes and a pot of coffee had slowly emptied behind her.

More tractor trailers had been followed, shipments examined. Three different helicopters that had left Natanz had also been tracked. Keyhole satellites, drones, and ground assets had come up empty. Fisher decided he had nothing to lose by calling on Kobin.

"Hey, asshole."

Kobin snorted. "I thought we loved each other now."

"I filed for divorce."

"Nice."

Fisher lifted his chin. "I need information."

"What else is new?"

"Your guy find out anything on the Snow Maiden yet?"

"Still waiting on him."

"Follow up. Right now we got a shipment out of Natanz we need to find."

"Don't be coy, Fisher. I know what you're looking for. I eavesdrop on everything."

"Then you already got something for me."

"What the fuck? You think I got a guy in every city? A guy in Iran for God's sake?"

"Why not? You sold weapons to the Blacklist Engineers. You didn't care about that." Fisher scowled.

Kobin took a step back, thought it over, opened his mouth, hesitated, then finally stammered and said, "Look, I got one guy down in Bandar Abbas, but that port's pretty far south. Not sure why they'd send the container all the way down there. I'll give him a call, but listen, I don't think I have shit on this one. Wish I did."

"Make the call."

"Okay. And hey, I've been doing a lot of thinking."

Fisher almost smiled. "You actually have brain cells left?"

"Seriously, for what it's worth, I'm sorry."

Fisher frowned.

"You know. For everything. The past is the past. I think we make a great team."

Fisher took a step toward Kobin, staring him down. "You know what I think? I think it's all about you. You're not sorry. You're just saving your ass here. What you've done for us is good. You helped us find Kasperov. Thank you. But let's agree to just use each other and keep the apologies and this fantasy you have about joining our team out of the equation. Right now you're a consultant—and that seems to work. Okay?"

"Damn, I'm just trying to make nice over here. Not exactly in a good mood, are we?"

"You make nice by calling your buddy."

Fisher left the man standing there by the servers. Yes, Kobin had been a great help, but his abduction of Sarah and desire to have Fisher killed meant that no amount of "making amends," "earning his keep," or anything else could fix what he'd done. Ever.

Before returning to the control room, Fisher took a moment to calm himself. That bastard had set his blood to boil, and he knew he'd take it out on the team if he didn't let go.

After a deep breath, he started forward. "Hey, Charlie, we get anything?"

"Perfect timing, because, yeah, I found a link I've been looking for." The kid swung around in his chair, rubbed his eyes, then waved his peanut butter spoon like Excalibur. "Come see this."

Grim and Briggs joined Fisher at Charlie's station.

"If this is another dead end . . ." Grim warned.

"Hell, no, boss," Charlie answered, pointing to satellite photos of a seaport labeled King Abdulaziz.

The port was in the city of Dammam along Saudi Arabia's east coast and about halfway down the Persian Gulf, between Kuwait City and Abu Dhabi. Fisher recalled that it was one of the largest in the entire gulf. A data window beside one image indicated that the port was a main gateway through which cargo entered the Eastern Province and moved on into the central provinces of Saudi Arabia and was strategically placed to service the oil industry. The port had its own administration offices; mechanical and marine workshops; electrical, telephone, and marine communication networks; and water treatment plants. A clinic, a fire department, and housing complex for employees with nearby mosques and supermarkets helped classify the surrounding harborage as a city within a city.

Was this the oligarchs' third target?

"Given our timetable, it's possible that our device could've been transported down to the southern coast like Sam said, then put on a ship—because three different Iranian ships called on the port within the last four hours."

"So they want to blow up the port?" Fisher asked.

Charlie shrugged. "The generator's a booster, yeah, but I'm thinking these guys are bolder than that. They'll bury it within a bigger shipment and try to slip it past security. They wouldn't worry about that if they wanted to blow the port. Hell, they could leave it on the ship and just detonate it there."

"Come over here," said Grim, crossing back to the SMI. "Great work, Charlie. You finally got something that points to Abqaiq. I'll take it now."

Charlie grinned. "I knew you would."

Grim zoomed in on a map of Saudi Arabia, the vast plains of desert stretching out across the display like a piece of tanned leather. She narrowed the image toward a splotch of gray, a birthmark on an otherwise unbroken flesh-colored stretch sixty miles southwest of the port. The image came into focus to detail a cookie-cutter community with adjacent industrial facility to the east. Photos popped up in a gallery to the left, along with more data bars that identified the region as Abqaiq— pronounced "Ab-cake."

While the overhead image showed circular storage tanks and rectangular buildings, the photos revealed an even vaster network of pipes—like the exposed bowels of some metallic beast—along with huge columns of smoke backlit by flames shooting skyward in long, thin tongues.

This wasn't just an oil well. This was an oil processing facility, and it was located within a gated community of thirty thousand owned by Saudi Aramco, a Saudi Arabian national oil and natural gas company based in Dhahran.

"You're looking at one of the largest oil processors in the world," said Grim. "This facility handles more than half of Saudi Arabia's daily oil exports. It's a key node in the global energy pipeline. The main thing they do here is remove hydrogen sulfide from the crude oil so it doesn't spontaneously explode during shipping."

Grim tapped one data window to bring up a list of news stories. "Al-Qaeda launched an attack on Abqaiq back in 2006. They tried to get two cars carrying a ton of ammonium nitrate close to the processing plants, but the Saudis shut that down pretty quickly. They have security and entrances set up like an old medieval castle, where after you cross the gate, there's a wide open area nearly a mile long that allows the second tier of forces to take you out. Since then, there have been hundreds more attempts, all of them small and barely worth mentioning. The Saudis have increased security—higher fences, electronic surveillance, and a garrison of over thirty-five thousand troops. They have operators from the Special Security Forces, Special Emergency Forces, the General Security Service, as well as local reps from fire and police. The bigger players include specialized brigades of the Saudi Arabian National Guard, the Royal Saudi Navy, and even the Coast Guard. They have a contingency plan for hijacked aircraft being flown into the plant, with F-15s from their nearest base on continual standby."

"Tighter than Fort Knox," said Briggs.

"And the Russians know it," Charlie added.

"So what're you thinking, Grim?" asked Fisher. "They're smuggling the device into the processing plant?"

"There are two equipment warehouses on the east

side in an area called Material Supply." Grim spread her thumb and forefinger apart, coming in tight on the buildings. "The device could be hidden within some larger shipment and move through security. Some of those neutron generators—not all of them but some— emit radiation, and they're expected to do so. I'm not sure the fluctuations or increase in readings would be picked up by those security teams when they're already expecting some radiation—and I think that's what the oligarchs are counting on."

Fisher snickered. "So we won't find a nose-cone-shaped warhead with a ticking clock on it, huh?"

Grim rolled her eyes and typed something on the touch keyboard. The screens faded to expose another map of the region with concentric circles of devastation flashing in crimson red, along with data bars popping up all over the screen to detail the destruction. "A fifteen kiloton nuclear explosion—about the size of the detonation in Hiroshima—would kill everyone at the plant and surrounding community, some 65,000 in all, including many American engineers." She flicked her glance between Fisher and the SMI. "Within the first two to four months of the bombing, the acute effects of Hiroshima killed 90,000 to 166,000 people, with roughly half of the deaths occurring on the first day. The Hiroshima prefecture health department estimated that, of the people who died on the day of the explosion, sixty percent died from flash or flame burns, thirty percent from falling debris, and ten percent from other causes. Now take a look at this." Grim brought up another series of windows with charts, graphs, and tables. "This data comes from conflicting sources, and the Saudis are always giving us the best-case scenario and boast that they've got enough backup supplies, reserves, facilities, and personnel to take a major blow like this and come out unaffected."

"No way," Briggs said.

"Yeah, I know," said Grim. "Shutting down Abqaiq could take up to fifty percent of Saudi oil off the market for years and with it, much of the world's spare capacity."

"To hell with the oil. There are too many lives at stake—including Americans," Fisher said. "And we lose credibility if the world learns assets were in place and we didn't act. Let's get on the horn right now."

Grim's expression grew tentative. "We need to be careful. We can't run in there and cry wolf."

"I know," Fisher said. "But the Saudis need to suck it up and understand what's at stake here."

"I agree, Sam, but we can't forget that the Saudis are a very proud people. We lose credibility as an organization and as a nation if we're not absolutely sure about this. We know Abqaiq is a likely target. We have three Iranian ships that ported at Dammam within our time frame . . . but I'm concerned that's not enough for us to impose our will on them. We can alert them, sure, we'll do that, but I know you'll want to go in, and I know they'll want to handle this themselves."

Fisher looked at Charlie, who shrugged.

Briggs pursed his lips. "Iranian ships stop at that port all the time."

"We only need to be wrong once," said Fisher. "And that's not good enough for me. I'd rather piss off the Saudis and cry wolf than play games. We need to be there. We need to inspect anything that goes through there ourselves."

"But if we just had a little more," Briggs said. "Because you're right—we only need to be wrong once. And if we're sitting there at Abqaiq and a bomb goes off some-place else . . ."

"We need more?" Fisher asked, raising his voice in frustration. "All right, damn it, I'll get us more." He whirled and rushed off toward the infirmary.

As he opened the hatch, a dark thought crossed his mind: He could use Kobin to lie for him.

Fisher was not prepared to tiptoe around political interests. That wasn't happening. Not on his watch. Kobin would make up a story. Charlie would falsify the contacts. It'd all look plausible to Grim and Briggs. He understood their reservations, but he didn't have to agree with them. Abqaiq was the target with the highest strategic value. That was a fact.

Then again, maybe Fisher was more like Kasperov than he cared to admit: a man with a conscience.

Damn, what was he thinking? He couldn't do that to his team. They deserved better.

He'd take up the Russian's offer. Kasperov still had contacts. While it was true Grim had kept much of the intel away from him in the interest of national security, they didn't need to hand over much: A nuclear device might have been smuggled into Abqaiq, and did any of his contacts know anything about that or could they confirm any connection to the processing plant?

After giving the man a capsule summary, Fisher sighed and said, "Can you help?"

"I need a computer," Kasperov said.

Fisher called Charlie, who came down with a laptop and remained there, watching.

"Damn, you're calling him," said Charlie.

"Yes, I am," Kasperov answered, speaking in English for Charlie's benefit.

"And you know where he is?"

"Of course, I've always known. He's been right hand, ace in hole, as you say, for long time. He is at risk right now, but I think he will understand."

Fisher caught sight of a name on the screen: Kannonball.

Kasperov was in an encrypted chat session with his former employee, and they were now chatting in Cyrillic.

"Can you read any of that?" Fisher asked Charlie.

"Not really."

"They're typing too fast. Mr. Kasperov? What're you saying?"

"I'm letting him know about problem."

"What's he saying?"

"Several of oligarchs have GRU agents on payroll now, and Kannonball has hacked into GRU network. He says one GRU agent sent to Dammam with orders to intercept another agent on ground. No IDs yet because information wasn't being transmitted until pursuing agent arrived on target."

"What's this about?"

"It's about one agent killing another."

"They're cleaning up a mess."

"Exactly."

"On whose order?"

"Kannonball thinks maybe President Treskayev or Izotov from GRU ordered execution."

"Who does the rogue agent work for? One of the names on our list?"

"Correct. Recently hired. Rogue agent might be at port to receive shipment."

That left Fisher puzzled. "Why would they do that? If the agent is caught, that pins it back to the oligarchs. They're taking a big risk."

"Oligarchs would hire Iranians, yes. Train them, yes. But trust them entirely with something like this? No way. They would demand agent oversee operation, agent on suicide mission who either knows about bomb or does not."

"I think he's right," said Charlie. "And if that's the case, then maybe we've got enough."

"I'm taking this to Grim," said Fisher. "It'll *have* to be enough."

Within seconds he was back in the control room and sharing the news.

And when he was finished, Grim took a moment to mull it over, then said, "I'm proud of you, Sam."

"Excuse me?"

"You're making sure we have more evidence before we move."

"Yeah, well, you and Briggs are right. It helps."

She nodded. "The truth is, my gut was already telling me Abqaiq is the target, and yes, I said we have to be careful, but I think I would've pulled the trigger right there."

"Are you kidding me?"

"No. But I'm glad I didn't say anything—because it seems like we're rubbing off on each other."

"Yeah, finally. In a good way."

She smiled at him.

He smiled back.

She glanced away. "Okay, awkward moment. I'll call over to the processing plant right now."

Fisher headed over to Briggs, unable to repress his smile. "Let's get packed."

32

WITH Abqaiq finally ID'd as their next destination, the pilots filed for the city's local airport, only to discover that the lone runway had been abandoned fourteen years prior and was no longer usable. The processing plant did boast an active helipad intended for medevac and visiting Saudi royal family tours. Consequently, Fisher and Briggs chartered a small, four-passenger Bell 206 JetRanger helicopter from Dubai, a trip that took approximately 2.5 hours. They set down on the northwest helipad a few minutes after sunset. Their pilot would wait for them for the return trip out, but he warned of bad weather on the way.

They were met by Prince Al Shammari, a heavyset man in his forties dressed in a brown woolen *thawb* flowing in deep creases to his ankles. On his head was the traditional small white cap called a *taqiyah*. The cap prevented his much larger scarf-like *ghutra* from slipping off. The long *ghutra* was bound by a doubled black cord fitting tightly across his forehead. When visiting an Arab country, Fisher sometimes chose to dress like the locals, but when he didn't, conservative clothes were the order of the day. Fisher and Briggs wore simple business casual shirts and slacks—one size too large because beneath them were hidden their tac-suits.

Shammari was already waving his hands and booming a welcome from across the well-lit pad. In addition to his security duties he was the assistant interior minister of the country and had been educated in California, so his English was excellent, if not tinged by a little Los Angeles slang. Grim had warned Fisher that he was a devoted technophile, addicted to his social media outlets and smartphone, and he'd demanded that Fisher video-conference with him before they met in person.

As Fisher climbed out of the chopper, he crinkled his nose over the strong scent of crude oil. He'd heard from those who worked around such facilities that the stench eventually vanished because you became used to it, not that it ever truly went away.

Shammari was accompanied by two squads from the Special Security Force. These were highly trained and heavily armed counterterrorism troops wearing perma-nent scowls and desert camouflage utilities. They cross-trained with special forces from all over the world, including Navy SEALs. The entire party had arrived in four Humvees whose diesel engines chugged behind them.

Fisher lifted his voice above the chopper's rotors as they spun down. "Prince Shammari, we appreciate you allowing us into your processing plant. We need to move as quickly as possible."

"Relax. As I said, I'll indulge your hunch because I want to show you how absolutely secure we are here. I don't believe that we are suddenly going to explode this very minute. Boom!" He waved his hands in the air, then glanced back at the troops, who broke out in laughter.

Briggs gave Fisher a look, as if to say, *Famous last words . . .*

"You told me you were bringing weapons and equipment. We'll need to see them now."

Briggs and Fisher turned over their duffel bags, and the squad leaders came forward and picked through their pistols, trifocals, and pair of SIG MPX submachine guns they were toting. Briggs said the trifocals were just prototype night-vision goggles, and the troops dismissed them. They did admire the MPXs because they were shaped like miniature assault rifles with curved thirty-round magazines and were the only submachine guns in the world that allowed the operator to change barrel length, caliber, and stock configuration in the field to meet mission requirements.

"You come to shoot bears," said the prince. "But I told you, all we have here is oil!"

"I understand. Just a precaution."

The prince made a face, looked at the troops, who

nodded okay, then he turned and waved everyone back toward the Humvees.

Shouldering their duffel bags, they followed Shammari and boarded the lead truck. They drove off toward a large tower where a ball of flame lit the night.

"Burn-off," Shammari said, flicking a finger in that direction. "Beautiful, isn't it?"

"Do you have the radiation equipment we requested, along with the schedule of deliveries?"

"You can meet with our security team at the main gate. They'll have all the information you want to see. But do trust me, I've looked over that schedule myself, and as I told you earlier, there's nothing out of the ordinary for us."

"Let's hope so," said Fisher.

"There are over thirty thousand employees here who've entrusted their lives to me and my security forces. I would never let them down."

"I don't doubt that for a second," said Fisher.

"Then why are you here?"

"Because the men I'm dealing with are very determined, and I think they're smart enough to fool us if we're not careful. So let's be careful—and check it out."

"All right, then, there's the main gate ahead. Go ahead and check it out."

There was no mistaking the prince's sarcasm, and Fisher guessed he might act the same way were the tables turned. The Saudis had transformed the place into a fortress, and Fourth Echelon's presence implied that the prince's "impenetrable" security force had been summarily scrutinized and found wanting, which in turn had bruised his ego.

The Humvee pulled to a halt even as a pair of broad, wrought-iron gates bordered by black-and-yellow stripes yawned inward. A guardhouse stood on either side of the gates, with riflemen posted at each. More bearded guards wearing traditional security uniforms came out to greet Fisher and Briggs, who were introduced to the officer in charge and taken over to a computer terminal, where the logs were stored.

Although Fisher had requested that those logs be sent electronically to the team, the prince had declined, saying they were confidential but that Fisher was welcome to take a look at them in person. Fisher began surreptitiously snapping photos of the log with his OPSAT and transmitting them back to Charlie and Grim.

"Got them, Sam," said Charlie.

"We receive fifty, sometimes one hundred shipments per day," said the officer in charge. "Packages and equipment of all kinds."

Fisher squinted and scanned through the long list in 10-point type, the items identified in a mishmash of English and Arabic.

He scrolled down, tapped his finger on the screen, and moved back so that Briggs could have a look.

An invoice indicated the arrival three hours earlier of seven thousand feet of pipe and four new drill heads.

"What do you think?" asked Briggs.

"I think we should check it out."

They returned to the Humvee, and Fisher said,

"Prince Shammari, there is a delivery you received earlier that we'd like to examine."

"You think my personnel missed something?"

"No, sir."

"Then we can take you back to your helicopter."

"We'd rather inspect the shipment ourselves—only because the timing is right."

Shammari made a face and called out to the driver. The convoy moved forward, through the gates, and onto a road leading out toward four silver spheres looming in the distance.

"And can you tell the driver to get us there as fast as he can?" Fisher added.

"Of course I'll tell him. But first, look over there."

Shammari pointed to the lines of Al Fahd Armoured Personnel Carriers on either side of the road, some armed with .40mm cannons, others with .50-caliber machine guns mounted above their cabs. Some troops manned the fifties while others stood on lookout in the turret-top cupolas to the rear.

The prince went on: "If anything were to bypass the gates, these men would cut them down in a second. Do you have any idea how many eyes and ears we have on this processing plant? How at this very moment we're being monitored by cameras, by motion detectors, by drones flying over our heads? Do you know how many rounds of ammunition we can put on a target in a single minute? It's truly incredible."

Fisher closed his eyes and steeled himself. "Yes, it is."

"But still you question our security."

"Didn't the king, your uncle, say it was better to have a thousand enemies outside your tent than one inside?"

"He did. But you've just crossed into one of the most secure places in the world."

Fisher considered a retort, then thought better of it.

The pair of warehouses Grim had mentioned earlier began rising from the twilit gloom ahead. At least the driver had taken his cue and raced ahead with a heavy foot and clear sense of urgency.

They pulled up outside the first warehouse, a rectangular two-story building about the length of an entire football field. Several guards were posted outside the doors, and a few more along the rear dock and loading ramps.

While Shammari strode from the Humvees, Fisher and Briggs jogged away with the security team hustling up behind them. Seeing what was happening, the warehouse guards moved aside, and the lead troop, a sergeant, slid a key card across a scanner, opening the side door. They charged inside.

Massive halogen lights suspended from the iron rafters cast broad puddles of light across the concrete floor. To their left, oversized racks rising some eight meters held bundles of pipes of various lengths and diameters. To their right towered literally hundreds more racks with thousands more pipes, fittings, clamps, and dozens of other parts, some recognizable, some completely foreign to Fisher. Placards in Arabic and English identified sections as DESALTER, VACUUM DISTILLATION, NAPHTHA HYDROTREATER, CATALYTIC REFORMER, and FLUID CATALYTIC CRACKER, among many others.

In sum, the warehouse was an overwhelming maze of drilling and oil refining equipment, each aisle a labyrinth of rubber, copper, steel, and aluminum. Without knowing exactly where the recent pipe and drill shipment had been stored, it could take them an eternity just to get near it. Moreover, it was after hours, and the warehouse foremen had gone home for the evening.

"The most recent large shipment," Fisher told one of the sergeants in Arabic, reciting the invoice number he'd memorized. "Delivered today."

The troop had a schematic of the warehouse and delivery schedule displayed on an iPad mini. He called up the route, pointed toward a long row between racks on their right, and once more, the group took off jogging, with the prince bringing up the rear.

They rounded a corner, and the sergeant called for a halt to once more consult his tablet. He glanced up at the storage racks, numbered 329, 330, 331 . . . then his gaze panned downward to more labels. He began walking up the row several more meters, then spun and stopped. "It'll all be here," he said, pointing to the bundles of pipes and cone-shaped drill heads sitting atop pallets covered in shrink-wrap.

"Grim, are you seeing this?" Fisher muttered.

"Got everything. I don't see anything that looks like a generator there."

Fisher turned back to the troops. "Who's got the radiation equipment? We need this scanned."

Two soldiers dropped their packs and fished out their portable radiation survey detection meters and wands.

Prince Shammari lumbered up behind the group and said, "What do you think of our warehouse?"

Fisher wasn't sure how to answer. "Nice."

"And this is the delivery you're so worried about?"

"Yes, it is." Fisher called for some more light, and the troops directed their flashlights onto the pipes and within them.

"I can assure you," said the prince, parading up to Fisher and getting in his face. "This delivery has been thoroughly inspected by three of my engineers, by my radiological teams, and by anyone else we deemed necessary to ensure it is not, and I repeat, *not* some kind of explosive device that you and your people suggest may be en route here. These items were ordered months ago, and the company verifies the shipment and invoices through their own security personnel, and then those items come through our very rigorous process. And I remind you, even after Ms. Grimsdóttir called, we searched this entire facility, just as a precaution. I was very explicit about that. You're wasting your time with these radiation detectors and with this whole nonsense. No one got past my security. No one can get past it. I hope you and your people understand that now."

Fisher stood there.

Part of him felt deeply embarrassed, the other part ready to commit murder.

Shammari bared his teeth, but his lips curled into a grin.

Fisher averted his gaze. "We'll be leaving now."

33

BEFORE climbing into the Humvee, Fisher stole a moment to have a word with Grim, who'd been monitoring the conversation he'd had with Prince Shammari.

The wind was beginning to howl in his ears as he listened to her through his subdermal: "I don't know, Sam, I was positive all the dots were connecting."

"They still are."

"Maybe Abqaiq's not the target."

"Then why are those Russians in Dammam?"

"Maybe it's been the port all along. Or maybe the capital. Maybe it's Riyadh. That's only two hundred miles southwest."

Fisher mouthed a curse and said, "We're heading over

to Dammam. We'll see what we can pick up there. You keep working with Kasperov and his right-hand guy. I'll be in touch."

As they drove away from the warehouse, Prince Shammari glanced up from his surfboard-sized smartphone and announced that out to the west, a thunderstorm traveling at up to 45 knots was beginning to collapse and dump torrents. Wind directions were reversing and gusting outward from the storm. Reports from Riyadh said a haboob was beginning to form and that everyone should seek cover.

"Haboob" was an amusing word for a very deadly and intense sandstorm common on the Arabian peninsula.

"Where are you headed now?" Shammari asked Fisher.

"Dammam."

"Then you'd best hurry."

"We will. I'm sorry we wasted your time. Your security is impressive."

"As I've demonstrated."

"Your deliveries here, they all come in by truck?"

"And by rail. With a few small ones by helicopter."

"The oil is shipped by pipeline up to Dammam."

"That's correct."

Fisher sat there, considering that.

"I hope for our sakes that you're wrong," said Shammari. "There is no plot. There is no bomb. I know we've been talking about terrorists with nuclear weapons for years, but the world cannot afford it. Not ever."

"I agree. But I've been doing this for a long time."

Fisher glanced out the window. "There's a bomb out there. And we're going to find it."

BY the time they hit the helipad, the chopper was already warm since Fisher had called ahead to the pilot. They bid their tense and somewhat awkward good-byes to the prince and his troops, then started for the helicopter.

While stars shimmered directly overhead, the western sky was no more than a churning brown wave that consumed the entire horizon. Briggs pointed, and they both gasped.

This could be the largest and most formidable haboob Fisher had ever seen, and that was saying something because he'd spent enough time in Arab countries to ride out his share of storms. This bad weather could buy them some time. If the storm extended all the way up to the port it could shut down operations, perhaps delaying the oligarchs' plan.

They climbed into the chopper, Briggs taking one of the backseats, Fisher up front with the pilot. They rolled shut the door, and just as they were lifting off, Grim called.

"Sam, I've got new intel from Kasperov. He called one of the oligarchs directly. Kargin, the guy who was talking to Chern. Kasperov threatened to unleash the Calamity Jane virus on the man's company and holdings if he didn't call off the attack."

"Then it's over?"

"Kasperov thinks Kargin killed himself while he was on the line. The guy said it's too late. There's nothing that can stop them now."

"Aw, shit. Did he get anything else?"

"He didn't, but his partner Kannonball did. More intercepted comms between the GRU and an agent in Dammam. Best we can tell there are four Iranian MOIS agents at the port. They've linked up with the rogue GRU agent and were ordered to meet up with a railcar broker."

Fisher's OPSAT flashed as Grim sent him a satellite map of the desert between Dammam and Abqaiq, with a flashing red line between the two. Fisher zoomed in on that line to expose a set of railroad tracks, noting how the railway left Dammam, ran right through Abqaiq between the Saudi Aramco compound and the processing plant, then arrowed farther south to Riyadh.

"Grim, what if they—"

"I'm ahead of you. The Saudis have GID agents at the port, and I confirmed with them that one of the Iranian ships offloaded an HEP car."

"A what?"

"An HEP car. These are high-end power cars that sit directly behind the locomotives. They look like engines sitting backward and they generate extra power needed for refrigerator cars and tractor trailer cooling units. The Saudis have some older diesel locomotives and still use some of these power cars on their lines. There was nothing unusual about this shipment, and all the paperwork checked out with the railway."

"So why are we interested?"

"Because that HEP car was attached to a locomotive carrying oil containers, twenty-one in all, and it's the only shipment scheduled to run through Abqaiq this evening. It's number 116."

"So you're saying they don't use HEP cars with oil container trains."

"No—but they attached one anyway because they wanted that car to move out tonight."

"Tell me why oil is being shipped down by train when there's pipeline from Abqaiq to Dammam."

"That oil is headed for Riyadh. They still need to ship the processed oil back down to the city by rail, and as you've seen, that railroad passes right through Abqaiq."

"So they got past security at the port and the bomb's inside the HEP car."

"It has to be."

"So the bomb *is* part of a larger shipment."

"Yeah," said Grim. "We weren't thinking big enough."

"So now all they have to do is wait until the train passes through the processing facility and detonate it for maximum impact. Just like the thorium operation, they either have a spotter in Abqaiq or like Kasperov said, they'll have someone to trigger it manually, someone on a suicide mission."

"Plus they have the storm to cover them. No way they could've planned that, but they'll take advantage of it."

"Call Shammari. Tell him to stop the train."

"I already did," she said. "The train's still coming. It's

been hijacked. Just a single rail between Abqaiq and Dammam. No way to divert it."

"What's our ETA to the train?"

"About fifteen minutes."

"Backup?"

"Shammari's troops are leaving the compound now, but his F-15s have been grounded. He says he's got some light helicopter gunships en route."

"Tell him to hold back those gunships until I give the order—otherwise they could spook the triggerman."

"Roger that. And, Sam, once the storm hits we'll lose the satellite feed and maybe the rest of our comms."

"That's all right. We know what to do now."

"Sam, I, uh . . . I think this time we're right."

"Is your gut telling you that?"

"It is."

"Good. Mine, too." He closed his eyes and could almost see her face. She wore the barest hint of a smile.

He wanted to say something else, something more meaningful because she was right, this was it—possibly the last conversation they'd ever have after years of working together.

"Grim?"

"Yeah?"

He stammered. "We'll be okay."

After a long pause, she answered, "Talk to you soon, Sam."

Briggs, who'd been listening in on the conversation via the chopper's intercom system, reached over and proffered his hand.

"What's this?" Fisher asked.

"Just in case," said Briggs. They shook firmly. "Someday, when I grow up, I'm gonna be just like you."

Fisher shoved Briggs and smiled. "Let's go kick some ass."

34

THE chopper pilot from Dubai, who'd introduced himself as Hammad, knew some English—enough to deal with tourists—but that wasn't an issue since Fisher and Briggs spoke Arabic.

However, convincing the thirty-year-old man with closely cropped beard to engage in the unthinkable with his rotary wing aircraft was the real challenge.

"We just need a ride to the train," Fisher said over the intercom.

"To the train? The storm's coming. We can't do that. Besides, why there? How were you planning on boarding?"

Fisher sighed. "Very carefully. You'll take us to the train. Now."

"I'm sorry, sir, but I won't."

"Then you can hop out right now, and my buddy will take over."

Briggs reached in beside the man and began to open the side door.

"What're you doing?" The pilot swatted away Briggs's hand and cried, "You're crazy! Crazy! We have the storm. We have to get back to the port and get under cover!"

"Hammad, we need you," said Briggs, who looked to Fisher for approval and got it. "We're talking about terrorists on board that train."

"I'll put it to you this way," Fisher interjected. "If you don't help us, we won't kill you—but what they have on that train will."

The pilot hesitated. "What do you mean?"

Fisher sloughed off his shirt to expose his tac-suit. Behind him, Briggs held up their machine guns. "Our business isn't exactly oil."

Hammad's eyes flared. "Holy shit, holy shit."

"Exactly," said Briggs. "We're just asking for a little help."

"Don't shoot me. Please."

Fisher snorted. "Are you kidding? Today's your day to be a hero. You up for it or what?"

Hammad was visibly trembling now. "My boss will kill me if I put even a scratch on the helicopter."

"It's cool," said Briggs. "I know you can do this."

Hammad gestured to a picture of two little girls taped just above his instrument panel, two gems about five and six years old. "They need their father!"

"I know," Fisher said. "So do we."

The man's eyes were burning now. "Who are you?"

Fisher tensed. "We're the passengers you'll never forget."

"Maybe *you're* the terrorists!"

Fisher tapped a few keys on his OPSAT, bringing up some digital photographs of his daughter Sarah when she was nine. He held up his wrist for the pilot to see. "That's my daughter. She's all grown up now, but she still needs her father. And her father needs you. So let's get this done. For all of them. Okay?"

Hammad pursed his lips, swallowed, then took another look at Briggs and Fisher.

Briggs put his hand on the pilot's shoulder. "We have faith in you, Hammad. More than you know."

After taking a deep breath and reaching out to touch the photograph of his girls, Hammad said, "I don't want to die."

"You won't," Fisher assured him. "Now take us a mile or two south, and get us up high, another thousand feet."

"I can't believe I'm doing this," the pilot muttered, banking sharply, then gaining altitude, the chopper buffeted hard by a sudden gust that left Fisher's stomach about thirty feet below.

"Continue nice and wide," said Fisher. "Anyone on the train spots us, they'll think we're heading to the port."

"I understand," said Hammad. "You're not the terrorists, then, right?"

"I know it's hard to tell who the good guys are these days, but Allah's on your side."

"Yes, always."

Hammad kept several pairs of binoculars on board for sightseers. Fisher grabbed a pair and focused on the train, just a metallic serpent chugging forward across the broad plains of desert. Twin headlights reached out into the gathering dust. Fisher panned up toward the haboob and regretted that decision.

The storm was a living, breathing creature of wind and sand, consumed by hunger and unaffected by politics, religion, or any other differences men used to justify killing each other. It was motivated only by the laws of physics, a perfect killer.

"All right," Fisher told Hammad, shaking off the thought. "Come back around and descend hard and fast. You're like an old fighter pilot in World War II, coming in to strafe the enemy, got it?"

"Holy shit, yes. I got it."

Briggs had finished stripping down to his tac-suit and was double-checking their pistols and spare magazines. He handed Fisher his Five-seveN and SIG P226, then holstered his own weapons. Next he handed Fisher his submachine gun with attached sling and clutched his own tightly to his chest.

"Good to go," Briggs said over the intercom. "Nothing beats the smell of factory-fresh ammo in the evening."

Fisher almost smiled, then glanced to Hammad. "You're doing great. Keep descending. Okay, now over there, we need to get lower, that's right, bank right . . . right . . . descend again! You see it now?"

Hammad swooped down like a vulture, then he pitched the nose and descended even more aggressively. Fisher found himself clutching the seat with one hand as they came within five meters of the desert floor before Hammad pulled up and leveled off to check his altitude. Not two seconds later, he descended a few more meters.

"That's how to do it," Fisher said. "That's perfect. You could be a military pilot."

"Yeah, man," said Hammad, sounding only half as confident as Fisher.

The helicopter was on a straight and level path directly behind the train, with the rail ties ticking by. Despite being jarred by the train's wash, Hammad kept them less than two meters above the railway, with only the caboose container's tiny red taillights as a reference point.

Their approach was about as stealthy as Fisher could've hoped for, but he still wasn't sure how loud the locomotive and HEP car were and if they'd been noisy enough to conceal the chopper's engine and rotors to anyone posted outside the train. The plan, of course, was to go in ghost.

Fisher lifted his binoculars. The tank cars themselves were as expected—long black cylinders with well-rusted bellies and ladders both fore and aft. There were grab irons mounted to the sides and narrow, flat upper decks with railings that allowed maintenance workers to pass from car to car.

"Okay, great job, Hammad," he said. "Stand by to get us up top."

As Fisher unbuckled and climbed toward the backseat, ready to give Hammad his final instructions, gunfire ripped across the canopy—

And suddenly Hammad was jerking the stick, throwing Fisher backward.

"Get above the last car!" shouted Briggs. "Don't pull away!"

"He's shooting at us!" cried Hammad.

Fisher crashed into the backseat and then whipped his head around, catching the barest glimpse of a man posted between the caboose and the next tank car. He repeatedly swung out from the side of the train, single-handedly firing his rifle, the muzzle flashing—but oddly not a single round struck the chopper. Was he the world's worst shot?

Fisher squinted for a better look.

"Oh, you're kidding me!" cried Briggs.

In that instant oil began spraying across the canopy, mixing with the swirling dust and clouding Hammad's view as the agent continued spraying the oil container with bullets, releasing more streams of oil.

"Pull up now!" Fisher cried.

Hammad shook his head. "I can't see!"

The oil kept splashing and bleeding off, the streaks beginning to blur like a kaleidoscope. One false move by the pilot, and they'd either plow into the back of the train or smash into the tracks—and Fisher's imagination took him through both of those scenarios in an instant.

"Come on, Hammad, do it!" Fisher cried, slapping his palm on top of the pilot's and ready to take over if Hammad backed out.

Hammad's eyes bulged. "Okay, I got it!" He gasped, shuddered, then pulled back and brought them above the oil spray, coming directly above the container car. He was leaning forward now, staring through a meager opening on the canopy no more than twelve inches wide and not yet stained with oil.

"Here," shouted Briggs, handing Fisher his pair of trifocals.

With his goggles on, Briggs threw the latch and yanked open the door.

The wind literally screamed into the compartment.

And the sand came in needle-like torrents.

Hammad coughed and cried, "Hurry!"

"Just hold position!" Fisher told him. "You're a hero today, my friend!"

"Holy shit, yes!"

Briggs leaped from the chopper and hit the container hard, falling forward, sliding for a second, then latching onto one of the railings. One hand slid loose and he was thrown back by both the train's velocity and the storm, but he leaned forward and returned that hand to the rail.

Ignoring the desert blurring by and the sand beginning to rip through the rotors, Fisher couldn't help himself. He chanced a look at the sandstorm—perhaps a quarter mile away and barreling toward them.

Oh my God . . .

The diminutive train and even tinier chopper lay

directly in the path of what resembled a thousand-foot-tall tidal wave as murky and thick as the ocean itself.

Chilled, Fisher flicked his gaze back on the oil container, focusing on his upper deck landing zone.

Then, with a curse that really meant *no, I'm not too old for this shit*, he pushed away from the helicopter and plunged two meters to the top deck.

As his boots made impact, they gave way on a thin coating of oil that had whipped up from the rotor wash and was dripping off the railings.

He hit hard on his rump and began slipping off the deck, a hairsbreadth from being blown right off the container—when Briggs's hand latched onto his, just as Fisher went swinging off the side and across the oil-slick surface.

Suspended now, Fisher caught another glimpse of the man who'd been firing at them, illuminated in the pale green glow of his trifocals. He was an Iranian MOIS agent, Fisher assumed, with balaclava tugged over his head, Kevlar vest strapped tightly at his chest and waist, and baggy combat trousers. Two pistols were holstered on his right side, one at the waist, the other on his lower hip. The rifle was an AK-47—and it popped again as Briggs dragged Fisher up and onto the deck.

Another salvo cracked from the AK, and Fisher swung back toward the chopper.

Hammad was just pulling away, taking heavy fire now from the agent, rounds sparking and ricocheting off the fuselage, a few punching into the side window.

Salvo after salvo tracked him.

He banked hard to the right. Too hard. Blood splashed across the side window. He lost control of the bird—

And before Fisher could open his mouth, the helicopter flipped onto its back, pitched slightly, then crashed with a thundering explosion into the desert behind them, the flickering fireball sweeping into the rising gale. Secondary explosions lifted into the first, with contrails of black smoke instantly shredded by the sand.

With the picture of Hammad's little girls abruptly and permanently etched in Fisher's memory, he gritted his teeth and sprang to his feet.

Thoughts of payback did not blind him with rage, but the anger did trigger a massive adrenaline rush. There wasn't a combatant in the world who could stop him now.

He raced across the top of the container car, reached the end, and just as the agent glanced up from his perch at the foot of the ladder, Fisher unleashed a volley of 9mm NATO rounds directly into the bastard's head, punching him back and sending him tumbling off the train.

"Sam, duck!" cried Briggs.

Fisher dropped to his haunches as more gunfire whirred over his head. Two cars up, another agent had mounted the ladder, placed his elbows on the top of the container, and begun trading fire with Briggs, whose submachine gun fire drove the man back behind the tank.

"Keep him busy," cried Fisher, who crawled forward, slid under the upper deck railing, seized one of the grab irons, then allowed himself to slide down, off the right side of the container. He descended on two more grab irons until he was able to latch both hands onto the base of the upper deck railing. Now, with his legs dangling freely, he worked himself sideways across the deck, concealed from the agent's view, while Briggs squeezed off another volley of suppressing fire, the MPX booming over the rattle and clack of the train.

Fisher continued slipping across the container until he reached the end and once more shifted down to the grab irons. He lowered himself between the cars, crossing over the coupler receiver hitch and reaching the next ladder.

Three more rounds cracked overhead, these from the agent, and Briggs answered with another triplet of fire.

"Almost there," Fisher told Briggs.

"Roger, let me know."

Fisher scaled the ladder and once more began skimming his way across the side of the container—

But without warning the train lurched forward, thundering at what must be full speed now, the diesel locomotive running at least sixty-five miles per hour. Fisher felt his grip falter and he tensed, fighting to pull himself higher and keep moving, each release of his gloved hands coming in smooth, practiced strokes. All those pull-ups and all that French Parkour training focusing on using momentum to breach obstacles always paid off.

"Sam, if you can still hear me, the train's only about ten minutes away from Abqaiq," Grim said. "We're running out of time here!"

"Okay. We're on the train. We'll get it done."

"You're breaking up now. I didn't get—"

Static broke over the subdermal as a gust wrapped around the tank, rattling the undercarriage.

When he was about two-thirds of the way down the container, he took a deep breath. "All right, Briggs. Hold fire."

"Holding."

Fisher reached up, slapped a gloved hand on the bottom rung of the upper deck's railing, then, hanging by one hand, he drew his Five-seveN and swung up a leg, latching it around a support post. As he forced himself back onto the upper deck, sliding on his belly, he brought up his pistol and watched as the agent chanced another look.

Bang. Fisher shot him in the eye. "Briggs, move up!"

The wind was so fierce now, the sand battering them so violently, that Briggs could only stagger his way across the deck, keeping both hands latched onto the railing.

"We're too slow!" Fisher shouted.

"I know! I know!"

Four MOIS agents and one rogue GRU agent. That was Fisher's initial threat assessment. Two down. There should only be three remaining, but there was no telling yet if the MOIS agents had brought in more recruits.

That was until the next three began firing at them, even as they descended the next ladder to continue moving up the train.

"That's not the rest of them," Briggs shouted.

"No, we've got more than we thought."

"Shit. Let me get an active sonar reading. Okay, there

it is. Picked up those three, maybe a few more near the front, but the signal's weak, too much downtime between bursts."

"We're nine minutes from Abqaiq," said Fisher.

"Then we get up there, and it's guns blazing! We got no choice," Briggs said.

"There's another railing that runs low along the wheels," said Fisher. "I think I can make better time using that one. Same deal. You cover, I move up."

"All right, but my way's faster."

"I agree. Your way will get us killed faster."

Briggs frowned.

"Let's do it." Fisher slid around the side of the container and stepped onto the lower railing, merely a thin bar and protective skirt for the wheels. The grab irons were too high to reach, and there was no way he could balance himself on that rail without hand supports and with the train dieseling hard at sixty-five miles an hour, so he clutched the rail, then allowed himself to fall forward, swinging beneath it, ankles latched, and he began a swift, hand-over-hand approach, with the cacophony of the wheels at his side until he reached the midsection, the wind passing under the container and coming in short bursts, the sand hissing and getting into his mouth, ears, and nose. Ignoring the blood rushing into his head and the fire in his pectoral muscles, he grimaced and slid even faster.

Briggs's machine gun cracked another announcement, but then footfalls thundered across the top of the container, followed by another exchange of gunfire—

And suddenly, one, two, three agents were dropping away from the train, smashing into the dirt, wiping out below Fisher, and flailing into the darkness.

"Three down. Let's keep moving," said Briggs through the subdermal.

"I told you, same plan," Fisher snapped.

"I know. I accidently killed them as I was trying to distract them."

"Yeah, right, hang on, I'm coming." Fisher reached the end of the container, then swung himself up between the cars as Briggs descended the ladder to join him.

"It's a long way to the front," said Briggs. "But we're clear for at least another five cars. Visibility is shit. Come on, come on."

Fisher hauled himself up the next ladder and clutched the railing with both hands. His boots actually lifted from the tank several times, and it felt as though a construction worker were holding a sandblaster to his cheeks. When he glanced to the right, he couldn't see anything save for the swirling phosphorescent sand via his night vision, and he wouldn't dare remove the goggles.

Briggs was right behind him, hunkered down, pistol in one hand, the other sliding across the railing.

The next gust slammed Fisher into the railing . . .

And when he looked back to check on Briggs, the man was gone.

35

SHOUTING his partner's name was a reflex action. Fisher didn't expect to find the man. He'd already assumed that Briggs had been swept off the train.

But then he was glad he'd called out—because a voice came from near his boots:

"Sam! Down here! Little help!"

Fisher lifted his chin to glance over the side of the oil tank.

There was Briggs, both hands locked onto a grab iron. He must've slid down the container and seized the iron as he smashed into it. Time to repay the earlier favor. Fisher got on his haunches and reached over, taking Briggs's hand, then, raging aloud in exertion, he hauled his teammate back onto the deck.

Coughing and spitting out sand, Briggs nodded, and they got back up and forged on, the train moving relentlessly through the storm now, the containers—despite being weighed down with oil—beginning to shimmy as though threatening to fall apart.

They neared the next car, and Fisher's impatience got the best of him. He gave a hand signal to Briggs then took off running. He made a flying leap over the gap between cars, then hit the deck and flung out his hands to seize the railing. Briggs bounded forward, made his jump, and landed behind Fisher. They both crouched down to spy the end of the tank. No response from anyone ahead. Now they would make some time.

Yet before they reached the end of the tank, something very odd happened, something that had them standing more upright and glancing around, their gazes lifting to the skies . . .

The din of howling winds and hissing sand faded, as though they were passing through some strange boulevard deep in the heart of purgatory, soft whispers coming on the air, the sand falling in light flurries like snow, the clinking of the train more distinct.

They took advantage of this lull and raced across two more containers. En route, Fisher spoke quickly into his SVT: "Grim? Charlie? Can you read me?"

"We got you, Sam," answered Charlie. "Looks like you're in some sort of pocket."

"Roger that. We're almost there."

"And, Sam, we got some new intel on that rogue Russian agent with the group."

"You got an ID?"

"Yeah, and—"

Charlie's voice dissolved into a rush of static accompanied by a blast of wind and sand that struck with a vengeance, slamming Fisher and Briggs into the opposite railing.

He could barely see his gloved hands now, and while reaching the HEP car and locomotive would take more time, the storm would, for the most part, conceal their approach until the very last second. He doubted the MOIS agents were equipped with protective gear, so they might've retreated inside. The reduced visibility could actually work in Fisher's favor, adding precious time to their remaining six minutes. The trigger man's top priority was to ensure the bomb was physically in the Abqaiq compound before completing the firing circuit. Right now he was presumably as blind as Fisher.

The next connection between cars required them to descend and ascend the ladders since the gusts—coming in erratic salvos like gunfire—made it far too risky to jump. Fisher took another sonar reading as they came within two containers of the HEP car. He glimpsed right through the oil-filled container to detect the shimmering white outlines of a pair of agents huddling against the wind between cars, ready to ambush them. There was another one inside the locomotive serving as engineer, and two more inside the HEP car.

So the Iranians had, indeed, picked up a few reinforcements. The GRU agent would more than likely be in the HEP car with the bomb.

Before they could climb up, ready to ambush the ambushers, a reverberation worked through the oil tank and into the ladder. Fisher ascended a few rungs, then caught the barest thump of footfalls. He turned back to Briggs, issued a hand signal, and Briggs gave a curt nod, ready.

Just as the agent above neared the edge of the railing and spotted Briggs, who was acting as the bait, a word came through Fisher's subdermal, just a whisper from his partner: "Now."

Clutching the ladder with one hand, his pistol jammed tightly in the other, Fisher pushed up from his current rung, leaned back, and shot the agent point-blank beneath the chin just as the agent was bringing his rifle to bear.

As he shrank back onto the deck, Fisher continued his ascent, slapping his arm across the dead agent's knees in order to target the Iranian's partner, who'd dropped to his belly about two meters ahead and had propped himself on his elbows.

Yet before either of them could get off a shot, what seemed like a long chute of sand—a twister tipped on its side—ripped across the train, sweeping the first agent's body right out from beneath Fisher, who seized the railing at the last second.

When he looked up again, the other agent was hurling through the air, writhing against invisible claws and firing wildly in a reflex response, the rounds drumming into the tank, a few ricocheting off the rails.

"Briggs?"

"Right behind you. No plans to slip again."

"We're clear to move. You get up there past the HEP car and take out the engineer."

"Roger. I'll need to check that windshield first to make sure they can't see us."

"Good call. We're down to five minutes here."

Fisher struggled up the ladder and hooked his arm completely over the railing, driving it into the crook. He clutched his wrist, using his arms like a carabiner clip to fasten himself to the deck. Briggs shifted past him, then Fisher carefully unhooked his arm and fell in behind, taking another sonar reading.

"Hold up," he ordered Briggs.

"Shit, what now?"

One of the agents inside the HEP car was not there. He took another reading, and the image came up indistinct, suggesting that maybe the two agents were so close together that he couldn't tell them apart.

"What?" Briggs.

"Forget it. Keep going!"

They left the last tanker car and then Briggs motioned them onto their bellies. They crawled forward so that Briggs could get a more furtive glance at the HEP car's operator's booth, which was facing toward them.

"Can't see much," said Briggs. "Let's do it."

As they clambered to their feet, rings of light appeared in the distance, like fireflies buzzing in a tight orbit, sparking and tinkling, with smaller, perpendicular pairs flashing in a random sequence of yellow and white behind them.

Next came the whomping. And Fisher's jaw dropped.

The twin silhouettes of Shammari's AH-6 light gunships burst from the gloom. The prince had ignored Fisher's request to keep them on standby and had sent them directly into the storm. As they approached, the shimmering rings became brighter and resembled Fourth of July sparklers spun by overzealous children. The effect was created by their rotor blades, as the air had turned into 80 grit sandpaper rubbing against their surfaces.

The first chopper knifed through more draperies of dust, and its pilot opened up on Fisher and Briggs, laying down a bead of 7.62mm rounds fired from a pair of miniguns. Rounds stitched their way up, across the tank container, cutting a line right over the deck between them.

Fisher dove forward, with Briggs crossing the path of fire as the second bird came in behind the first, swooping down and tipping forward, its rotors mere meters above them.

"What's he doing?" cried Briggs.

"Grim, if you can hear me, you need to call off these choppers!" hollered Fisher.

Automatic weapons fire cracked from the HEP car, and the fuselage of the chopper came alive. The pilot broke off and banked away at a steep angle, sure to come around for another pass.

Ironically, the agents inside the HEP car had driven off the bird—and that allowed Fisher and Briggs to reach the ladder.

The HEP car's windows were darkly tinted, so they

couldn't see the agents who'd just slid open the side door and leaned out to fire. Out of options, Fisher and Briggs descended anyway, rushing down between the cars, then Briggs climbed along the front of the HEP to remain low, beneath the windshield. From there, he'd claw his way above it, reaching the upper deck of the HEP from the storm side. That was the best path to the locomotive.

"Make it fast, buddy. Those birds are coming back, and our triggerman's got to be nervous now."

"Don't worry about me."

They banged fists, and Briggs tested his purchase on the HEP, then hauled himself away. There was no upper deck on the HEP car, just a series of rungs across the top not meant for climbing. Once he scaled his way up there, the gauntlet to the locomotive would prove, in a word, interesting.

Meanwhile, Fisher took one more sonar reading, and the image brought a curse to his lips.

Just a single occupant inside the HEP car. Clean reading. Where was the other agent?

"Briggs, we're missing one. Stay sharp."

"Yeah," the man answered, his voice burred by what had to be an intense physical effort. "I'll be ready."

Fisher shot a look to the sky: He couldn't see the choppers, but their rotor wash was suddenly stronger than the storm and blowing directly down on him.

Grim and Charlie were still unreachable.

As the pair of AH-6s continued around once more, Fisher peered alongside the HEP car, then looked up, zooming in with his trifocals.

Abqaiq rose like some otherworldly oasis from the swirling night, the once-bright security lights muted to soft candles, the chutes of burn-off bent sideways, the spherical tanks futilely barricading walls of sand that broke into tendrils and reared back like cobras ready to strike. Despite the sandstorm's best efforts to disguise it, the processing plant was still out there, waiting for them, and they were racing headlong toward it.

Pursing his lips, Fisher hauled himself up along the back side of the HEP car, reaching the operator's door and clinging to it against the high wind. He tried the lock. No, it wouldn't be that easy.

Clutching the door's handle with one hand, he leaned back and opted to shoot out the window. Three rounds chewed through, then he busted free the rest of the glass with his elbow and levered himself up and onto the sill, shoving in his pistol hand and ready to fire. Clear. He hauled himself inside, collapsing onto the car's floor.

Fighting for breath, he rolled, pushed up onto his hands and knees, then stood, spinning back toward the controls.

They were gone. Stripped. Nothing here but bundles of wires jutting from empty consoles. Some of the cables had been neatly cut, others torn free.

A small hallway ahead dropped down three steps to another door, this one made of aluminum or steel and seemingly retrofitted to the car. No window. Iron bar handle. Two locks. Dead bolt, no doubt.

"Sam, watch out! I think I see—"

36

FISHER never heard the rest of Briggs's warning. A pair of black boots had flown through the shattered window and connected with the side of his head. He flew back against the opposite door with such force that the window cracked behind him.

He reached for his weapon.

Never made it.

Two more blows struck him in the cheek and chin, a third to the neck.

He finally touched his holster. The weapon was gone.

He reached farther down to his secondary.

Gone.

Suddenly, his trifocals were torn from his head. He

blinked hard, tried to focus. The barrel of a .40-caliber pistol was poised six inches from the tip of his nose.

His eyes still weren't fully focused, but that was no matter; the voice came first.

And it was enough.

"I don't believe it. No, not you!" she cried.

Fisher had briefly entertained the idea that yes, it might be possible that their "favorite" GRU agent was in Dammam, but conventional thinking had him and the rest of the team focusing on a handful of other Russian operators who'd gone rogue over the years, including Kestrel.

But no, it was her.

Major Viktoria Kolosov. Snegurochka. The Snow Maiden. Fisher's pistols were tucked into her waistband. Yes, his MPX was still strapped around his back, but he'd never reach the machine gun in time.

He raised his voice above the incessant hum of the diesel engine and spoke to the wild-haired woman in Russian. "You missed a very nice helicopter ride!"

"I'm sure I did! What're you doing here?"

"Same question."

"No more talk. Say good-bye."

"You won't do it. You already had your chance back in Peru. I think you like me."

She took a step back, clutching her pistol with both hands. "What's so important that they sent you after us?" She gestured toward the door. "It can't be just the gun in there."

"The gun?" Fisher asked. "Is that what they told you? What's your mission?"

She snorted, as though she'd never share that.

"Look, you don't have to talk, but if this train gets to Abqaiq, nothing will matter."

"What do you mean?"

Fisher suddenly widened his eyes and screamed at her: "What's your goddamned mission!"

"I'm here to babysit the gun and make sure it reaches Riyadh. They're paying me a lot to do it."

"There's another guy in there, right? Have you seen him?"

"No. The door's been locked."

"That guy's an Iranian, the triggerman. That thing you're calling a gun? It's a nuke they built in Natanz. They want to blow up the oil processing station. Your Russian bosses sent you on a one-way mission."

"I'm supposed to believe that? Listen to me, asshole, you ruined my life! I lost Nadia and I lost Kasperov. I couldn't even go back to the GRU. Failures like me, we disappear. Do you understand? I had to take this job. And now you what? You want to save me?"

"I don't care about you. I just need to get through that door. Now get out of my way—"

"Oh, yes, me and the gun pointed at your head will let you come on through. Now shut up and take off your fancy little rifle."

Fisher reached up, slid a thumb under the MPX's sling, then pulled it over his head, his gaze never leaving hers.

"Now throw it out the window."

He smiled, thought about it.

"Do it!"

Now it was Fisher's turn to snicker. He tossed the gun over her shoulder and out of the train.

He was about to make his move on her weapon when a pair of deafening explosions resounded from outside, twin bursts so powerful that the ground and car quaked and the cracked window behind him shattered.

Not a second later the windshield blew inward with a horrific crash and burst into thousands of pieces that sent both of them ducking.

Next came a squealing of the train's wheels as they locked up, the force throwing the Snow Maiden forward, into the stripped console, with Fisher caroming off the panels beside her. He was already reaching out to seize her pistol when the windows had blown, and now he had it—

But she was reaching for his Five-seveN at her waist. He went for it.

But her grip went slack. And so did his.

Because the rumbling, shrieking, and groaning noises coming from outside, along with the shattering of more glass, meant only one thing: the train had derailed.

He couldn't be sure what happened next, judging it all based upon what he could hear and feel. His gaze was still locked on the Snow Maiden's, the ferocity on her face turned to utter shock.

He threw her pistol behind him while reaching for his Five-seveN. He seized it—

But now she had his secondary, the P226, pressed to his forehead.

This standoff lasted barely a second more before a

massive wave of sand, perhaps dug up by the locomotive as it buried itself into the desert, came rushing through the shattered windshield and drove both of them backward and into the hall and stairwell.

Even as the sand flowed in as though poured from a dump truck, the entire train heaved and creaked, iron scraping against iron, undercarriages wailing as wheels cut at wrong angles across the tracks. Another explosion rocked from somewhere outside, followed by a harsh cracking that sounded as though the hitches between container cars were being forced apart and snapped in two.

The operator's booth continued filling with sand, the walls buckling, and just as Fisher was slapping his hand on the wall, groping for purchase—

The entire HEP car smashed onto its side and continued skidding across the desert floor, more dirt and rocks and other debris coming in from the side door window, with the Snow Maiden now crawling backward toward the steel door at the bottom of the steps.

Summoning up a scream, Fisher forced himself up through the oncoming sand and dove onto the Snow Maiden, freeing the SIG from her grip before she kneed him in the chest, then brought her boot around and side-kicked him in the neck.

They both fell back as the side of the car, now their ceiling, began rumbling and smashing inward to a chorus of much louder scrapes and echoing booms. Fisher suspected that one or more of the oil container cars was ramming and tumbling over them, the entire train folding up like an accordion and rolling over itself, the tanks splaying across the earth like a box of cigars let slip from the hand of a drunken oligarch.

Perhaps only the train's collision could stop the triggerman from detonating the weapon—and any second's delay was either fate glancing kindly on Fisher or cruel irony baiting him with the idea that he still had a chance.

Barely finishing that thought, he and the Snow Maiden were thrown once more into the opposite wall as the HEP car fishtailed brutally to the right, booted by more cars piling up behind it, the reverberation like a legion of thunderheads vying for attention and drumming across the tracks.

More sand spat into their faces, and Fisher was momentarily blinded, reaching out now for the Snow Maiden, wary that she might have another pistol or knife at the ready.

A short bang came from nearby, shaking the car; it was followed by a collision that must've broken open one of the containers because now the air reeked of oil. A guttural hiss pierced the wind, as though pressure were being released from something, and that racket lasted a second more before the car rolled up, onto its roof, burying Fisher and the Snow Maiden under the sand.

But then the car's momentum kept it rolling and it smashed down onto its opposite side, the sand now drawing away from them, the explosions and near-human howls and shrieks of mangled metal still rising into the night.

It was all happening around them now, the car beginning to grow steady, the vibrations coming up through the ground, and yet there was nothing else striking them. The impacts were more distant now, like mortar fire half stifled by a mountainside.

Fisher coughed and clawed his way down toward the door, with the sand rising up to just below the first lock.

They'd stopped.

Shielding his face, he fired two rounds, the lock blowing off to reveal a hole.

He lifted the pistol to the higher lock.

That's when an arm slipped under his neck and a hand forced away his pistol.

The Snow Maiden leaned in close and wrapped her teeth around the top of his ear.

"Sam, can you hear me?" cried Grim in his subdermal.

"Come on, Sam, give us a shout," added Charlie.

He loved his team—but they usually had better timing. Fisher wrenched himself forward, freeing his ear as she was about to clamp down on it. He broke her grip on the pistol and whirled back to shove it into her head and pin her back down, onto the sand. "Nice try," he muttered, pressing the muzzle deeper into her skin.

"Just do it. I got nothing now."

"What do you mean you got nothing? You got me and my government as your new best friends. We'll have some really enlightening conversations about all your operations—past, present, and future."

He rolled his pistol back, striking her on the side of the head. The blow was enough to stun her and buy him time to fish out some zipper cuffs and bind her wrists in front.

Leaving her there, still groaning, he elbowed his way back toward the door and blew off the second lock. He turned around and walked crab-like to get in position. Then, resting on his rump, he lifted both legs in a powerful dropkick. As the door creaked open, he went sliding into the back of the car, riding the crest of falling sand.

At the bottom he rolled and stood, then tugged free an LED penlight from his tac-suit's breast pocket and aimed it at the back of the car.

If you lacked a military background or hadn't spent the bulk of your adult life shooting, evading, or destroying military weapons, you wouldn't recognize it for what is was—

But Fisher did.

It weighed close to six tons and at nearly twelve feet long took up the space ordinarily reserved for both the locomotive diesel and its electrical generator. For Fisher, the giveaway was the Sa'ir KS-19 gun breech.

In layman's terms he was staring at a stripped-down version of a 100mm antiaircraft gun. All the electronics and computer interfacing was gone—removed because the Iranians were fearful of an accident or premature detonation due to a crash, fire, or electrical short. The business end of the sawed-off barrel terminated into a larger cylinder roughly nine feet long and two feet in diameter, the whole contraption mounted to the AA gun's original four-wheel base, now collapsed onto its side. The gun was part of the bomb, of course, and they were using it to trigger the nuclear reaction.

The Sa'ir, Fisher knew, could deliver a projectile with

a muzzle velocity of about six hundred meters per second, much faster than the trigger speed used to detonate "Little Boy" over Hiroshima. If two pieces of subcritical material were not brought together fast enough, nuclear predetonation or "fizzle" could occur, with just a very small explosion, blowing the bulk of the material apart.

He couldn't see the neutron generator yet. It was either on the other side or underneath, out of sight, but he felt certain it was there.

The triggerman himself, a fey-looking agent in his sixties whose eyes shone like sapphires in the penlight, was trapped under all six tons of the device, blood pouring from his mouth as he reached for the gun's breech lanyard. It was clear the Iranian had already locked the breech on the 76.2mm discarding sabot projectile, allowing the three-inch projectile to be fired from a four-inch gun. All he had to do now was tug down on that black lanyard to manually trigger the bomb.

However, he couldn't reach it, his fingertips barely brushing the nylon.

Fisher thought of shooting him, but with a hundred pounds of weaponized uranium within spitting distance, there were "safer" ways of neutralizing him. Fisher rushed to the bomb, swung the lanyard away, then crouched down.

"Praise be to Allah," the man said in Farsi.

"You're going to die here," Fisher said, using the man's native tongue. "Just tell me, who hired you?"

The man opened his mouth, but then his eyes grew vague and his head slumped.

Fisher checked his neck for a pulse and found none. He stood back and began taking a video of the bomb with his OPSAT. "Grim, you getting this?"

"Receiving now, Sam."

"Is this thing stable?"

"They designed it to ensure that. If it survived a train wreck without going off . . ."

"All right. Have you heard from Briggs?"

"Nothing so far."

"Damn, I'm going up for him. You notify the POTUS and coordinate with the prince. We'll need a team in here to dismantle this thing."

"We're on it."

Fisher sighed and bounded back up the pile of sand to where the Snow Maiden was still lying. As he began to lift her, Briggs appeared in the shattered door window above them, his face half obscured by the penlight he directed into the booth. "Sam?"

"I'm here. You okay? What the hell happened?"

"Those choppers launched Hellfires at the tracks. The engineer's dead. I jumped off like a second before it all went to hell." Briggs shifted his light. "Oh my God, is that—"

"Yeah," said Fisher. "It's her."

"She tracked us?"

"No, they hired her."

"Well, that's some bad luck for her—and payback for us."

"Yeah. Come around through the window. See if you can help me get her out of here."

"On my way."

As Fisher checked the Snow Maiden's zipper cuffs to be sure they were still fastened, her eyes flickered open. "Kiss me," she said.

"What?"

"You heard me. You'll send me away. Who knows when I'll ever feel a kiss again."

"Sorry, honey, you're not my type."

"Oh, yes I am. And you owe me."

"For what?"

"For like you said, not killing you back in Peru."

Fisher rolled his eyes. "You really are a crazy bitch, aren't you?"

She wriggled her brows. "Come here."

He leaned toward her. She did smell magnificent. She was beautiful in a terribly sinister way. His lips did lock onto hers—

But then she grabbed his bottom lip with her teeth and bit down hard, just as Briggs caught them together.

Fisher cursed and pulled up, his lip beginning to bleed as he gaped at his teammate.

"Everything okay, boss?"

Fisher hesitated. His gaze averted to the Snow Maiden, who lay there, smiling daggers.

37

FISHER, Briggs, and the Snow Maiden were evacuated from the crash site by a squad of Shammari's troops. They remained inside a Humvee parked about a quarter kilometer south of the train, waiting out the sandstorm. A medic came by and treated Briggs for some lacerations on his arm and neck. The prince himself drove up and climbed into the passenger's seat of the Humvee, then sat with them a moment.

"My security here at the processing station is very effective," he said. "But we still have a lot of work to do at the port."

Fisher wasn't one to gloat or pretend he had all the answers. He just shrugged. "Too many leaks, too many bribes. And sometimes you can't watch everything."

"But we do our best," he said.

"Yeah. So it looks like nothing will be flying for a while." Fisher rapped a knuckle on the window. "Any chance of us getting a ride to Dubai?"

"My men will take you. But she stays with us."

"You'd better call your uncle on that. We have orders to take her back."

Grim had already worked with President Caldwell to ensure that the Snow Maiden did not leave their custody and would be extradited to the United States. The plan was to turn her over to CIA officers operating from the Naval Support Activity Bahrain, Fifth Fleet, in Juffair, Bahrain. The Saudis, of course, weren't happy about that, but Caldwell had already negotiated those terms.

Shammari made the call, and his expression changed less than fifteen seconds into the discussion. "All right, then, I'll say my good-byes. Safe journey back. And thank you."

The prince shielded his face from the wind and returned to his own Humvee. Five minutes later, a new driver and another troop entered their Humvee with orders to take them to Dubai. They rumbled off.

Fisher glanced over at the Snow Maiden, whose eyes were closed, head bowed. This was not resignation, Fisher feared. More like plotting. He never let his guard down. Not around her.

For just a moment, Fisher caught site of Hammad's helicopter as the driver headed northwest across the rutted desert to pick up Highway 615. Fisher had promised the poor pilot that he wouldn't die, but now those little girls had lost their father. These moments, when ordinary citizens rose to the occasion and wound up sacrificing themselves for the greater good, were the ones that weighed most heavily on him. Fisher suspected he'd be taking many more helicopter rides in his nightmares, with the reluctant Hammad at the stick. Being sorry was never enough.

MORE than nine hours later, after a refueling stop and a chance to grab something to eat, they arrived at the airport and were dropped off beside Paladin One's loading ramp.

"Hey, Fisher!" cried Kobin as he strode toward them. "I finally got some intel on that Russian agent you've been looking for. My guy says . . ." He broke off as Fisher and Briggs approached with the Snow Maiden cuffed between them. "Aw, fuck, I'm a day late and a dollar short."

"Get your crap out of the cell," Fisher said. "She needs to borrow it for a little while."

Kobin's brows rose as the Snow Maiden faced him. "We can share the cell. I promise to be good."

Briggs burst out laughing. "Dude, she'll tear you apart like a pit bull."

"You wouldn't hurt me, sweetheart, would you?"

The Snow Maiden glanced at Kobin as though he were her next meal. "Let's find out."

* * *

THEY were still prepping for takeoff, and Fisher was cleaning the sand out of his ears, when President Caldwell contacted them with an intel update. Fisher rushed from the infirmary and stood in the control room with the rest of the team.

"I've just gotten off the phone with President Treskayev, and he wanted to express his thanks," Caldwell began.

"We'll send him the bill," said Fisher.

Caldwell nearly grinned. "He claims they've arrested nearly a hundred individuals who they say aided or abetted the oligarchs. Those who they believe masterminded the plot are still out of the country. He confirmed that Kargin did commit suicide, as Kasperov reported. In an interesting sidebar, Kargin also left some bank files open on his computer that suggest he and the others may have been helping to finance the Blacklist Engineers. I can't get anything more definitive because they refuse to turn over the files."

"So where are these *businessmen* now?" asked Grim.

"Still in hiding, presumably in those foreign capitals with banking systems that help harbor their assets. Right now, Treskayev has his hands full cleaning out the corruption in his inner circle. He's already fired a few career Kremlin underlings who were on the oligarchs' payroll and have been complicit in attempting to discredit him. Unfortunately, the oligarchs themselves have enough money to rent years of delaying tactics from their newly adopted countries. They're safe until their money runs out or the national governments declare them persona non grata."

Fisher snickered. "We've still got more work to do."

"Madame President, what about the bomb?" Grim asked.

"We flew in the NSA Bahrain, Fifth Fleet, EOD team to dismantle the bomb and take possession of the uranium, which we only need long enough to sample a fingerprint of the material. Treskayev's sending the old heavy cruiser *Admiral Ushakov* to pick up the material in Bahrain. Meanwhile, back here, the FBI has already taken into custody several individuals involved in the thorium attack. These are Iranian nationals who claim they worked with a Russian sleeper cell in the United States who infiltrated security at the storage site to smuggle the C-4 into the thorium shipments."

"There's still one more loose end," said Fisher. "And that's the virus. Kasperov still has it, and if we piss him off, he could play that card against us."

"I know," said Caldwell. "And I've already spoken to him privately about this. The Office of the National Counterintelligence Executive wants the software turned over to them. They plan to study it."

"Has he agreed?" asked Fisher.

"Not yet. I suspect the negotiations will be long on this one. Anyway, I want to thank you all. We're in your debt—and don't think for a minute that we ever forget that. The work you do is vital to national security, and

I'm honored that you've all accepted this important and extremely difficult job. I mean that. And I'll be in touch."

The screen went blank, and Fisher faced the team. "I'd like to say something, too."

Grim looked at him expectantly.

Briggs was waiting.

Charlie's mouth began to open.

Fisher began to squirm. "Ah, forget it." He hurried back toward their living quarters.

THIRTY minutes later they were at cruising altitude and finally heading back to Virginia.

Kasperov and Fisher were standing near the infirmary door, gazing out across the control room, where Grim and Briggs stood at the SMI. Nearby, Charlie sat at his station, showing Ollie and two other analysts diagrams of his early work on the SMI.

"Your team and its mission remind me of a trip I once took," Kasperov began. "I visited your CIA headquarters, and I remember the wall of stars, all those heroes with no public recognition."

"We don't do it for that. Or the money."

"Then why?"

"Because we can. Because somebody has to . . . and it's the right thing to do."

"It's that simple?"

Fisher grinned. "If it were any more complicated, they'd have to find a smarter man than me."

"You underestimate yourself, Mr. Fisher."

"No, I've just . . . changed."

"I guess it's a brave new world for both of us."

Fisher beamed. "There was a rumor that one of your bodyguards smuggled some vodka on board my plane."

"Rumor? Nonsense. Let's have a drink!"

Before leaving the control room, Fisher glanced back at his team, at the new Fourth Echelon.

Yes, he was Sam Fisher. Splinter Cell.

But now he was something even more.